By K.C. Wells

BFF
Bromantically Yours
First
Love Lessons Learned
Step by Step
Waiting For You

DREAMSPUN DESIRES
The Senator's Secret
Out of the Shadows
My Fair Brady
Under the Covers

LEARNING TO LOVE
Michael & Sean
Evan & Daniel
Josh & Chris
Final Exam

LIONS & TIGERS & BEARS
A Growl, a Roar, and a Purr
A Snarl, a Splash, and a Shock

LOVE, UNEXPECTED
Debt
Burden

MERRYCHURCH MYSTERIES
Truth Will Out
Roots of Evil
A Novel Murder

SENSUAL BONDS
A Bond of Three
A Bond of Truth

With Parker Williams

COLLARS & CUFFS
An Unlocked Heart
Trusting Thomas
Someone to Keep Me
A Dance with Domination
Damian's Discipline
Make Me Soar
Dom of Ages
Endings and Beginnings

SECRETS
Before You Break
An Unlocked Mind
Threepeat
On the Same Page

Published by DSP Publications
SECOND SIGHT
In His Sights
In Plain Sight

Published by DREAMSPINNER PRESS
www.dreamspinnerpress.com

IN PLAIN SIGHT

K.C. WELLS

DSP PUBLICATIONS

Published by

DSP Publications

5032 Capital Circle SW, Suite 2, PMB# 279, Tallahassee, FL 32305-7886 USA
www.dsppublications.com

In Plain Sight
© 2023 K.C. Wells

Cover Art
© 2023 L.C. Chase
http://www.lcchase.com
Cover content is for illustrative purposes only and any person depicted on the cover is a model.

Trade Paperback ISBN: 978-1-64108-567-0
Digital ISBN: 978-1-64108-566-3
Trade PaperbackS published October 2023
v. 1.0

Printed in the United States of America
∞
This paper meets the requirements of
ANSI/NISO Z39.48-1992 (Permanence of Paper).

This book is dedicated to two men.
The first is my husband, Andrew, who sat with me and plotted every scene, every twist and turn. That man has the patience of a saint.
The second is my dear friend Jack Parton, who in the course of a Skype conversation, presented me with two ideas—and I had my book….

Acknowledgments

As always, thanks to my beta team. I really put them through the wringer with this one. Special thanks to Jason Mitchell for his advice from start to finish.

IN PLAIN SIGHT

K.C. WELLS

PROLOGUE

Boston, MA, Monday, July 10, 2006
11:45 p.m.

FORENSIC PATHOLOGIST Del Maddox drove up to the barrier across the entrance to the Fort Point Channel Tunnel, where lights had been set up to illuminate the site. Judging by the amount of traffic he'd passed to get there, Boston was going to have more than its usual amount of pissed-off motorists—the tunnel connected with the Ted Williams tunnel that headed out to Logan airport. On the other side of the barrier were fire trucks, police vehicles, and two ambulances, and from deeper within the tunnel came the sharp grind of cutting tools and raised voices.

Del sighed. *Welcome to Boston PD.* His first day, and it seemed he already had customers for his table.

An officer approached his car, armed with a flashlight, and Del wound his window down. He grabbed his badge from where he'd stowed it under the visor and held it open. Not that he needed it—Medical Examiner emblazoned on the car door was a bit of a giveaway.

The cop aimed the flashlight's beam at Del's credentials, then at Del's face, causing him to squint. He frowned as he lowered the flashlight. "Wait a minute. You're not Mike."

Del arched his eyebrows. "And who might Mike be?"

"Mike Harrison, the medical examiner."

"Then there can only be two possible explanations. Either I murdered Mike, stole his car, copied his ID, and added my own details to fool everyone into thinking I was a medical examiner—or I could actually be the *new* medical examiner, because the previous one retired last week." He smiled. "I'll leave you to work it out. In the meantime, can you move this barrier, please, and let me do my job?"

Way to go, Del. Ever heard the phrase, "You never get a second chance to make a first impression?"

He blamed it on the job. His clients never told him if he was being rude.

The officer scowled but hoisted the barrier out of the way. "Mike was way more of a laugh," he murmured as Del drove past him.

"Good for him," Del muttered. He drove as far as he could into the mouth of the tunnel, then switched off the engine. He grabbed his bag from the passenger seat and got out. Then he opened his door again and rooted in the glove box for a flashlight. His safety hat was in the trunk.

The dark mouth of the tunnel sloped downward, and the site of the collapse was maybe fifty feet ahead of him, lit by emergency lamps. Del walked toward the yellow tape that marked off a portion of the road. Huge concrete panels had been moved by mechanical lifters, revealing the crushed form of a Honda Civic, surrounded by rubble. Above, a large hole gaped in the ceiling, the width of two panels. Men in safety hats and reflective jackets stood around talking in low voices, and Del counted about four police officers.

One officer approached him, flashlight in hand. "You the medical examiner?"

Del nodded. "How many casualties?"

The officer grimaced. "Two. One fatality and one guy badly injured. He was driving. He's on his way to the hospital already. The tiles completely crushed the passenger side of the vehicle. His partner was killed instantly, we think. We haven't removed her body from the wreckage yet, although the firefighters have just cut through to take the roof off."

Del gave a nod of approval. He signaled to the paramedics waiting beside the wreckage, and together they walked solemnly to the crushed car. It didn't take long to lift and place her in a body bag. Del watched as they carried her away from the wreck to where the ambulance waited.

"Who is in charge of the scene?"

The officer pointed toward the fire truck. "Sergeant Michaels. He's over there."

Del glanced at the amount of debris. "How much concrete do they think fell?" He peered at the officer's badge. "Officer Mitchell."

"They estimate about twenty-four thousand pounds." He pointed up. "The tiles are reinforced concrete slabs, suspended from girders bolted to the ceiling roof. It seems the anchor bolts ripped loose." Officer Mitchell bit his lip. "Except they weren't the only things that fell." He crooked his finger. "This is where things get a little weird."

Del followed him. Officer Mitchell crouched beside another black body bag covering a heap on the ground. Del froze. "I thought you said there were only two casualties."

Mitchell's eyes sparkled in the strong emergency lights. "Strictly speaking, there were. But I have no idea what caused *this* casualty—well, apart from the obvious." He removed the bag, and Del's breathing hitched.

A skeleton lay on sheets of plastic, partially covered. Mitchell's remark about the possible cause of death suddenly made sense.

There was no head.

The remains had obviously been there a while, judging by the complete decomposition. Del guessed at more than a decade. He studied the body, noting the pelvis.

"I don't suppose it's possible to tell right away if this person was male or female," Mitchell murmured. "Unless the Bible is correct and males have one less set of ribs than females."

"I hate to disillusion you, but we all have twelve pairs—though some people are born with eleven or thirteen. Doesn't appear to afford them any ill effects, however. But yes, it's possible to tell." Del pointed to the subpubic angle where the two bones met. "This was almost certainly male. The female pelvis tends to be wider." He straightened. "I can see why you'd think this a weird situation. Is the theory that the body had been stowed above us, placed there when the tunnel was constructed?"

"Yes. That was the early nineties. I checked."

Del hunkered down next to the remains. "The plastic didn't mummify the body. If anything, it created the ideal environment for bacteria—warm and moist." He took a closer look. "Interesting, though. Because of the air exchange, the initial decomposition went all the way to skeletonization."

"Even wrapped in plastic?"

Del arched his eyebrows. "As we all know, meat wrapped in plastic still goes bad." He stood, glancing up to the gaping hole in the ceiling. "A very weird situation indeed."

"But that's not the strangest part." Mitchell carefully drew back the two flaps of plastic that partially covered the skeleton.

Del blinked. "I see what you mean." Nestled within the wrapping were what resembled two vinyl pouches—very familiar pouches….

"Are they what I think they are?"

Del nodded. "Our unknown dead male had silicone breast implants."

His first day in Boston, and he already had a mystery to solve.

CHAPTER ONE

Monday, July 9, 2018

"Do I look nervous?" Detective Gary Mitchell fingered the collar of his dark blue shirt, then adjusted his tie knot for what had to be the fifteenth time that morning.

Dan Porter rolled his eyes. "Will you quit fidgeting? And seeing as you've asked, yes. The more you fidget, the more nervous you appear. It's only roll call, for God's sake."

It was way more than that, and they both knew it. Dan appeared calm. Actually he was immaculate, from his closely shaven square jawline to his characteristic quiff. His hair was swept up off his face, the warm brown tones matching his eyes, and his dark blue suit was impeccable with its matching shirt and purple brocade waistcoat.

As if he'd read Gary's thoughts, Dan speared him with a look. "And if anyone should be nervous, it's me. Right?"

Gary shoved aside his selfish qualms, his stomach clenching. "I'm sorry. You're right." Dan had nailed it. Lieutenant Travers's announcement at the end of May that a psychic would be consulting on the case of a serial killer had been met mostly with incredulity and ill-disguised skepticism. It didn't matter that Dan had subsequently helped them find the killer. Many of Gary's coworkers dismissed the role Dan had played in catching him, but paradoxically they wouldn't forget what Dan had revealed about one of their own.

Travers's about-to-be-revealed news was sure to be met with yet more incredulity and derision.

Dan's face glowed. "And that's what I love about you—you admit when you're at fault. Do you know what a rare trait that is?" He inched closer, his voice dropping to a whisper. "And if we weren't about to go out there, I'd show you exactly how much I love you."

Gary's chest tightened. "I'm not ready." It was still so new. Breathtaking, exciting, and stomach-churningly new. There were mornings when he woke to find Dan's arms wrapped around him and had to pinch himself in reassurance that this was no dream.

Hearing Dan say he loved him made it an awesome dream.

"Ready for what?"

"For everyone to… know about us. About me." Except he was pretty sure some people already knew.

Warm hands cupped his face. "You don't have to tell anyone *anything*, okay? It isn't a law, you know, that you have to come out as bisexual. It's *your* decision, no one else's."

"Riley knows." And in recent weeks, Gary had become increasingly aware of inquiring glances as he strolled through the precinct.

"But Riley won't say a word, and you know it. Hell, he said as much last month. That night you rode in on your white horse and rescued me, remember?" Dan placed his hands on Gary's shoulders. "And you *know* I won't do anything to make life awkward or uncomfortable for you. As far as I'm concerned, I'm here to do a job." His eyes gleamed. "Let's save everything else for when we're alone. And while we might be alone at the moment…." He removed his hands. "Just in case someone walks in unexpectedly."

"Good idea. Most of the people I work with don't believe in knocking." Then he added, "Except for Riley."

There was a knock at the door, and Detective Riley Watson stuck his head around it. "You guys ready?"

Despite the butterflies in his stomach, Gary laughed. "Your timing is amazing."

Riley entered the room and let out a low whistle as his gaze took in its contents. "I'm impressed. When you said Travers had found you an office, I expected something along the lines of the closet we were using." It wasn't huge by any means, but it had everything they needed—two desks with PCs, a printer-copier, a couple of filing cabinets, a free-standing whiteboard, and four chairs. No window, but Gary didn't mind that.

Gary snorted. "What a difference a month makes. Plus a lot of support from the chief."

And let's hope that support is enough. Gary expected opposition.

"We'd better get out there. I saw Travers on his way just now." Riley smirked. "I hope you two are prepared, because it looks as if the cat's out of the bag already."

"What do you mean?" Gary hadn't heard a whisper, at least not about his new role.

Riley opened the door and removed something from the outside. He handed the sheet of paper to Gary, who groaned.

"Great. Who talked?" Someone had drawn a cartoon of him and Dan seated at their desks, both frozen in blocks of ice. Below it they'd written Cold Cases Department.

Dan took it from him and chuckled. "This is really good. We should frame it." He scanned the office walls. "Did you keep the Cereal Killer one? That was great."

Gary knew better than to accept Dan's attempt at forced humor. "I guess we'd better go and let Travers make it official." He grabbed his jacket, attempting to put it on as he strode through the hallways, Dan and Riley behind him.

With every step he took, the churning in his stomach increased.

Gary didn't give a damn what his fellow detectives thought of him. But he sure as hell didn't want them giving Dan a hard time.

"THAT'S EVERYTHING." Sergeant Rob Michaels closed the folder on the lectern in front of him. He cleared his throat. "But before you all disappear, the lieutenant would like a word."

Murmurs rumbled through the assembled officers and detectives, and Gary's fears were confirmed.

They know what's coming.

Lieutenant Travers stepped up to the lectern, looking at them over his glasses. "I'm sure I don't need to remind you how valuable Mr. Porter's contribution was last month in helping us apprehend a serial killer, one who'd eluded us for some time." The rumbles increased, and Travers's eyes grew flinty. "Regardless of what you think about the aftermath of that arrest, justice was served. And that's why we're all here, isn't it? To see justice served?"

A hush fell over the room.

Travers nodded. "Well, the chief has decided we should be paying more attention to our cold cases. And there are a great many of them, some dating back decades. You know, in the days before you could send a sample off to a lab for DNA testing." He grinned. "And then complain about how long it takes to get the results." That raised a few chuckles. "So yes, times have changed. We have the gift of technology." He glanced toward Dan at the back of the room, seated next to Gary. "And now we have other gifts at our disposal." Travers squared his broad shoulders. "Imagine if someone you loved had died or disappeared in unexplained circumstances. You'd want closure, even if it happened years ago. As I see it, a cold case is one where we had to admit defeat. Well, no one likes to do that. And with that in mind, as of today, Detective Gary Mitchell and Mr. Dan Porter will be working together exclusively on cold cases." That steel gaze was back. "I expect them to be given every cooperation."

"What makes you think they'll be able to turn up anything new?" That was Detective Will Freeman. Gary had figured he'd be the first voice of dissent.

Travers arched his eyebrows and gave Gary an inquiring glance. No words passed between them, but Gary knew the lieutenant well enough to decipher that look.

You *can deal with this, Detective.*

Gary coughed, and chair legs scraped over the floor as the assembled officers and detectives turned to stare at him with expressions of both amusement and disbelief.

Gary met their gazes, his shoulders squared. "Mr. Porter's involvement may give us access to new information."

"You said 'may.'" Will stared at Gary. "That implies you have doubts about his abilities."

"He's not like one of those fortune-telling machines you find in arcades, all right?" Riley's face reddened. "You can't just put your money in the slot and out pops the bad guy. It doesn't work like that." Gary laid his hand on Riley's arm, and Riley expelled a breath. "Sorry." He glared at his coworkers. "But you guys haven't seen him at work—I have. And he's no fake. Ludlow started killing in 2014, and ten days after we brought Dan in on the case, we stopped him. Ten days."

Travers cleared his throat once more, and heads swiveled in his direction. "Do I have to repeat myself about offering cooperation?" Another silence fell, and he nodded. "Good. Because if you don't like this new initiative, I suggest you take it up with the chief. He loved the idea." And with that, he marched out of the room. As soon as he was out of sight, the murmurs began again, only louder.

Barely seconds later, Will Freeman marched over to where Gary, Dan, and Riley stood. That was all it took for others to follow.

Here we go.

Will came to a halt in front of them, his arms folded. "All that stuff in the media about the Ludlow case," he began, "it was all hype, right?"

Gary opened his mouth to tell Will where to get off, but Dan got there first. He held out his hand. "Give me your watch."

Will frowned. "Why do you want my watch?"

"Because you work with Gary, and he needs you to have his back. And the only way forward is to prove to you that what the media reported was the truth." He held his head high. "So give me your watch, and I can help you put all your doubts aside."

Will arched his eyebrows. "And what if you don't… *feel* anything?"

Around them the officers and detectives were all unusually quiet, their attention focused on the scene before them.

Dan has an audience. Gary hoped to God it wouldn't be a bust. He knew from experience Dan couldn't turn his visions on and off like a faucet.

Dan shrugged. "Then we'll try with something else until I do." His palm faced upward. "Your watch, please."

Will hesitated for a moment, then unclasped the stainless-steel bracelet and placed it in Dan's hand. Dan covered it with his other hand and closed his eyes. The room was silent, and Gary could hear nothing but the slow intake and exhalation of air.

Will refolded his arms. "Don't get excited, guys. Nothing's gonna happen."

Gary prayed Will was about to eat his words.

After a minute or two, Dan opened his eyes. He handed the watch back, and Will fastened the clasp. "So? What did you discover?" He stuck out his chin. "Gonna tell me what I had for breakfast?" He grinned at the audience surrounding them, raising a few chuckles.

Dan regarded him with a sympathetic gaze. "Your father gave you that watch for your twenty-first birthday."

Will blinked. "H-how did you know that?" Then he breathed easier, his usual brash demeanor returning. "You're good, I'll give you that. You saw the inscription on the back."

Dan shook his head. "Did you see me look at the back, even once? No, you didn't. So let me give you something else. He mentioned the watch the last time you saw him. Not that I'm about to mention where you were at the time. That's no one's business but yours."

Will's eyes widened, and his mouth fell open. "But... you couldn't...." He turned and pushed through the throng gathered around them, heading for the door, cries following his exit.

"Hey, Will, what's up?"

"Well? Did he get it right?"

"Aren't you going to tell us?"

"Show's over, guys." Rob Michaels called out from the front of the room. "You've all got work to do." Little by little the crowd dispersed, until only Gary, Dan, and Riley remained.

Dan glanced at Gary. "I don't think he'll give us any more trouble." His expression grew uneasy. "I didn't want to do that, but I've learned from experience that some people don't believe a word I say—until I show them. And then they're either fascinated, like Riley was when we first met, or scared shitless of what I'll see next."

"What *did* you see?" Riley asked.

Dan shook his head. "I'm sorry. It's not for me to say." He gestured toward the door. "Let's go to our office."

Riley patted him on the back. "Good luck. And in case I forgot to mention it...." His smile lit up his face. "Welcome aboard."

"Thanks."

They headed back to the office, and Gary closed the door.

"Okay, that was pretty much how I thought it would go down." He gave Dan an inquiring glance. "You okay?" He knew from experience that using his gift exhausted him.

"I'm fine, honest. That didn't take a lot out of me." Dan peered toward the door. "I think it took more out of Will." He looked at the pile of folders on one of the desks. "Are those cold cases?"

Gary nodded. "They're a real mix. Missing persons, kidnapping, death.... Travers sent them. To be honest, I'm not sure where to begin."

"Maybe we should spread them out, blindfold one of us, and stick a pin in one of them," Dan suggested. Then he stilled. "Is Brad's case going to be one of them?"

Gary's throat seized. He shook his head.

"That's probably a good thing. I can't see Travers being happy about us tackling that one. Talk about a conflict of interests. And especially with all the media hype following our recent success—and my involvement. The press would have a field day. I mean, can you imagine the headlines? 'Cop Uses Psychic to Investigate His Own Brother's Murder While Other

Cases Go Unsolved. Your Tax Dollars at Work.'" His hand went to Gary's back. "I said I'd try, and I meant it. We don't need to involve Travers. We'll do whatever we have to on our own time."

Relief flooded through him. "Thank you."

A rap on the door had Dan dropping his hand quickly. An officer poked his head into the room. "Detective Mitchell? You have a visitor, a Mrs. Sebring. I've put her in Interview Room One."

"Thanks. I'll be there directly."

The officer hesitated. "But she's asking to see Mr. Porter too. She was very insistent about that."

Dan raised his eyebrows but said nothing.

"We'll *both* be there directly, then." The officer withdrew, and Gary expelled a long breath. "I'm okay now. And this isn't the time or the place to discuss Brad. How about we go see our visitor?"

They left the office and walked through the crowded hallways filled with people and noise. Gary did his best to ignore the stares and murmurs, but he knew Dan would have a harder time doing that.

Maybe by the time we've got a few successes under our belt, they'll have warmed to the idea.

He wasn't going to hold his breath.

Mrs. Sebring stood as they entered the interview room, and Gary's first impression was of a very weary woman, maybe in her forties, pale, with shadows under her eyes. Her hair was scraped back and secured with a clip, and her face was devoid of makeup.

She headed straight for Dan. "You're the psychic, aren't you? The one I read about in the paper."

He smiled. "Yes, I'm Dan Porter."

"I'm here because of you. To be honest, you're my last hope." She didn't speak loudly, but Gary couldn't miss the note of desperation.

"What can we do for you, Mrs. Sebring?" He gestured to her chair. "Please, sit down." They sat facing her.

She lowered herself into the chair, studying their faces as if she was trying to reach a decision. Her forehead creased.

"First thing I need to know is… was it all true? Did you really find that serial killer?"

The edge of desperation in her voice grew more obvious.

Dan nodded. "I helped the police, yes."

Her expression hardened. "You never know these days. There's so much hype, disinformation… truth seems to have gone out of style."

"Mr. Porter provided valuable information that led us to the killer," Gary assured her. "So… why are you here?"

Mrs. Sebring's gaze flicked from Gary to Dan and back to Gary.

"Okay, then." She shuddered out a breath. "My husband died in 2016. An accident, they said. But I know different. I *know* he was murdered." She met their stares. "And I want you to prove it."

Chapter Two

For a moment Gary was too stunned to react. Then he regained his composure. He grabbed a notepad and pen from the table. "You'll have to give me some details so I can look the case up in our system."

She nodded as though she'd been expecting that. "His name was James Oliver Sebring. Born October twenty-first, 1980, in Dorchester. Worked his whole life in different places around the state. He died June twenty-fourth, 2016."

Gary scribbled notes, then started tapping on the keyboard, aware of Dan's soothing tone.

"You said your husband's death was ruled accidental," Dan said.

"Yes. But it wasn't. I know it."

"But *how* can you know that?" He fixed her with a keen glance.

"Because I knew *him*. He spent his whole working life being careful. He knew what he was doing."

Gary frowned at the monitor screen. "According to our records, your husband was working on a construction site."

"That's right. He was a joiner and carpenter. He was building houses at the time."

Gary quickly scanned the information on the screen. "And he fell off a roof while working. Well, the roof rafters." Gary's chest grew tight. "I'm sorry, Mrs. Sebring," he said in an apologetic voice, "but I don't see how we can help you. It was an open-and-shut case."

"But it *wasn't*," she wailed. "And I've been saying this for the last two years to anyone who would listen." Her eyes glistened.

Dan removed a dark blue folded handkerchief from his waistcoat pocket and pressed it into her hand. "Hey," he said softly. "*We're* going to listen to you, okay?" He covered her hand with his own, then froze.

Gary knew what that meant. And he had to know more.

"Mrs. Sebring, can I get you some coffee? Tea?"

She eased her hand from Dan's grasp and wiped her eyes. "Tea would be good. And please, call me Linda."

"I'm sure I can find some." He gave Dan a meaningful stare, then inclined his head toward the door. "We'll be right back."

Dan took the hint and rose to follow Gary from the room. Outside the door, Gary gave him an inquiring glance.

"What did you pick up on?"

Dan's brow furrowed. "I… I'm not sure. She's desperate, I know that much."

"Yeah, well, that hadn't escaped me either."

Dan shook his head. "It's more than that. She's utterly convinced she's telling us the truth. So I guess my question is… would Travers agree to us looking into it?"

Gary laid his hand on Dan's arm. "Can I point out a couple of things here? One, it's not a cold case—it's a *done-and-dusted* case, with nothing indicating any outcome other than the official one. Two, I'm pretty certain Travers would think this would be a total waste of our time."

Dan stared into his eyes. "But what if she's right?"

"When all the evidence points to it being an accident? I checked. There wasn't *one* eyewitness account of someone throwing him off those rafters. As far as I can make out, he was *alone* up there." One glance at Dan's solemn expression stopped him in his tracks. "Did you sense something else?"

Dan glanced at the door. "I can't explain why, but she… she really shook me. I think we need to look into this."

"You trust your senses that much?" Then he reasoned that was a dumb question.

Dan's senses hadn't steered them wrong yet.

A slow nod. "They don't lie, Gary. Okay, they might lead me off in weird directions sometimes, but at the heart of everything, I'm… shown there's an inescapable truth." He stared once more at the door to the interview room. "And I need to know what her truth is."

Gary gazed at him in silence, then pulled his phone from his pocket and called Travers. "Sir? Something's come up." He relayed what they had so far.

"This doesn't sound as if it would be a good use of your valuable time," Travers commented dryly. "In fact, it sounds a lot like a wild goose chase."

Dan grabbed his arm and locked gazes with him. *Please*, he mouthed.

"One moment, sir." Gary pressed his phone to his chest. "You said it yourself. You don't have anything to go on."

"You think I don't *know* that? This is what's bugging me about the situation. *Everything* in me is screaming not to let this go."

If it was a choice between provoking Travers's ire and following his own instincts….

Gary held his phone to his ear. "Sir, Dan feels there's something that needs to be investigated. And if you want my opinion? I think we should see where this leads us."

Travers fell silent, and Gary's heart sank. *He's not going to go for it.*

At last he spoke. "You have until Friday. After that, I expect you both to be hard at work solving a cold case. Is that clear?"

"Yes, sir."

"And keep me informed if you find anything." He hung up.

Dan gazed at him expectantly. "Well?"

"We've got until Friday. So I guess I'd better find some tea."

The glow in Dan's eyes made Gary feel like a million bucks. "You backed me up."

"I did."

Dan bit his lip. "Remind me to show you my gratitude tonight."

Warmth spread through Gary's chest. "I'll hold you to that."

GARY PLACED a cup of tea in front of Linda, then picked his pen up once more. "Okay, tell us more about James."

She sipped the fragrant amber liquid, and Gary could almost see the layer of calm that descended, settling on her like a shawl, her shoulders relaxing.

"What do you want to know?"

"A little of his background."

She leaned back. "James worked with wood since before he was sixteen. That was when we met, when we were both in high school." She smiled. "I used to say his hands were magic."

The light in her eyes made her seem more alive.

"So he always knew what he wanted to do in life?" Dan asked.

She nodded. "When he was seventeen, he got a job as a carpenter with a company who planned to train him. He was good at what he did, a fast learner. He must have been, because the company kept him on, moving him from carpentry to house building."

"He stayed with the same company?" Gary made notes.

"Well, different companies, but they were all part of the same group."

"Which group?"

"DFF."

Gary's pen stilled.

She frowned. "You must've heard of them. I mean, they're everywhere in Boston."

"Yes, I've heard of them." *For all the wrong reasons.*

"Well, James was working for them when he died." She fixed Gary with a hard stare. "Aren't you going to write that down?"

Gary dragged his pen across the page. It wasn't a name he could forget.

"So what happens now?" Linda asked. "Because I don't think there's anything else I can tell you."

"We'll look at the case again, but you have to be prepared." Gary didn't want to raise her hopes. "We might not turn up anything new."

She took a deep breath. "But you will. I know it." She pushed her chair back. "I guess it's up to you now."

She wasn't looking at Gary, but at Dan.

Gary wasn't under any illusions. She was relying on Dan's gift to provide new leads.

He hoped Dan's instincts were correct.

They shook hands, and Gary assured Linda they'd be in contact. Whatever happened. He opened the door to call for an officer to accompany her from the building.

"Thanks for listening," she said as she walked over to where the officer stood patiently.

"That's what we do," Gary told her with a hopefully reassuring smile. He removed a card from his wallet and handed it to her. "This is my phone number. You can reach me at any time." He waited until she was no longer in sight, then came back into the room.

"Why the frown?" Dan asked.

"You're not from Boston, so you've probably never heard of the DFF group. Not a good company to be associated with."

"What's wrong with them?"

Gary leaned against the table. "Let's see. Dodgy deals, bad press, scandal, corruption…. And all the companies are under the control of one family—the DiFanettis."

Dan chuckled. "With a name like that, we could be talking organized crime. You know, like the Mafia."

Gary didn't say a word.

Dan gazed at him openmouthed. "Oh my God. Seriously?"

"Maybe I'm doing them an injustice—they definitely had that kinda rep back in the day. But then again, I'm a firm believer that leopards do *not* change their spots. But enough of them. I think the only way forward with this is to interview James's coworkers again. The ones who were there the day he died."

"Are you expecting different results?"

Gary smiled. "Yes, I am. Because this time, we have you." From the moment Travers had proposed the two of them working on cold cases, Gary had felt an undercurrent of excitement. It hadn't been cut and dried at that point—they'd had to wait for approval from the chief—but something told him the addition of Dan's gifts could make a real difference.

And if thoughts of finding Brad's killer occurred, that was only because Gary was human.

Dan moved closer. "There's something I've been meaning to discuss with you."

"And what's that?"

"When I changed the calendar in the kitchen last week, I noticed something."

"Ah. You noticed I hadn't changed the page. It happens a lot."

Dan chuckled. "Whereas I'm usually good at stuff like that. The fact that I missed it only goes to prove one thing—you addle my brain."

Gary preened. "Damn, I'm good."

"But that isn't what I wanted to talk about. You'd circled a date last month—the twenty-third, I think—and you'd written 'lunch' underneath. But you didn't have a lunch date. I remember because that was the Sunday I moved in with you." He peered at Gary. "Did you have to miss something because of me?"

Answering that question was going to open up a can of worms Gary would rather leave sealed, but he knew they had to talk about it sometime.

"One Sunday every month, I have lunch with my parents."

"So what excuse did you give them for missing that particular Sunday?"

He cleared his throat. "I told them I was helping a friend move house."

Dan's eyebrows shot up. "So I'm a friend? And I'm guessing you didn't tell them whose house I was moving into." Before Gary could respond, Dan held his hand up. "You know what? It's okay. They don't need to know, not if you're not ready to tell them."

"You don't mind?"

Dan rolled his eyes. "What did I say to you right before roll call? You don't have to tell anyone anything, and yes, that includes your parents." His face flushed. "I'm sorry I reacted so badly just now. I wasn't thinking."

"I *will* tell them, okay? About our relationship, the fact you're living with me. But not yet."

"That's okay." Dan smiled. "I'm not going anywhere. Now how about we sit down, go through the original statements, and draw up a list of James's coworkers? Because it's going to take us a few days to locate them all, and we only have until Friday, right?"

"Then what are we waiting for?"

Work was better than thinking about his parents' reaction when he finally shared his news. Gary knew what lay at the root of his reluctance to tell them the truth was not fear of them rejecting his assertion that he was bi. No, what he feared was that they wouldn't react at all, that his words would crash into the wall they'd built around their hearts and fall to the ground to be forgotten.

Chapter Three

Wednesday, July 11, 2018

"I'm beginning to think this is a waste of time," Gary muttered as he locked the car.

Dan was inclined to think the same thing. So far they'd interviewed four of the men who'd been present on the day James Sebring died, and not one of them had anything illuminating to add to their original statement. Gary had suggested not mentioning Dan's psychic abilities for fear they might prove reluctant to shake hands with him, which was sort of the point. Luck was on their side—no one seemed to recognize Dan, which was a miracle after all the media attention that had ensued that summer.

Shaking hands had been a bust too, at least as far as their case was concerned. On the other hand, Dan had gotten a quick glimpse into some of their minds and had retreated just as fast from a couple of them. Nothing dark or dangerous, but very private.

There were times when his gift made him feel like a shabby peeping tom, although he knew that was an exaggeration. On those infrequent occasions, he beat a hasty retreat.

He peered at the wire fence separating them from the construction site. Beyond it, men were hard at work, carrying planks, sawing, talking loudly, laughing, and calling out to others. "So who are we here to see?"

"Luke Weiss," Gary informed him. "He's the last one on the list for today. Still haven't managed to locate Chris Reed. We're seeing Dex Forrest tomorrow. He was the foreman." He walked up to the metal gate and waited.

A guy in a safety hat approached them. "You from the police?"

Gary nodded. "I called yesterday." He flashed his badge.

"Yeah, I took the call. You wanna see Luke, right? He's on a break right now." He pointed to a mobile office. "You can talk to him in there. I'll send him to you."

Gary thanked him, and they opened the door to the mobile building and stepped inside. It obviously served as an office: A desk sat at one end, covered in blueprints and sheaves of paper. Three chairs stood in front of it.

Dan took one of them and sat. "I hope this one knows more than the others."

"You and me both."

A moment later the door opened and a guy entered, wearing dirty jeans, a stained white tee, a denim jacket, and heavy boots. He was maybe in his late thirties, with a crop of straggly dark blond hair that covered his eyes, his jawline rough with stubble. He stood there, his hands thrust into his pockets. "You wanna talk about Al, right? We told the cops everything when it happened. And I can't tell you anything you haven't already heard from the other guys."

News travels fast.

"We're just reviewing the case," Gary told him. He gestured to a chair. "Please, take a seat. All we want is for you to tell us what happened that day."

"Fine, but I got nothing new to tell you." Luke flopped into the chair, hands still out of sight, his legs stretched out in front of him. "Okay. It was a totally normal day. We were on our lunch break. Al had finished eating and had wandered off someplace. I think he'd said something about having to make a call."

"Al? You keep saying Al. Do you mean James?"

Luke arched his eyebrows. "James. *No one* called him James, except maybe Chris Reed. He was always singing that song by Paul Simon, you know, 'You Can Call Me Al'? Well, it kinda stuck. I remember someone—Chris maybe—asked one time if he could call him Betty, you know, like in the song, and James said only if he wanted a new asshole. From then on, he was Al."

Gary made a note. "So Al wasn't with the others."

"No. We were working on a development of ten houses, and what we usually did was use one of the unfinished plots for our breaks. Well, that day we were sitting around plot seven on crates and piles of planks. Then Chris started looking for his newspaper. Figured he'd left it somewhere on plot three, where we'd been working, so he went to look for it."

"How long was he gone?" Gary scribbled on his notepad.

"A few minutes."

"Did he seem okay when he returned?" Dan inquired. The conversation had taken an interesting turn. None of the previous witnesses had mentioned Chris leaving them.

Luke's brow wrinkled. "Funny you should ask that. Chris sat back down with his paper, but… I don't think he was really reading it, you know? He seemed kinda distracted." Then he widened his eyes. "Hey, wait a minute. He didn't stroll back to us after pushing Al off the rafters, if that's what you're thinking. Those two were neighbors, buddies even. And Chris is no killer."

"What happened then?" Gary asked.

"Not long after that, Dex—he was the foreman—told us all to get our asses back to work, so we headed to plot three."

"How much time elapsed between Chris returning and you going back to work, do you think?"

Luke scrunched up his eyebrows. "Ten minutes, maybe? No more than that." He paused. "And then we found Al. Lying on the ground, his neck at a funny angle. Matt checked for a pulse, but you only had to look at Al to know he was dead." Luke swallowed. "He was the last person you'd expect to have an accident."

"Why do you say that?" Dan leaned forward.

Luke huffed. "Because Al was the OSHA guy on site. He was always riding us about taking precautions, staying safe, not taking any risks…."

"OSHA?"

"Occupational Safety and Health Administration," Gary told Dan. He focused his attention on Luke. "What did you do then?"

"We went to find the boss in the mobile office. We thought he was ripping someone a new one when we got closer, but when Dex peered in the window, the boss was on the phone. *Someone* was getting a lot of grief. We waited till he'd finished—Al wasn't going anywhere, was he?—then we knocked and went in. The boss was the one who called the paramedics."

That part of the account had varied little, all the witnesses recounting the same thing.

"We're seeing Dex tomorrow," Gary informed Luke.

"Then that's it? You've interviewed all of us?"

"Not quite. We haven't managed to contact Chris Reed yet." Gary slipped his notepad into his pocket.

Luke's face fell. "Well, if you wanna talk to Chris, you're gonna need to be quick about it."

Gary frowned. "What do you mean?"

"Did none of the others tell you? Chris got diagnosed with lung cancer couple of years ago. Turns out he hasn't got long left. Poor bastard."

"Do you know where we can find him?"

"Sure. He's in some community care place near Newton. Good Shepherd, I think it's called." Luke's face tightened. "I've only visited him the one time, last month. I know these kinda places are good at what they do, but honestly it felt awful seeing him with a load of people waiting to die."

Dan held out his hand. "Thanks for talking to us, Luke."

"You're welcome. Sorry I couldn't help." They shook, and Luke stood.

"What do *you* think happened?" Dan asked him as he headed for the door.

Luke shrugged. "The only thing I can think of is something distracted him and he lost his footing. But that doesn't answer the one question we've all been asking ourselves since it happened."

"And what's that?"

"What was he doing up on the roof rafters in the first place?" He inclined his head toward the door. "Can I go now?"

Gary nodded. "Thanks again for your time. Sorry if our visit robbed you of a break."

Luke waved a hand. "You probably saved me from losing a packet. Some of these guys play cards during their breaks, and my luck's been crap lately." With a final nod to both of them, Luke stepped out into the sunlight and closed the door after him.

Gary gave Dan a speculative glance. "Well?"

"He seems genuine enough, but then they all did. No one's hiding anything—at least nothing to do with our case."

Interest flickered in Gary's eyes. "That sounds intriguing."

"It can sound as intriguing as you like. I'm not about to share what I saw." Then warmth flooded through him when Gary squeezed his hand.

"Which only goes to confirm what I already knew. You're an honorable man, Dan Porter." Gary released Dan's hand, then scraped his fingers through his red hair, pushing it back from his forehead. "What I found interesting about *this* interview was that the only person we haven't talked to is the one person who left the others that day."

"We haven't spoken to the foreman yet, but I agree. No one else mentioned Chris leaving them at any time." He gazed inquiringly at Gary. "You think Chris could've gone back to plot three, pushed James off the rafters, then returned to the others and continued eating his lunch?" Dan folded his arms. "Does that sound likely?"

Gary stroked his beard. "Ten minutes, Luke said, between Chris returning and them discovering the body. No one heard James call out when he fell, did they? They have no idea when he died. For all they knew, he could already have been dead when Chris went back to the plot."

"I'm not saying you're wrong, but…." It was no use. Something didn't add up. "Luke didn't believe Chris to be capable of murder. And he worked construction for *years* with no issues. But I do realize we have to cover every possibility, so maybe we should pay him a visit tomorrow. How far is Newton from the precinct?"

"Less than twenty minutes, given favorable traffic. And if it *was* Chris, then it looks as if fate has caught up with him."

They stepped out of the mobile office and walked toward the metal gate where they'd entered. The guy in the safety hat caught up with them.

"Everything okay?"

Gary nodded. "Thanks for your help."

"No problem." He opened the gate for them, and they headed for Gary's car.

As they drew nearer, Gary's phone rang. He pulled it from his jacket pocket and frowned. "Unknown number." He stabbed at the screen. "Hello?" Gary listened for a moment. "I'm with Dan right now. I'll put you on speaker." He glanced at Dan. "It's Linda Sebring."

"Hi, Linda," Dan greeted her. "Everything okay?"

"You've been interviewing the guys who worked with James, haven't you?"

"Yes. That's standard procedure," Gary told her.

"Well, I've just had a call from a friend of mine, Carla Reed. Her husband worked with James. She told me one of the men you interviewed came to see Chris last night at the hospice, and Chris became very agitated. Carla and Chris are our neighbors. We've known them a long time."

Dan blinked at the coincidence.

"I still don't understand why you're calling," Gary said in a patient tone.

"You need to visit Chris. You need to talk to him about that day."

"Linda, we've spoken with most of the men who were there. None of them have a clue what happened."

"You haven't talked to all of them, have you? You haven't talked to Chris."

"But we *are* going to interview him," Gary assured her. "What makes you think he'll tell us anything different?"

"I'm getting to that. Carla called to tell me that after what she just heard, she doesn't think James's death was an accident either."

Chapter Four

Thursday, July 12, 2018

DAN STARED at the gray bricks of the Good Shepherd Community Care facility. The only splash of color in sight was the stylized swirl of red that represented the letters *G* and *S*. Trees grew around the building, breaking up its outline.

"Want to tell me what's on your mind?"

He gave a start. Gary stood beside the car, gazing intently at him.

"What makes you think I've got something on my mind?"

Gary rolled his shoulder in a slight shrug. "You haven't said a word since we left the precinct." His eyes sparkled. "You didn't even notice when I told you how good you looked today."

Despite his churning stomach, Dan managed a wry smile. "I look good, do I?"

"And now you're just fishing. Not to mention avoiding the question." Gary smiled back. "By the way, you always look good."

The compliment skimmed over the top of Dan's head.

It's no use. I have to tell him.

"Look… before we go in there…."

Gary froze. "Something's wrong."

"Not exactly, but…." He took a deep breath. "I'm not comfortable using my gift where Chris Reed is concerned." He swallowed. "We know he's dying. Using my gift in these circumstances feels—at least it does to me—as though it would be a gross invasion of privacy. Put it this way. I wouldn't want someone inside *my* head if the roles were reversed." He held his hands up. "I know by doing this I'm cutting off an avenue of investigation, but taking a step back is the more ethical thing to do."

Gary's gaze held nothing but compassion. "Then that's what you should do."

"You're okay with that?" Except part of him had known Gary would support him, and it had nothing to do with the fact that they were in a— fledgling—relationship.

It had everything to do with the kind of man Gary was.

"Of course. So before we get in there…. You're my coworker, okay? Ask whatever you like."

"Thank you." The tension that had crept across Dan's shoulders on the way there had already begun to dissipate. He followed Gary to the entrance and stood back while Gary explained their visit. He'd informed the facility the previous evening as soon as Linda Sebring had finished her call.

The nurse—Rebecca, according to her name tag—checked her monitor. "Okay, what you both need to know is, Mr. Reed is on BiPAP. This is an assistive device that requires a mask, and it allows him to stay awake and speak. Right now he's exhausted and in pain, but he's insisting we hold off on his medication until he's spoken with you."

"But why?" Gary asked.

"It makes him sleep, too foggy to think straight. What I *will* tell you is this. Someone in his condition has to be damned determined to use whatever strength he has to participate in what sounds as if it's going to be an emotionally and physically taxing conversation." She looked Gary in the eye. "Whatever he has to tell you must be really important." Rebecca pointed ahead of them. "Keep going that way. Mr. Reed's room is right before you reach the garden. His wife will meet you."

The hallways were quiet but for the music playing in the background, low and unobtrusive. Dan tried not to glimpse through open doorways, conscious of his heightened senses. He was aware of so many differing emotions assaulting him from all sides, some sharp enough to bring tears to his eyes. There was acceptance, resignation, but underlying it was a strong current of trepidation.

None of us knows what lies beyond.

Finally they reached Chris Reed's room, to be greeted by his wife, Carla. Dan took her hand without thinking, and was ill-prepared for the jolt the contact gave to his senses. He couldn't speak, his throat tight, his stomach clenched.

Life, why do you have to be such a fucking bitch *sometimes?*

Carla regarded them, her expression neutral. "I guess Linda called you, right?" She inclined her head toward the door. "He knows you're coming. I told him last night. I don't think he slept much, and he's been agitated all morning." She hesitated. "I didn't know, okay? I didn't know *any* of this. He never said a word. And if I hadn't listened when his buddy came over, I'd *still* be in the dark. All I know is he has to tell someone before… before it kills him." She gave a sharp swallow. "I'm playing dumb. All he told me was he had to speak to the police. Didn't say why. And when I called Linda, she didn't hesitate. She said you were the ones he needed to see."

Before either of them could get a word out, she pushed the door open and led them into the pale lemon room, dominated by a single bed with monitors on both sides, the air filled with the whisper of the BiPAP machine.

Chris Reed was ashen, his breathing harsh behind the mask that covered his nose and mouth. He tried to sit up in bed, but Carla stopped him. She grabbed the button that lay on his bed and pushed it, raising the pillow end into the air.

"Mr. Reed, I'm Detective Gary Mitchell, and this is Dan Porter. We're here because—"

Chris waved his hand. "I know that part." He glanced at Carla. "Honey… can you…?"

She leaned over and kissed his forehead. "I need coffee anyway." With a nod to Gary, she walked out of the room and closed the door behind her.

Chris sagged into the pillows. "I don't… want her involved. She doesn't need… to know." He inhaled deeply. "She's got enough… on her plate without… me adding to it."

That part Dan understood all too well.

"You and James Sebring were good friends, I understand." Gary's notebook and pen had come out.

Chris nodded. "We'd known each other… for years. He could be… a real pain in the ass… sometimes, especially when… it came to OSHA stuff…. I think he slept… with the regulation folder… under his pillow." He gave a half smile, but then his face fell. "All you guys need… to know about his death was… it wasn't an accident."

"How do you know that? Did you see something that day when you—"

Another wave of his hand. "My story. Need to… tell it my way… all right?"

Gary nodded.

Chris clutched his mask, sucking air into his lungs. At last he spoke. "About a month before… James died, I got my diagnosis. I told him the next day. Just him. I was still kinda numb." A pause. "Anyhow.... Two weeks later... he came to work... and he was a mess."

"You were still working?" Dan inquired.

"Yeah. Bills weren't gonna... pay themselves, right?"

"Why was James a mess?" Gary asked in a low voice.

Pain flickered across Chris's face. "Linda got diagnosed. They found a... shadow on her lung. A woman who never... smoked her whole life."

Gary's breathing hitched. "She didn't mention that."

"We didn't know at the time... if it was terminal or not." He sucked in more air. "I've... been around stuff, okay? You come into contact... with all sorts of shit... in my trade... I was a smoker too... but *Linda*?"

"It must have hit him very hard," Dan murmured. "First you, then his wife."

Chris gave a nod. "The four of us... were neighbors. And for two weeks after... man, he was on a... downward slide. He was always such... a positive guy, but... this rocked him. And then in June... he came to see me." Another hard-won breath. "I can still see him... sitting at my kitchen table... telling me...." He met Dan's gaze. "He said... he knew why I was sick... why Linda was sick... and whose fault it was."

Friday, June 3, 2016

CHRIS STARED at James. "The *boss*? What does he have to do with me having lung cancer? Or Linda, for that matter?"

James took a long drink from his cup of coffee. "You know about radon, right?"

"Radon?" Chris froze. "Wait, are you saying—"

"I had tests done, okay?" James blurted. "Independent air-quality tests. On *both* our houses."

Chris blinked. "You mean the houses we helped build? Without a word to me?"

"I had them test for radon." James's face contorted. "I don't have to tell you what the results were, do I?"

"But why test at all? What made you do it?"

"It was a hunch. And it paid off. So now...." James set his jaw. "I'm gonna put the bite on the boss."

Chris's stomach roiled. "You're not making sense. I know you're upset about Linda—hell, I would be too—and you're looking for someone to blame, but…."

James leaned forward. "Do you remember when the legislation came in? Last year, right? Radon barriers to be fitted to all new builds."

"But our houses were built *before* that came in."

James nodded. "I did a little snooping around some of the latest building projects. You know, the stuff we're working on right now. Wanna know what I discovered?"

"Just *tell* me, okay?" Chris's guts were in turmoil.

"He hasn't fitted radon barriers. In *any* of the new houses. So this is what I'm gonna do. Those barriers can be retrofitted for all builds now. I'm gonna insist he retrofits our houses and that he helps us financially—well, helps *you*. Because now you've gotta think about Carla, dude. You know… when you're… not around anymore."

Thursday, July 12, 2018

"THAT SOUNDS a lot like blackmail," Dan observed. "'Fit the barriers, pay up, or word gets out.'"

"He wasn't doing it… for himself—he was doing it for me. He wanted to make… mine and Carla's life comfortable." He shivered. "He was that kinda guy. And it worked."

"Did the boss do as he was asked?" Gary inquired.

"Yeah, he did. I got a check in the mail… about a week after James died."

Gary lowered his pen. "So what you're saying is your boss did everything James asked of him? That sounds like the actions of an honorable man. Okay, maybe he wouldn't have done it if James hadn't gone to him. But I still don't understand why—"

Chris started coughing, and the sound made Dan's heart ache for him. "Can we get you anything? A nurse?"

Chris waved his hand agitatedly, and they waited until he'd stopped coughing. He took a moment to draw air into his lungs.

"Listen to me. There is no doubt… in my mind… he threw James off those rafters."

Chapter Five

Gary stared at Chris. "Surely if that were true, you'd have said something at the time. But there's nothing like this in your statement to the police."

"I had my reasons," Chris wheezed.

"What reason could there be that warrants covering up what you believe to be murder?"

Chris studied him for a moment. "I was afraid... I'd end up like James."

"You really thought your boss was a murderer?" Dan appeared incredulous.

Chris's chest heaved. "Do you live in... Boston, Mr. Porter?" Dan shook his head, and Chris gave a single nod. "Because if you did... you'd know the name Gianni DiFanetti... unless you lived under a rock. I was scared... for my job, my wife...."

"But how do you know he did it?" Gary demanded. "Did you *see* him push James off that roof?"

"No, but... I heard their conversation."

Gary shook his head. "All your coworkers stated the boss was in his on-site office on the phone when they went to get him after discovering James had fallen. Nowhere near the building plot where James was found."

Dan's voice was gentle. "Tell us what you heard."

Friday June 24, 2016

Chris went through the open space that would soon be someone's front door and scanned the ground for his newspaper. He was certain he'd last seen it around there. A rectangular hole in the joists above his head marked where the staircase would be, a ladder propped against one of them. Some of the second floor had already been laid, cutting off his view of the roof rafters, making the interior a little darker.

His head was still reeling. *They can cure it, right?* He'd read so much stuff online in the last month about lung cancer, and most of it made him feel sick. And as for James's revelations…. They'd only spoken of it once since that day. James had put together all the things he wanted to say to the boss.

Chris thought James was crazy. Demanding money from Gianni DiFanetti was a surefire way to end up in Boston Harbor wearing concrete boots. He'd begged James to reconsider, but James had been adamant.

Then he realized he could hear the murmur of voices above him, as though the speakers were up on the rafters. Chris went to the foot of the ladder and listened. He couldn't see anyone, but he recognized the speakers. He froze.

"You're gonna do this, you hear?"

Aw fuck, James.

Chris would know the boss's snort anywhere. "Ya think? You can't make me."

He listened intently, but James's voice dropped to a mumble, and he couldn't catch the words. Whatever he'd said had evidently struck a nerve. The boss sounded pissed.

No, James, don't piss him off. You know *who you're dealing with, right?*

James mumbled again, and then silence fell, a quiet that chilled Chris to the bone. Then the boss spoke, delivering his words in a flat tone loaded with menace.

"You know fuck all about that fucking painter freak."

Thursday, July 12, 2018

"WHAT DID that mean?" Gary asked. The rasp in Chris's voice, the whisper of the BiPAP machine; all of it sent a shiver through him.

"No idea. Made no sense to me." Chris's eyes were full of pain. "I… I'm not a brave man…. I didn't want the boss… to know I was there." He breathed deeply. "So yeah, I picked up my paper… and scurried out of there… like a frightened rat. I hurried back… to the others."

"And said nothing," Dan observed.

"Yeah. I tried to act normal. I read my paper… waiting for… James to join us… so I could… find out the rest… only… he never came back.

Then Dex started yelling… and we packed up… all our stuff… and went back to plot three." He swallowed.

"Where you found James on the ground, dead," Gary concluded.

Chris nodded. "Neck broken. And no sign of the boss." He shivered. "I've thought a lot… about this. I figure I was gone… maybe ten minutes. Plenty of time for… the boss to push him, climb down… and head back to his office."

"You don't think James would've cried out if that were true?"

"Not if… the boss knocked him… out first with a… piece of wood… then shoved him off."

"Was DiFanetti strong enough to do that?"

Chris nodded. "Big guy. Then when we got to… his office, he was… on the phone. Said he'd been… talking for a half hour."

Dan glanced at Gary. "Wouldn't the police have checked up on that? Phone records or something?"

"Why would they?" Gary said. "As far as they were concerned, James was just a carpenter who'd fallen off a roof. It was an accidental death, substantiated by witness statements."

Dan stroked his smooth jaw. "Something I have to ask. This was two years ago. Why tell us now?"

Chris's face darkened, and he inclined his head toward the door. "Because Carla has lung cancer too."

Gary's breathing caught. "Oh, I'm so sorry."

"So that's both of us dying. We don't have kids. No way the guy can… hurt us anymore." He clutched the sheet tightly. "I've felt so guilty. If I'd made a noise… said something… the boss would've known he… had an audience… and maybe James would still… be alive. I had to… set the record straight… before… before it's too late."

Gary rose, and Dan joined him. "Thank you, Mr. Reed."

Chris reached out and grabbed Gary's hand. "Wait. One more thing." They stilled, and he released Gary. "James told me what… he was going to say… to the boss."

"You mentioned that," Gary told him.

He nodded. "But that stuff about a painter? James had to have… said something about it… to get that reaction. Only…." He locked gazes with Gary. "That wasn't in the script."

The door opened, and Carla came back into the room, carrying a cup. "I think my husband has talked for long enough, don't you?"

"We're done now," Gary informed her.

"I had to… tell someone, honey."

Her face tightened. "I know. And now that you have, maybe you'll sleep a little easier. Let the police deal with it."

They thanked the couple, then left the room, walking slowly toward the exit, Gary going over Chris's words in his head.

"I knew about his wife's cancer," Dan said quietly. "But I couldn't say anything, not without giving the game away." He paused. "It doesn't add up, does it?"

"No, it doesn't," Gary admitted. "So he was going to confront his boss. But *radon levels*? That's not enough to get him killed. If Chris is right—and I see no reason to doubt him—and those barriers *can* be retrofitted for all builds after 2016, then what was the problem?" He pursed his lips. "No, it feels wrong. There had to be something else."

"I agree. Maybe the key to all this is 'that fucking painter freak.'"

Gary had a feeling he might be right. "And who the hell knows what *that* meant?"

As they neared the car, Gary got his phone out and dialed. "Mrs. Sebring? Detective Mitchell here. Just to inform you we've been to see Chris Reed."

"And? What did you find out?"

"He's given us new information that I can't discuss right now. But we *will* look into it."

The problem was Gary had no idea where to start.

"There *is* one thing I'd like to know. Mr. Reed talked about *your* diagnosis."

A sigh filled his ear. "Yeah. I'm receiving treatment. They removed a third of my lung, and so far I'm doing okay. Fingers crossed, right? Thank God the medical bills get covered. I was sure my insurance wouldn't stretch that far, but James's old boss told me he'd take care of it. He's been awesome."

You wouldn't be saying that if you'd been in that room with us just now.

"I didn't say so before, but…. Something was going on with James in the weeks before he died. He wasn't himself. It was like there was something eating away at him, and he wouldn't tell me what it was."

"Mrs. Sebring, when we have more definite news, we'll share it, okay?" Gary assured her. "In the meantime, look after yourself."

"Did I do the right thing, coming to you? I-I couldn't let it go."

James would've been proud of her.

Gary did his best to reassure her, then said goodbye and hung up. He stood next to the car, fingering his keys in his pocket.

"What's wrong?"

"I didn't want to say it, but I don't think this will go anywhere." No sooner had he said this than his phone buzzed, and he glanced at the screen. He sighed.

"Travers wants to see us."

DAN WALKED into their office and removed his jacket, then hung it over the back of a chair. "I'll make us some coffee." He picked up the pot and went to the door, almost colliding with Travers on his way in. Dan replaced the pot.

Coffee would have to wait.

Travers closed the door behind him. "Well? Any luck? Or was it a giant fishing expedition?"

Dan listened as Gary recounted what they'd discovered. When he revealed the name of James's boss, Travers whistled.

"Wow. Much as I would *love* for Gianni DiFanetti to turn out to be a killer, I don't think there's enough evidence to pursue this."

"I'm inclined to agree," Gary remarked. "Which makes me feel sorry for James's wife."

Dan had been intrigued since Gary's first mention of the DiFanetti family. "Who is he?"

Travers sat, leaning on the arm of the chair. "He *says* he's a businessman, but everyone knows he's up to his armpits in some shady stuff. His dad, Bruno, is the head of the family. Haven't heard much about him, but I suspect the apple doesn't fall too far from the tree."

"Are we talking organized crime?" Dan had thought stuff like that had died out years ago.

"In the forties and fifties, the DiFanettis were into a whole load of shit—gambling, prostitution, narcotics, smuggling, you name it. Still up to no good in the sixties. Nowadays, though?" Travers rolled his eyes. "They've got a PR campaign painting them as pillars of the community, but you know what? I'd bet if you dug down deep enough, you'd still come up with the same shit." He got up, went to the desk, and peered at the folders Gary had placed there. "You want my advice? You've gone as far as you can with this. Leave it alone, and tomorrow get started on a cold case. In fact if I might make a suggestion…." He tapped one of the folders with a long finger. "Start with a case from 2006. The body in the tunnel." His eyes glittered. "That should test your powers, Mr. Porter."

Dan blinked. "A body in a tunnel?"

"Part of the Fort Point Channel Tunnel collapsed in July 2006, killing a motorist and injuring her partner," Gary told him. "City got sued—successfully—for millions. But what made it weird was the skeleton that turned up in the debris, wrapped in plastic, with no head. I was there."

Travers widened his eyes. "Really?"

Gary nodded. "I was about to undergo more training to become a detective. But yeah, I was the one who showed Del Maddox the body."

Something was tugging at Dan's senses. "Lieutenant? Why do you think we should start with that case?"

Travers looked him in the eye. "Because I don't believe in coincidence."

CHAPTER SIX

As soon as Travers had gone and the door closed, Dan couldn't rein in his curiosity a moment longer.

"What did he mean about coincidence?"

Gary sat at the desk and opened the folder. "The company involved in the construction of the tunnel, from 1991 to 1994, was part of the DFF group, which was run by Bruno DiFanetti."

Dan stared at him. "This family keeps cropping up, doesn't it? What caused the tunnel collapse?"

Gary leaned back, the folder open in his lap. "There was an inquiry, of course. The collapse was eventually found to be the result of the epoxy used in the construction of the hanging ceiling system. The epoxy wasn't up to standard, so the anchors embedded in the tunnel's roof slab began to creep. Bolts were too short. Basically, it was a chain reaction that ended up with twenty-six tons of concrete on the roadway below." His eyes gleamed. "And the company in charge of the tunnel construction, the one that contracted the suppliers of the epoxy, was run by… Gianni DiFanetti."

Travers had certainly nailed it.

"Then how come that wasn't the end of the company?"

Gary barked out a laugh. "Maybe they had friends in high places. Not that they came away without a blemish. They were fined, and they had to pay out millions to the family of the deceased. Not long after that, Gianni took over the running of the housing construction company." He bit his lip. "Guess his dad thought he needed a change of career."

"What about the mystery body? Could it be identified?"

"Yes—again, eventually. And this is where things got interesting. The body was that of a male, but it was found with the remains of silicone breast implants. Given the dates of construction, a search was made for missing persons from that time. Dental records were out, obviously."

"You think that's why the head was removed? To prevent identification?"

"Whoever stowed that body in the space above the ceiling tiles clearly hoped it would never be discovered, but just in case? Yeah. In the end identification came down to a steel pin in the leg, which led us to only one person—Cheryl Somers, last seen late August 1992."

Dan blinked. "Cheryl? Was she trans?"

"Yes. Born Benjamin Raskin, 1964. She'd been living as Cheryl since the age of twenty-one, in 1985. According to her medical records, the only surgeries she underwent were the insertion of that steel pin in her leg and the breast implants."

"Who reported her missing?"

Gary peered at the notes. "Her father, Pete Raskin, and also…." He widened his eyes. "Wow. Talk about friends in high places. Senator William Cain. Apparently she had a connection with the Cain family." He tapped on the keyboard for a moment.

"What are you doing?"

"Something I read in the notes made me curious. I just want to see…." Gary stared at the monitor. "Oh my."

"What is it?"

"She was an artist." He crooked his finger. "Come take a look at this. Her work is stunning."

Dan walked around the desk and peered at the monitor. Gary scrolled, revealing amazing portraiture. There were individuals, couples, a family group, but all imbued with such vitality that they took Dan's breath away.

"I see what you mean. So much talent." He stiffened.

"What just occurred to you?"

Dan gazed at the screen. "It's just a thought, but… might someone who's worked in construction refer to a trans artist as 'that fucking painter freak'?"

Gary's mouth fell open. "It's a very *good* thought."

"Can I have a copy of the notes?"

"Of course." Gary got up and went over to the printer-copier to feed the sheets under its lid.

"Travers is right. This is a great case to start with."

Gary turned his head toward him and smiled. "It's got your interest, that's for sure." The copier spat out the sheets, Gary tapped them into a neat pile, then handed them to Dan.

He scanned the top copy. "How far back do these go? Does she turn up in any police records before her death?"

Gary shuffled through the sheets. "Yes, in 1989. She was assaulted while on a date. Apparently the guy, one Aiden Reynolds, took exception to her being trans." Gary glanced at the sheet. "He was twenty-seven. Worked in construction."

Dan grinned. "Oh really? I suppose it's too much to hope he worked for the DFF group. On a certain tunnel?"

"Yeah, wouldn't *that* be fortunate?" Gary chuckled. "Don't get carried away looking for more coincidences, okay?" He went back to the notes. "It says here Cheryl didn't want to press charges but was persuaded to do so by Senator Cain. Except this was a couple of years before he became a senator."

Dan's mind suddenly shifted into gear. "Maybe that's how she died. Another date, but one that went wrong? Or maybe Aiden Reynolds decided he hadn't gone far enough and came back to finish the job."

Gary gazed at him with wide eyes. "Three years later? I think that might be a bit of a stretch."

Dan shrugged. "He might be the type who bears a grudge. I still think we should interview him. In fact we need to interview everyone we can find who was connected to her. People who knew her from college, friends. And here's another idea." Dan cocked his head to one side. "Does Benjamin Raskin appear in police records?"

"Let's take a look." Gary tapped on the keyboard, then stared at the monitor. "Yes, in 1983. There was a traffic accident involving two vehicles. Raskin was driving one of them. The other driver, Connor Brightmore, was killed at the scene. Raskin received injuries to his right leg and was in bad shape, but he pulled through. According to all the witnesses, Brightmore was at fault." He frowned. "Brightmore. I recognize that name. An old Boston family, I think. I recall seeing that name in the local news."

"Is that all we have so far?" Gary nodded, and Dan straightened the sheaf of notes. "Then maybe our first port of call is Cheryl's father."

"As soon as we've located him, yes." Gary smiled. "You're enjoying this, aren't you?"

"I wasn't sure what to expect, but this case has grabbed my interest."

"Just don't get your hopes up. There will be much more mundane cases to solve, I'm sure."

As far as Dan was concerned, Travers's suggestion had been perfect, and he couldn't wait to get started. His thoughts went back to their visit to the hospice. "You know what would be wonderful? If Travers is right, and it turns out this case and the death of James Sebring *are* linked. And I don't mean wonderful because it would sew everything up in a neat little bow. I was thinking of Linda Sebring."

"I know what you mean, but I think you might be asking a little too much. Let's concentrate on locating anyone who knew Cheryl Somers and see where that leads us."

"Starting tomorrow." Dan placed the notes on the desk. "But for tonight? No more work talk. You're all mine."

Gary's eyes sparkled. "I like the sound of that."

DAN STACKED the dishes and carried them into the kitchen. "Coffee?" he called out to Gary in the living room.

"Please."

He set up the coffeepot, then loaded the dishwasher.

"Dinner was delicious, by the way." Gary stood in the doorway, leaning against the frame.

Dan smiled. "Anyone can cook pasta."

Gary chuckled. "You wouldn't say that if you'd been on the receiving end of some of Brad's first attempts at cooking."

Dan had a feeling the mention of Brad wasn't altogether coincidental.

He closed the dishwasher and turned to lean against the sink. "I've been meaning to talk about him. I'm sorry I haven't been able to tell you much, except for the emotions connected to his sweater."

Gary swallowed. "I think you told me plenty, don't you?"

"I only told you he'd known the person who killed him. And I *so* wanted to tell you more than that. Perhaps…." He clammed up. He didn't want to push.

"Perhaps what?"

"It might help if I could touch things that had belonged to him." Except Dan knew what that would entail, how much turmoil that would subject Gary to.

I don't want to put him through the wringer.

Gary became still, and Dan knew he'd pushed him too far. "That would mean a visit to my parents, and I don't think I'm ready for that yet."

"I can wait," Dan assured him before adding, "as long as you can."

Gary walked over to the coffeepot and grabbed two cups from the cabinet above it. "Had any visions lately?"

Dan managed a smile, despite his quaking heart. "What you really want to know is do I still get the vision of you and me making love?"

"Do you?"

Dan shook his head. "Not for a while now. I guess it served its purpose. It prepared me to meet you, opened my eyes to show me who you were. And as for other visions… not as such, no. But have you ever woken up with something in your head, and it won't leave you?"

Gary huffed. "Sure. Usually song lyrics."

Dan shook his head. "This is a movie. It's one I'm familiar with, but I have no idea why I keep thinking of it."

"So what's the movie?"

"*Cape Fear.*"

Gary frowned. "Not sure if I've ever seen it."

Dan shivered. "It's a really creepy cat-and-mouse kinda movie. You know, one of those where you're sure the bad guy has bought the farm, but then he turns up alive again and twice as dangerous as before."

"And you keep dreaming about it?"

"Yeah. Not scenes from it. It's more like… seeing it on the cover of a DVD or a movie poster." Another shiver trickled through him. "I think I need that coffee."

Gary filled the cups, then handed one to him. "Can I ask…? Why do I keep finding Brad's sweater out of its drawer?"

Dan sighed. "Because now and again I sit with it, trying to see if I can pick up anything else other than the knowledge that Brad knew his killer."

"And can you?"

Lord, the hope in Gary's eyes….

"You know better than to ask that. I would never hide anything from you. Not now." He understood the question. They were still feeling their way around each other, learning the ground rules. Gary was coming to terms with the fact that he wasn't straight, but bisexual.

Dan was coming to terms with the idea that some higher power had determined he and Gary were meant to be together, something which he found both exhilarating and scary as fuck in equal measure.

"You're right. I do know that." Then Gary took him by the hand, and a surge of desire crashed over him, leaving him aroused and trembling, in no doubt as to what was coming next.

"Yes." The word left his lips in a breathless whisper.

Gary stilled. "Yes what?"

Dan closed the gap between them until he could feel the warmth radiating from Gary's body, the need rolling off him in waves. "I want you too. Now. Inside me."

All thoughts of skeletons, cancer, corruption, and tunnel collapses were swept away as Gary led him to their bed. Work would still be there in the morning.

The night belonged to them.

Chapter Seven

Friday, July 13, 2018

"This is a retirement home?"

Gary chuckled. "I know, right?" Springhouse Senior Living Community was nothing like he'd expected. As they followed the driveway that led to reception, all he could see were trees, flowers, and elegant white buildings.

"It must cost a fortune to live here," Dan commented.

Gary approached the circular area at the end of the driveway and switched off the engine. It hadn't taken long to track down Pete Raskin the previous evening, and Gary had called ahead to make sure they'd be okay to visit. Pete had been a resident of the community since his retirement and was now seventy-six.

They entered the building, and Gary was struck by how light and airy the interior was. A couple of residents smiled as they approached the reception desk, which was located near the entrance, and a young woman greeted them with a warm smile. When they told her they were looking for Mr. Raskin, her smile widened.

"You won't find him indoors on a glorious day like this. This property is situated on thirteen acres, and Pete helps take care of the gardens." Her eyes twinkled. "We've even tried to pay him for his services, but he won't hear of it." She pointed toward the door they'd used. "Go back that way, turn left, and follow the signs to the fountain. He won't be far away."

They thanked her and exited the building. Gary couldn't get over the lushness of the lawns surrounding the accommodation. A path led them to a low stone wall circling a pond where water trickled down over tall rocks, and all around was the delicious fragrance of summer flowers heavy with perfume.

"This is a beautiful place," Dan murmured.

"It is, isn't it?" An elderly man knelt on a thick mat in front of a flower bed, his hands full of weeds. He tossed them into a dark blue sack and struggled to his feet, wiping his hands on the apron he wore about his waist. His hair was all but gone, but his eyes were still bright, a piercing blue that gave his face a youthful appearance.

"Mr. Raskin?"

He nodded. "You here to see me? They said I was to expect visitors. I don't get many of 'em. And call me Pete."

"I'm Detective Gary Mitchell from Boston PD, and this is Dan Porter. We're—"

"You're here because of Cheryl, aren't you?" Before they could confirm it, tears spilled onto his wrinkled cheeks. He reached into his deep pocket and removed a handkerchief, then dabbed his eyes, sniffing. "Sorry about that. Don't know what came over me."

Gary pointed to the rustic bench beside the fountain. "Let's sit, and we can talk."

Pete sat, his breathing still hitching now and then. "You *are* here about Cheryl, aren't you?" He paused, staring at Dan, and his eyes widened. "I know your face. You're that psychic who helped the police catch that serial killer last month. Are you working with them to find out what happened to Cheryl?"

Dan smiled. "Yes. I'm part of Boston PD's cold cases department now. And—"

"Thank you, thank you, both of you." Fresh tears streaked Pete's face. "I always dreamed one day I'd learn the truth, but to be honest I'd given up hope. So do you know who killed her?"

Gary sighed. "Not yet. We've only just begun to look at the case, and you're the first person we're talking to. Do you think you could answer some questions?" He joined Pete on the bench, and Dan perched on the low fountain wall.

Pete squared his bony shoulders. "If it helps you find out how she died, I'll answer as many questions as you like."

Gary took out his notepad. "When was the last time you saw her?"

Pete didn't hesitate. "August twenty-eighth, 1992. Back then I was the head gardener for Senator Cain, at the Cain residence in Lenox. Cheryl lived there with me, in the cottage provided by the family. Well, she did until 1987. After that, she got a place in Boston, where she worked."

"How long did you work there?" Dan asked.

Pete scratched his head. "I started there in 1958, when I was sixteen. The senator was only four years old then." He smiled. "He used to run after me, demanding that I play with him. Then I met Rachel—my wife—and we married in sixty-one. Cheryl came along in sixty-four." He glanced at them. "You wanna know why she will always be Cheryl for me?" His Adam's apple bobbed. "It's a sort of… penance. Because I didn't get it, not at the time, when she said she'd always felt like a woman in a man's body. I-I wasn't the most tolerant of men back then. But you grow older, wiser. And when I saw how much happier she was as Cheryl, well, I had to accept her decision. Her mom, on the other hand… it drove a wedge between them."

"Where is your wife?" Dan's voice was soft.

"She died four years ago. Heart attack." Another hard swallow. "She gave up hope of ever finding out what happened."

"Where did you last see Cheryl?" Gary asked.

"At the senator's house in Lenox. She turned up that morning to see me." He smiled. "She'd gotten into a habit of visiting every Friday during the summer months. I think it was because Friday was her regular day off. She came early and had breakfast with me. Then I went to work."

"Did you see her after that?"

"No, sir. I finished work at noon, and then the wife and I went to visit my mother-in-law. We stayed there until Sunday night."

"Do you know of anyone who saw her after August twenty-eighth?"

Pete shook his head. "No, not a soul. And you'd better believe we asked everyone. When the police contacted me in 2006 to say they'd found a body that might be Cheryl, I prayed they'd got it wrong, but that steel pin was the clincher. She had an accident when she was nineteen, you see. It made a mess of her leg, but they fixed her up."

"The car accident?" Dan proffered.

"You know about that?" When Dan nodded, Pete gave them a keen glance. "And what about all the stuff that came after? The death threats? The letters?"

Gary stilled. "What?"

Pete gave a slow nod. "For two years. Anonymous letters, phone calls, all saying the same thing—that she was to blame. I told her to go to the police about them, but she never did. I think the senator told her the same thing. And then they stopped."

"Do you have any idea why?" Gary asked.

He swallowed hard. "Yeah, I do. Because that was when Ben Raskin disappeared off the face of the earth and Cheryl Somers was born. She changed her name, her hair, her clothes, and suddenly I had a daughter instead of a son." He flushed. "I'm not proud of how I reacted at the time. I only hope I made it up to her in the years leading up to her disappearance."

"We saw her work. Her portraits." Dan's face glowed. "Such a talented artist."

Pete gave a wry chuckle. "I've got no idea where she got it from. Her mom and me, we were about as artistic as a road digger. Hard to believe the portraits were a sideline. I think she made more money from them than from her job."

"What did she do?" Dan asked.

"She was an art conservationist at a museum, but painting became her life. Her bedroom at home wasn't that big, and most of it was taken up with her painting gear. She said the light was good in there. And sometimes she'd go to museums and sit in front of famous paintings. She'd study them, copy them…."

"Did she study art at college?" Gary inquired.

"Yeah, but she'd never have done that without the senator. He paid for her tuition."

"That was very generous of him," Dan remarked.

"He wanted to help, and *we* couldn't afford it." A faraway look came into his eyes. "Cheryl and him, they used to talk about art all the time, even when she was a kid. He'd take her to the house and show her all those paintings his family had collected for generations. Maybe that was what got her started."

"So until her body showed up, she was a missing person?"

Pete gave another nod. "When she first went missing, the senator… I think he put a bit of pressure on the police department to give her case higher priority. They told him they were doing everything possible to find her. So then he hired private detectives, offered a reward. But there was no sign of her." He studied his clasped hands. "I tried to hold on to the tiniest hope that she was alive, but I think I knew deep down. Because if she'd been alive, she would've contacted me. And as more years went by, I accepted she was dead. Then that tunnel collapsed…."

Gary held his pen poised. "We're going to put together a list of everyone who knew her. Can you think of anyone we should definitely speak to?"

"First name that comes to mind is Lori. Can't remember her surname. She worked with Cheryl, and she was something to do with art. Maybe she was an art conservationist too. Then there was Rayne… she was a friend from college."

"We read the report on the assault in 1989. Aiden Reynolds."

Pete scowled. "That lowlife. But I suppose you need to talk to him too. If I think of anyone else, I'll let you know."

Gary removed a card from his wallet. "Here's my number."

Pete took it, thanking him. "Will you come back and let me know if you find anything?"

"Of course," Dan assured him. He glanced at their surroundings. "You live in a beautiful place."

Pete's face glowed. "And that's only because of the senator. If it wasn't for him, I'd…." He swallowed, then straightened. "Seeing as you're investigating, you might want to look into those anonymous letters. Maybe someone found her after all. Someone from that guy's family."

Gary had had the same idea. "Did she keep any of them?"

"No, not one. I suppose that means there's no evidence. Can't really investigate if you've got nothing to go on." He glanced at Dan. "Although I suppose *you* might find other evidence no one has even considered."

Dan smiled. "That's the plan."

Pete stood, walked over to Dan, and grasped his hands. "Then God bless you for being part of this."

Gary's chest tightened at the sight of tears sparkling in Dan's eyes, and he knew it was a reaction to whatever he'd felt during their contact. Gary might not have Dan's gift, but he felt Pete's grief as deeply as he felt his own. They had both lost someone precious.

No, *lost* was the wrong word. They'd both been robbed of someone they loved.

We're going to find out what happened to her. We'll do whatever it takes.

Chapter Eight

As soon as they got back to their office, Gary was on his keyboard, tapping away.

"I'll make coffee," Dan suggested, amused by Gary's noncommittal murmured reply. On the way to the precinct, the conversation with Pete Raskin played over and over in Dan's head. He hadn't given them much more to go on, and Dan was certain detectives would have interviewed Cheryl's friends once the identity of the body had been revealed. But that part about anonymous letters and death threats….

There has to be something *we can find out about those.* Connor Brightmore's family was an obvious start.

By the time he returned to the office with a pot full of water, Gary was leaning back in his chair and smiling.

Progress.

"What have you discovered?" Dan set up the machine and spooned coffee into the filter.

"I've been running checks on Aiden Reynolds, the guy who assaulted Cheryl while on a date." He peered at the notes he'd made. "Okay. He's got a background in civil engineering. Worked mostly in construction: roads, bridges, tunnels. What's interesting is who employed him at the time of his arrest."

Dan's skin prickled. "The DFF group, right? What did I tell you?" He grinned. "What was that you were saying about not getting carried away looking for more coincidences?"

"When you've finished patting yourself on the back…. Just because Reynolds worked for the same company who constructed the tunnel, that doesn't mean he was working on it when she disappeared." He held up his hand. "But I'll check his tax records too. You never know, right?" Gary resumed reading his notes. "He's got a history of arrests for violence. He also spent time in prison. Repeat offender."

"So how do we find him? Where's he working? If he does work."

"He's only fifty-seven, so let's assume he's got a job. Something else we can find out from his tax records. Leave it with me. And in the meantime, there's something I'd like you to do."

"Pour you a coffee? Give you a head rub, shoulder massage...." Dan bit his lip. "Unless you've got something else you'd like massaged."

Maybe it was the fact that Dan hadn't been intimate with anyone for a long time, but something in Gary brought out the wicked streak in him.

Dan was starting to like it.

"Down, boy. What I want *you* to do is search social media—Facebook, Instagram, Twitter—and see if Reynolds is out there, and if so, what he's saying."

Dan sat at the other desk, the coffee forgotten. It didn't take him long to come up with a couple of people who could possibly be their man, and when he narrowed it down to one, he shivered.

"I don't like this guy," he muttered.

"Is that your intuition talking, or what you see on the screen?"

"A bit of both, I suspect. Oh yes, we need to speak with Mr. Reynolds."

"I've found his current place of work." Gary glanced at the monitor. "He's the building supervisor in an apartment block overlooking the harbor. Remember that fancy place we went to on Liberty Drive? It's the apartment block next to it."

Dan frowned. "That was a pretty swanky neighborhood. How did someone with a criminal record end up with a job there?"

"Maybe friends in high places—or low ones—with a lot of influence."

Dan stilled. "What have you found?"

"According to his tax records, between 1991 and 1993, he was employed by a construction company." His gaze met Dan's. "The same company that was building a certain tunnel in August 1992."

That prickling sensation was back. "When you factor in what *I've* just found, it all adds up to one conclusion."

"Which is?"

"We're paying Mr. Reynolds a visit tomorrow."

Gary smiled. "On a Saturday? You're keen."

He expelled a breath. "Yes, I am. I'm keen to find something to tell Pete Raskin. Because he's counting on us."

Saturday July 14, 2018

GARY PARKED the car in a guest parking space and switched off the engine. He peered at the apartment building. "He might not want to talk to us."

"If he proves reluctant, then…." Dan shrugged.

"Then you do your thing?"

"Just don't let him *know* I'm doing my thing. Unless he recognizes me, of course." Dan pushed out a low grumble. "Thanks, Lewis."

Gary gazed at him in surprise. It was the first time Dan had mentioned Gary's former coworker in weeks. Gary could understand that. Dan had been instrumental in Lewis's departure from the police department. Lewis had also been the one to give the media details about Dan's involvement with Boston PD, putting him directly into the path of a serial killer. For a couple of weeks, Dan had been page one news.

All he wanted to do was help the police and stay out of the spotlight.

"How about I do most of the talking?" Gary suggested.

Dan nodded. He glanced toward the building. "Then let's go talk to him."

They got out of the car and walked to the glass doors at the front. Inside, Gary spied the sign that said Supervisor's Office. "We'll start there."

Dan rang the bell, and a moment later the door opened. Aiden Reynolds had to be almost six feet tall, a heavyset man with a shock of graying hair and gray eyes with no spark of warmth. He wore jeans, heavy boots, and a plaid shirt.

He frowned. "Can I help you?"

Gary flashed his badge, and Dan held up the credentials provided for him. "I'm Detective Gary Mitchell, and this is Dan Porter. We'd like to ask you some questions about Cheryl Somers. You went on a date with her once."

Reynolds's frown deepened. "Cheryl…." His eyes widened. "You have got to be fucking *kidding* me. You wanna talk about a date I went on—" He paused. "—almost thirty years ago, for Christ's sake."

"Can we talk about this in your office?" Dan asked in a polite tone. "Or do you really want to discuss this in the lobby?"

Reynolds stood aside, glaring at them. "I suppose you'd better come in."

They walked past him into a sparsely decorated square room with a desk, a chair, and a filing cabinet. Through an open doorway, Gary got a glimpse of a living room, the TV blaring a football game. Reynolds closed the door, then faced them, his arms folded. "I still can't believe you guys wanna talk about that freak after all this time."

Gary got out his notepad and pen. "We know from our records you were arrested on a charge of assault in June 1989. Can you tell us what led up to that arrest?"

"Why do you want to know? This is ancient history." Reynolds's scowl knitted his eyebrows together.

"We'll get to that part in a moment. Just tell us what you remember."

Reynolds flopped into the chair behind his desk. "Fucking freak. Should've told me."

Saturday, June 17, 1989

AIDEN REYNOLDS couldn't stop staring at his date. He couldn't put his finger on what was so different about her, but there was definitely something. Cheryl Somers had glossy shoulder-length brown hair, a sort of chestnut brown that matched her eyes. Not too much makeup, but then again she didn't need it. Fine cheekbones, clear skin… a natural beauty. Okay, so she was no catwalk model, but she had something. Unlike most of the girls he dated, she hadn't gone for a plunging neckline, which was a pity, because he badly wanted to see what was under that blouse. She talked about her work, something to do with art, and he pretended to listen, but all the while he kept thinking about what would come *after* dinner. Not that they'd made plans—she'd said dinner, and that was all— but Aiden's dick was like a rock in his pants. If he'd unzipped, it would've been smacking itself on the underside of the table.

He still couldn't believe she'd said yes. It had been one of those "eyes across a crowded coffee shop" moments, and he knew the minute she'd noticed him. Aiden wasn't one for false modesty. His job kept him fit and toned, and he spotted her giving him the once-over. So he'd struck up a conversation while they waited for the server to get their names wrong, and by the time they'd finished their coffee, he'd impulsively asked her to have dinner with him.

But now dinner was over, and Aiden's mind turned to other appetites.

They split the check, he tipped the server, and then they were out into the evening air. She told him she'd left her car near the public alley, and he offered to walk her to it. Still nothing to indicate if there'd be a second date. But once they entered the alley, Aiden's libido got the better of him.

He pushed her against the wall. "How about a good night kiss?"

Her breathing hitched. "Sorry, but I don't kiss on a first date. Not unless we've talked first. Now, would you please let me go?" She tried to sidestep out of the way, but he blocked her.

"We've talked all night," he ground out. "Besides, what is there to talk about?"

"Look, I need to tell you some—"

That was as far as he let her go before he smashed his mouth against hers, grinding against her, placing his hands on her breasts to—

What the fuck?

Saturday, July 14, 2018

"SHE DIDN'T get the chance to tell you she was trans," Dan observed. "According to your statement when you were arrested, you claimed she initiated sex, but that wasn't true. You did." The more words tumbled from Reynolds's lips, the less Dan liked him.

"I was horny, all right? I didn't wanna wait, so I went for the tits. Except that was when I discovered he didn't have any. Knew that the second I squeezed 'em."

"So you assaulted her. Beat her up, in fact. I saw the police photos." Gary's expression was grim.

"Consumer rights," Reynolds fired back at him. "If the product and label don't match, I got a right to complain."

Gary glared at him. "Not when you do it with your fists. And you've done that a lot."

"Was that the last time you saw her?" Dan inquired

Reynolds gaped at him. "You're really gonna keep calling him 'her'?"

"Yes," Gary told him. "Because that was how she saw herself."

Reynolds rolled his eyes. "Whatever. And no, it wasn't the last time. Saw *him* again a few years later. I was working in Boston at the time, on the Fort Point Channel Tunnel. The boss called, asked my supervisor if me and two other guys could go to Lenox to build a pool house."

Gary's pen came to a halt. "The boss?"

"Yeah. Gianni DiFanetti. Lemme tell you, when he said jump, you didn't even bother asking how fuckin' high. You just did as you were told."

"When was this?" Gary asked.

Reynolds stroked his stubble-covered chin. "Summer of '92, July maybe. Yeah, that was it. Anyhow, the three of us went over there. Fucking hot, it was. I remember stripping off and diving into the pool to cool off, only this guy came over and hollered at me to get the hell out of there. Think he was the gardener or maintenance man, something like that. Fucking asshole. What did he think I was gonna do, piss in it?" He paused. "We were there for a week. And on the last day, I saw the freak in the gardens, walking with the guy who owned the place. Some senator, I think."

Gary stared. "Senator Cain?"

"Yeah, that was him. Got a big place in the middle of acres of trees. Funky-looking house too."

"Did you speak to Cheryl?" Dan asked.

"No."

"As a matter of interest, where were you August twenty-eighth, 1992?" Gary's tone was even.

Reynolds blinked. "Excuse me while I check my diary…." He gave another eye roll. "Like I can remember a date twenty-six years ago." Then he narrowed his gaze. "Why that day?"

"That was the last time anyone saw her," Gary informed him.

"So? So what?"

"Then she turned up in 2006, in plastic, when she dropped from the roof of the Fort Point Channel Tunnel."

Reynolds's jaw dropped. "That was the freak?"

If it was an act, Dan was impressed.

"Uh-huh. And *you* were working on that tunnel when she disappeared." Gary didn't break eye contact.

Reynolds's eyes were huge. "Wait a sec. You think *I* killed him? Sure, I beat the crap out of him, but *murder*?"

"Plus you have a history of violence against women," Gary added.

"He wasn't a fucking woman!" Reynolds snarled.

Dan couldn't keep quiet any longer. "Your antitrans views are well documented. I've seen your posts on social media. Maybe the beating you gave her wasn't enough. You saw her that day, and that brought it all back, the resentment, the anger. Maybe you thought you'd find her again and finish the job. And don't tell me it was a long time ago. I can still hear the anger in your voice when you talk about her. Did she offend your masculinity or something?"

"I don't have to answer that. In fact, I don't even have to talk to you, unless you're arresting me. *Am* I under arrest?"

"No, you're just under suspicion," Gary said in a mild voice. Dan had never seen him so cool. "We'll be looking into it."

"Fine, you do that. So will I. You've got no way of proving I was anywhere near that tunnel, outside of work. And there's no need for a return visit, because you're not gonna find anything. I might not recall where I was on that date, but I know for sure I didn't kill *her*, okay?" Reynolds's eyes bulged, his face red, the cords of his neck standing proud. "Are we done?"

"For now." Gary opened the office door and went out into the lobby, Dan following. They crossed the marble-tiled floor, heading for the entrance.

"So he beats them up but doesn't go as far as killing them? As if assault is okay, but murder is somehow incomprehensible?"

"He's not off the hook yet." Gary's voice was low. "His job puts him at the scene. He saw Cheryl in July 1992. What if you nailed it? What if he went back to Lenox, looking for her—and found her? What's to stop him killing her and driving the body to Boston, then stowing it in the space above the concrete ceiling tiles? He'd have access."

Dan stopped at the threshold, his hand on the glass. "But cutting off her head? Isn't that a step too far?"

Gary gazed at him. "You don't think him capable of that? What do your senses tell you?"

"Nothing solid, but…." Dan shook his head. "No, I don't think he did it, unfortunately for us. But don't let that stop you. Don't put all your faith in my abilities."

Gary sighed. "We're way past that. I trust your senses. But yeah, we *will* still check up on Aiden's movements."

"So what now?" Dan asked as they walked out into the sunshine. "Are we going back to the precinct?"

Gary peered at him. "Why? Something you want to do there?"

Dan nodded. "I think we should look into the car accident. If someone went to the trouble of sending death threats, I don't think they would give up so easily just because they lost track of Ben."

"But seven years elapsed between the threats and Cheryl's disappearance."

Dan had thought about that. "Maybe it took them that long to find her." He gave Gary a beseeching glance. "Surely we can pay the family a visit, see what we can learn?"

"You mean, what *you* can learn." Gary chuckled. "You're getting a taste for detection, aren't you?"

Except it wasn't detection that provided motivation—it was the burning need to learn the truth.

Chapter Nine

DAN RETURNED from the restroom to find Gary making notes. "Did your digging turn anything up?"

Gary nodded. "Connor Brightmore was twenty when he died. College student from a wealthy family. But based on the eyewitness accounts and the examination of the wreckage, there's no doubt he caused the accident."

"So young," Dan murmured. "His poor parents."

"They still live in Boston. They have two houses, one on Marlborough Street and another on Cape Cod."

"I've heard a lot about Cape Cod. Do you know it at all? Did you ever go there on vacation?"

Gary smiled. "Once or twice. My mom used to say she'd love to have a summer house on the coast. My dad told her to start buying lottery tickets." He cocked his head. "How about a trip to Nantucket?"

"Okay, that's… random." Dan blinked. "Aren't we a little busy right now? Maybe once we've gotten a case solved, but—"

"While you were gone, I called Mr. Brightmore to arrange a meeting. He says he'll meet with us, but only if we come to their summer home—in Nantucket." His eyes twinkled. "I said yes. I didn't think you'd mind."

Dan grinned. "When do we go?"

"I asked if we could see him tomorrow, but he refused. Said it could wait until Monday. Which means we have a long day ahead of us. It's easily an hour and a quarter drive to Hyannis Port. Then we have choices. If we take the vehicle ferry, that's another two-plus hours. Or we can take the high-speed passenger ferry. That only takes an hour."

"We'd better have an early night Sunday, then. It sounds as if we're going to have an early start Monday."

Gary chuckled. "That only works in theory. Our early nights usually end up with both of us tired the following day."

No time like the present. "Actually? I have plans for tomorrow."

Gary's grin widened. "I like the sound of that. What do they involve?"

"To quote you—down, boy. I think it's time I finally got around to unpacking the rest of my stuff. I can't keep living out of boxes and suitcases. If you're serious about us living together...."

Dan didn't have to see Gary's expression or touch him to know a change had taken place—he could feel it in the air, feel Gary's focus on him.

"Of course I am. And you're right. It's time we made it your home too." Gary turned the monitor off. "And we're done. It's Saturday afternoon. Why don't we go grab some lunch, and then we'll go home." He smiled. "We can get started on your unpacking."

Dan couldn't resist. "Well, we don't have to start right away, do we?"

Monday, July 16, 2018

Gary and Dan walked up Broad Street toward the Whaling Museum, and took a right onto North Water Street. The one-hour ferry trip had served as a reminder how much Dan enjoyed being on the water. He'd grown up around boats: his dad had let him take the helm of the family yacht for the first time when he was fifteen. Nantucket Sound was full of boats, and the flap of sails, the dull murmur of engines, and the occasional burst of laughter or loud comments between boats had plunged him into pleasant memories.

North Water Street was narrow and lined with cobbles, the sidewalk done in red and gray blocks. On one side were red brick houses, and on the other, white mansions with porticos and vaulted roofs, upper decks surrounded by white railings, and trees that provided a splash of green against the white-cedar shakes. Then white gave way to gray, but the size of the houses didn't diminish. Cars were parked along one side, and white picket fences protected front yards filled with shrubs, trees, and twisting, clinging plants that crept over trellises and covered exterior walls.

Dan gazed at the properties with a smile. "It's like being home."

Gary chuckled. "I keep forgetting. You come from New Hampshire. I suppose you get a lot of summer visitors too."

"We get our fair share." The high-speed passenger ferry had brought back yet more memories. It had been packed with families and couples armed with vacation paraphernalia and all sporting sunglasses.

Gary stared at the huge, almost palatial houses on the left side of the street. "We are talking a *serious* amount of money here."

Dan said nothing. He came from such a background. His parents had expected him to lead a philanthropic life of fund-raising for charity, not to employ his strange gift to help others.

Not that they ever discussed his gift.

They came to a fork in the road, and Gary pointed to the left. Cliff Road was a collection of impressive properties, some of them guest houses or hotels. They hadn't gone far when Gary came to a stop. The house was set back on the right, its exterior walls covered in cedar shakes, a lawn stretching from the front door to the sidewalk, dissected by a rustic paved path. Dan figured the second-story windows had to provide great views of Nantucket Sound.

They made their way to the door, which was hidden beneath a porch covered with roses. As they approached, it opened, and an elegant woman with short white hair and gold-framed glasses stood there.

"Gentlemen, I'm Marie Brightmore. My husband is expecting you. Please, follow me."

They stepped into the light interior with oak floorboards, a staircase on the left, and glass-paned doors leading from the hallway. Mrs. Brightmore stopped in front of the farthest door. "I was about to make tea. Would you like some?"

"Thank you. That would be great," Gary told her. She pushed the door open, and they entered what looked like a sunroom, the walls and numerous window frames painted in a pleasant sage green, a colorful yet faded rug covering the wooden floor. Outside, Dan spied a deck with three sofas, surrounded by lawn.

Mr. Brightmore rose from his rocking chair to greet them. "Detective Mitchell?" Gary went over to him, and they shook. He introduced Dan, another shake of hands, and then Mr. Brightmore indicated the couch below the window.

Gary had mentioned that Roland Brightmore was seventy-seven years old, and his wife, seventy-five. Looking at the man who welcomed them, Dan had an impression of someone a lot older—someone who didn't indulge much in smiling.

"Thank you for agreeing to come out here. We spend the summer months here." Mr. Brightmore gestured to their surroundings. "This old house has been in the family for generations. I believe it was built in the early eighteen hundreds."

Gary crossed the room to the table that stood in one corner, draped in a white tablecloth. Its surface was covered in framed photos. Gary pointed to the ones in the front row. "Your children?"

Mr. Brightmore smiled. "Indeed." He joined Gary and picked up the nearest frame. "This is our daughter Rachel, her husband, their three children and their partners, and our great-grandchildren." He replaced it and picked up another. "And this is our daughter Louisa, her husband, their two children and their partners, and yet more great-grandchildren."

Dan joined them, peering at the happy, smiling people. "You have a beautiful family, Mr. Brightmore."

His lower lip trembled. "But we lost our son, so this is where the family line comes to an end. A family that can trace its lineage back to the nineteenth century." His face contorted in a grimace. "Except the result would probably have been the same had he lived."

Gary gave Dan an inquiring glance, but Dan hadn't understood the remark either.

Mr. Brightmore straightened. "But enough of that. I believe you said in your phone call that you're investigating a death. How does this concern us?"

"We're looking into the death of Cheryl Somers, who disappeared in 1992. Her body was later discovered in 2006, clearly a wrongful death."

Mr. Brightmore frowned. "I have no recollection of that name."

Gary's voice softened. "You would have known her under another name—Benjamin Raskin."

The only sound in the room was Mr. Brightmore's labored breathing, and the hairs on Dan's arms stood on end.

At last Mr. Brightmore cleared his throat. "In that case, justice was served." His voice quavered.

Dan studied his face, his body language. "You don't seem surprised by the news."

Mr. Brightmore managed a shrug. "That is because I'm not. I must admit, I had no idea of the name or… gender change, but I knew whoever was responsible for our son's death had met their Maker."

Dan's goose bumps would not quit.

Gary gave Mr. Brightmore a thoughtful glance. "How could you know that, sir?"

Another shrug. "I was informed."

"The reason we're here is because we discovered that for two years after your son's fatal accident, death threats were made against Cheryl—Benjamin." Gary kept his voice low.

"Ah, I see." Mr. Brightmore arched his sparse eyebrows. "And you want to know whether someone carried out those threats." He looked Gary in the eye. "I can assure you, though Connor's untimely death devastated us, no one in this family would ever resort to such an illegal and immoral act." He paused. "Clearly we have an avenging angel who is not hampered by such scruples."

"But avenging what?" Dan demanded. "Connor was to blame for the accident." Mr. Brightmore's eyes narrowed, and Dan gave a slow nod. "Unless they're avenging the fact that Cheryl survived and Connor didn't."

Mr. Brightmore's breathing caught, and Dan knew he'd touched a nerve.

"That's all you can tell us?" Gary asked.

A heavy sigh rolled from Mr. Brightmore's lips. "There is nothing to tell. And if that is all, gentlemen…." His wife appeared at the door, holding a tray, and he shook his head. "Our guests are not staying, Marie."

They had been dismissed.

Gary shook Mr. Brightmore's hand. "Thank you for your time, sir. I'm sorry to have brought back such painful memories."

Dan took the proffered hand and clasped it briefly, steadying himself for the onslaught of emotions he felt sure was about to overwhelm him.

What he felt was so much more powerful than he'd anticipated.

He waited until they were out of sight of the house before sharing his shock.

"Well, that was a wasted trip," Gary declared with a sigh. "That is, if we believe him. Please, tell me *you* learned something useful." They headed down the street toward the ferry.

Dan gripped his arm, forcing him to come to a halt. "Gary, he… he's… dead inside. Thirty-five years have passed since the accident, and I don't think he ever got over it."

Gary stared back at the house. "He might be dead now, but what about twenty-six years ago? What if he sent out that *avenging angel*? Or *paid* someone to be an avenging angel? Someone unconnected to the family? He did say that, right? No one in the family. And he's a man of means." His expression grew grim. "A car accident kills his only son. I'd say that's a pretty good motive for wanting the person responsible dead."

Dan couldn't help but agree. As they walked slowly to the ferry, all he could think about was the void he'd encountered.

A void he would never forget.

Chapter Ten

Tuesday, July 17, 2018

GARY GLANCED across the office to where Dan sat at his desk, drinking coffee and reading notes from Cheryl's file. Gary couldn't shake the feeling something was on Dan's mind. He'd seemed distracted ever since they caught the ferry back to Hyannis, and he'd been pretty quiet during the trip home.

Gary hadn't pushed. He was learning—slowly—that if whatever was bugging Dan was important, he'd share it.

Living with someone was a whole new ball game, yet another area where Gary was still finding his feet. Every day was different, bringing new experiences. For one thing, Dan slept naked, but that was a new custom Gary had gotten into with ease. Sharing a kitchen, a bathroom, however, had brought a few challenges. Gary had lived alone since he'd left college, and now here he was, two years shy of forty, learning to be part of a couple.

So far, he loved every single minute.

The knock at the door made them jump. Detective Will Freeman stuck his head into the room. "Can I come in?"

Gary resisted the urge to make a snarky remark; Will was never this polite. "Sure."

Will came inside and closed the door. He went over to Dan's desk, and Gary didn't need Dan's gift to feel the trickle of unease that had entered the room, an unseen visitor that had slipped in with Will.

He stood in front of the desk, hands at his sides. "I-I need to apologize."

Dan arched his eyebrows. "Oh?"

"Yeah. About last week… I was an asshole."

Gary couldn't hold back a second longer. "You've been an asshole since the day you walked into the precinct. Why should last week have been any different?"

Will turned his head to glance at Gary. "Okay, point taken."

Yet another departure from Will's usual barbed comments. Gary was starting to believe the Second Coming had been announced and he'd missed it.

"Look…." Will placed his hands on Dan's desk, putting his weight on them. "The thing is you kinda shook me. That demonstration of yours." He straightened. "I thought you were a fake, okay? But the stuff you came out with…. There was no way you could've known any of that. Because *no one* knows. I never told a soul." He stared at Dan. "But you knew. I don't know how, but…."

Dan's smile was warm. "Thanks for the apology. And as for what I saw, no one else will ever know, I swear."

Will swallowed. "Thanks." He peered at the coffeepot. "Can you spare a cup? I don't think I've hit my caffeine level yet this morning."

Gary found an empty cup and filled it. "Black okay?"

Will nodded. "There was another reason for me stopping by. Word is you're investigating that headless body they found in the tunnel back in 2006."

"That's right. Cheryl Somers." Gary handed Will the coffee.

Will cocked his head to one side. "Did you know there's another headless body on record? In Boston?"

Gary frowned. "Really?"

"Yeah. The victim was one Kevin Donaldson. It wasn't a cold case, though. The guy who did it is behind bars—a lifer. Guy named Frank Wyler. He went down for six murders."

"When was this?" Dan inquired. "I mean, when did the body turn up?"

"In 2007." Will shrugged. "Just seems like an awful big coincidence, having two headless bodies. I looked up the case. We questioned Wyler about the body in the tunnel, but there was no evidence to link him to it. But what if we got it wrong? This might not be a coincidence after all. Your killer could already be behind bars." He grinned. "Worth a visit to check it out? Now we've got a little extra help." He inclined his head toward Dan, then took a drink.

Gary stroked his beard. "Possibly. I don't like coincidences either."

"Wyler is serving time at FMC Devens."

Dan frowned. "FMC?"

"Federal medical center," Gary told him. "Don't let the name fool you—it's a federal prison. And it looks like we're going for another ride once I clear it with officials there." He glanced at Will. "Thanks for that."

"You're welcome." Will held his hand out to Dan. "And thank you." Dan took it, and they shook. Will held the cup up. "I'll bring this back when I'm done with it, promise." He left the office, closing the door behind him, and Dan expelled his breath.

"I'm glad he cleared the air. So that's one more person around here who I can rely on."

"Is that how it feels to you? That you don't have enough support?" Gary had known it wouldn't be easy, but apart from Will's initial hostility, there'd been little sign of animosity toward Dan since Travers's announcement.

Maybe that's because it's hidden.

He shivered.

Dan bit his lip. "It's early days. Let's get a few successes under our belts, and then people will come around."

"Then you do feel something?"

Dan gestured to the door. "Out there it's like wading through wave after wave of suspicion, fear, anger…." He got up from his chair and walked around the desk to where Gary stood. "You forget, though. I've been through this twice already. They *will* come around. You should have seen the detectives in Chicago when I helped them stop Jackson Perrault. I could've started a fan club."

"Yeah, but I'll bet a lot of that was down to guilt." Chicago PD had dropped the ball on that case, and Dan had ended up with a long, jagged scar across his chest when Perrault came after him.

Gary couldn't let anything like that happen again.

Dan cleared his throat. "So when can we get to see this Frank Wyler?"

"As soon as they say we can, which could be in a day or two."

"Good. That gives me time to read about his trial. I want to know as much as I can before we go in there."

Gary nodded. "And in the meantime, I'll draw up that list of Cheryl's contacts."

They'd be going over ground already well-trodden, but now they had Dan's gift, an ace up their sleeve, and one that could be a game changer.

He hoped.

Thursday, July 19, 2018
FMC Devens

GARY AND Dan sat at the bare table in the equally bare interview room. There was one window high up that let in a little natural light, but stark white tubes flooded the room, illuminating every corner.

The door opened, and a guy dressed in a khaki shirt and pants was escorted in. Frank Wyler was in his fifties, with cool blue eyes and hair peppered with gray. He was lean, and his sleeves clung to muscled upper arms. The guard with him closed the door, then stood beside it.

Wyler stared at Gary and Dan. "I haven't met either of you, have I? I've got a good memory for faces." He pulled the empty chair out and sat facing them, leaning back. "I don't get many visitors." His eyes twinkled. "Actually, I don't get *any* visitors. Only reason I agreed to see you. To break the monotony. So…." He folded his arms. "You're a detective, right?" Gary gave a nod. "Why are you here? What is it about me that could possibly interest you?"

Gary leaned forward, his hands clasped on the table. "You went down for six murders."

Wyler rolled his eyes. "Duh. I know that. I was there when they sentenced me to life imprisonment."

"We're investigating a cold case. A headless body that came to light when part of the ceiling of the Fort Point Channel Tunnel collapsed."

"Seriously?" Wyler snorted. "They tried to pin that one on me in 2007. Sorry to disappoint you, but it wasn't me." He twisted his lips into a thin smile. "Maybe I have a copycat."

"I read the trial transcripts," Dan announced. "I'll admit, I'm a little confused. You committed six murders. Five of your victims died as the result of strangulation. But the sixth, Kevin Donaldson, was the only one where you removed the head. Why?"

Wyler gave a shrug. "Maybe I didn't know my own strength." There was that twinkle again. "Maybe I squeezed so hard, his head popped right off."

Gary pushed his chair back and stood. "Then we have nothing more to discuss." He glanced at the guard. "You can take him—"

"Wait!" Wyler leaned forward, his eyes wide. "Don't be hasty." Gary didn't move, and Wyler sighed. "Like I said, I don't get visitors."

Dan placed his hand on Gary's arm. "We might still learn something."

Gary pretended to assess Dan's words and retook his seat.

Wyler relaxed. "Look, if you wanted information, you should've come prepared. You know, with an offer to sweeten the deal?" He grinned. "You could always smuggle in a woman. That would sure break up the monotony."

"Who says we didn't?" Dan reached into his jacket pocket, removed a packet of cigarettes, and pushed them across the table.

Wyler let out another derisive snort. "If there's a woman in there, she ain't gonna be good for much." He smirked. "You've been watching too many detective movies. One lousy pack of cigarettes? What decade do you think we're in—the fifties?" Another shrug. "Still, it's better than nothing." He grabbed them, but the guard intervened.

"You know the rules. No tobacco products allowed in prison." He gestured toward Dan. "Give them back to him."

Wyler held the packet to his chest. "Aw, come on. You could turn a blind eye just this once."

The guard's steady gaze told Gary that wasn't about to happen.

Wyler slid the packet across the table with a show of extreme reluctance. He scowled at Dan. "You're a regular tease, aren't you? No way am I gonna tell you anything now." Then he glared at the guard. "And you? You could've let me have *one*. It's not as if I'm worried about getting lung cancer—I'm gonna die in here."

Dan picked up the packet, holding it in both hands. He closed his eyes, and Gary held his breath. He knew Dan's gift didn't always come through, and sometimes it took its sweet time getting there, but….

Please, Lord. Let him see something.

Wyler chuckled. "Is he praying? I didn't realize you guys were gonna be *this* entertaining." Another glance at the guard. "You should've told me. I'd have brought popcorn and a soda."

Dan opened his eyes, smiled, and a tingle of electricity zapped through Gary.

Hallelujah.

"The sixth victim, Kevin Donaldson." Dan looked Wyler in the eye. "You didn't kill him."

Wyler gaped. "What the fuck are you talking about?"

"Watch your mouth," the guard murmured.

Dan didn't break eye contact. "It wasn't you. Sure, you put your hand up to it. But it wasn't you."

Wyler froze, his jaw slack. "Who are you?" he whispered. "You're not a cop."

Dan smiled. "No, I'm not. I'm a psychic who's working with the police."

"Psychic?" All of Wyler's swagger dissipated, and he stared at Dan with wide eyes. "Are you for fuckin' real?"

"What did I say about that mouth of yours?" The guard was starting to sound pissed off.

Dan nodded slowly. "Now why don't you tell us the truth? Especially the part about why you're so scared." His smile faded. "And don't bother denying it. Your fear is so tangible, I could almost taste it in the air."

Wyler swallowed. "You're bluffing. You've got nothing."

It was Dan's turn to fold his arms. "Really? So if I go to the DA and tell him I have doubts about that last murder, that maybe they have the wrong guy and need to look elsewhere? Because after what I did last month to help out Boston PD, you'd better believe he'll listen to me."

"No!" Wyler shouted.

"Quiet down." The guard fixed Wyler with a hard stare. "You do that again and I'll have you back in your cell before you know it."

Gary got his notepad and pen out. "Start talking." They needed to make some progress before Wyler got taken away.

Wyler gazed at them in silence, his mouth open. Then his shoulders slumped. "Boston PD had me bang to rights for five murders. There was no shortage of evidence, but I'm still amazed they caught me. I thought they couldn't find their own ass with a flashlight and a map."

"Get back to the point," Gary interjected.

Wyler laced his fingers, his gaze focused on the tabletop. "They had me locked up in Suffolk County, okay?" His voice was low. "While they were investigating, putting their case together…. Anyway, a visitor turned up. A friend, one I owed big-time." A shudder rippled through him. "And when those guys want to collect, you don't say no, you get me?"

"Which guys?" Gary demanded.

Wyler ignored him. "And he thought it was the perfect time to collect. It wasn't as if it was all that big a favor. I was facing life anyway, so what was one more?"

Gary stilled. "Are you telling me you confessed to a murder you didn't commit?"

Wyler nodded. "The cops were happy. One more case off their books."

Dan leaned forward. "So who asked the favor?"

Wyler shook his head. "Nope. You don't get that part. No way José."

"Why not?" Gary asked. "He can't harm you in here."

Wyler gaped at him, wide-eyed. "Are you kidding? That family would find me if I lived on the fuckin' *moon*."

Family....

"This friend… did *he* carry out the murder?" Dan kept his voice low and even.

"No idea. And I didn't ask, okay? It was real obvious he didn't want anyone linking Donaldson to him."

"And when was this?"

"I didn't make a note of the date, all right? Fall 2007, I think." Wyler leaned back, all the fight zapped out of him. "That's all there is. Are we done now?"

Gary nodded. "Thank you, Mr. Wyler. You've been very helpful."

Wyler scowled. "Just as long as you don't spread that part around, okay? You were never here. We never talked."

Dan was right; Wyler was scared to death.

They waited as Wyler was escorted from the interview room.

Dan stood with a sigh. "We didn't get a name. And I certainly didn't pick up on one."

"I think you did more than enough," Gary said warmly. "Besides, we don't need a name. If this 'friend' visited Wyler while he was locked up in the county jail, there'll be a record of it. I'll make a call."

His stomach was tight. Wyler's mention of family gave him an uneasy feeling.

"But I *can* tell you one thing," Dan added. "Wyler wasn't responsible for Cheryl's death. He was telling the truth on that score. So while it was a good idea, it's a dead end for our investigation."

They got back to the car, and Gary phoned Barry Davis, the clerk at Boston PD with a knack for sniffing out information. He told Barry what he needed, and Barry said he'd get back to them within ten minutes.

Gary hung up. "And now we wait." He squeezed Dan's shoulder. "You were amazing. And that part about going to the DA? Inspired."

"It worked, that's the main thing." Gary's phone rang, and Dan chuckled. "If that's Barry, he really is a whiz kid."

Gary clicked Answer and listened. "Thanks, Barry. I owe you."

"You can repay me by putting me on your team the next time we all go bowling."

Gary laughed. "Seriously?"

"Yeah. Your team always wins. My team sucks." He disconnected.

Gary took a deep breath. "This case just took an interesting turn. Wyler's visitor was Gianni DiFanetti."

Chapter Eleven

"That name keeps cropping up," Dan muttered as he got into the passenger seat. "Do we bring him in?"

Gary huffed. "For what? Visiting Wyler? No, not until we have more proof."

"Well, *Wyler* might not have been involved in Cheryl's death, but as for Gianni DiFanetti?" Dan got his phone out of his pocket and scrolled to where he'd written his notes. "It seems to me the proof is building up."

"Go on, then—present your evidence." Gary switched on the engine and pulled out of the parking space.

Dan studied his notes. "Okay. Between '91 and '94, Gianni's company procured the materials for the tunnel that collapsed and where a headless body turned up. In 2007, he asks Wyler to put his hand up to the murder of a headless victim. Then in 2016, he's heard arguing with his employee James Sebring, who ends up dead."

"And no witnesses other than Chris Reed to put him at the scene. No link to Cheryl—you know, the case we're investigating?"

"So we do nothing?" That felt so wrong.

"No, we investigate *our* case, and when we've resolved it—or not—we pass on all we've learned."

Dan couldn't help feeling there had to be more they could do.

"We've got a list of Cheryl's friends. Let's start by interviewing them. Maybe they can tell us more about her." Gary glanced at him. "And I think we should begin with Senator William Cain."

Dan blinked. "You don't think *he* had anything to do with her death, do you?"

Gary shrugged. "They were close, her dad said. The senator reported her missing, tried to locate her, offered a reward. We need to know if there's anything more."

Dan googled the senator and came up with an image of a man in maybe his sixties, with dark eyes and silver hair, a little gray still here and there. In his navy-blue suit, white shirt, and pale blue tie, arms folded, mouth locked in a smile, he looked every inch the politician. "How old is he?"

"Sixty-four, I think."

"What's he like?"

"He's a Republican. He's also popular, except with his party."

"Why not?"

"In the past he's voted in favor of stuff like gun laws, gambling restrictions, longer sentences for supplying drugs…."

Dan gazed at the image with interest. "Are you sure he's a Republican?"

Gary chuckled. "See if you can find a number for his office. They'll know where we can find him."

Dan's thumbs got busy, and it wasn't long before he'd found the number. A pleasant-sounding woman told him the senator was at his Boston residence in Louisburg Square, but that he would be returning to the family home on the coast on Saturday.

"Can we make an appointment to see the senator?" he asked her, after explaining they were with the police department.

"One moment, please."

Dan held the phone to his chest. "Just what are you hoping to discover?"

"I don't know if we *will* discover anything," Gary confessed. "But I'm not going to leave him off the list simply because he's a senator. We need to talk to *everyone* who knew her."

Dan put the phone to his ear just in time to hear that pleasant voice again. "The senator says he'll see you tomorrow at two o'clock." She reeled off the address.

Dan thanked her, then hung up. He went back to the image he'd found.

Gary glanced across. "Yeah, that's him."

Dan studied the senator's face. He was clean-shaven, his brow smooth. His most striking feature was undoubtedly his eyes, however. Then he noticed the senator's hands, tucked out of sight.

Why does he hide them?

Friday, July 20, 2018

DAN GAZED up at the townhouse that served as the senator's office. "Am I right in thinking this is a much-sought-after address?"

Gary nodded. "Beacon Hill is *the* place to live, if you can afford it."

The house stood on the sunny side of Louisburg Square, an imposing federal-style residence comprising at least five levels that Gary could see. In front of the second-floor full-length windows was a black iron balcony. All the townhouses in that row had one, and in each case the pattern of the scrollwork was different. Black shutters stood out against the red brick, and eight steps led up to the gleaming black-painted front door surrounded by glass decorated with thin black lead strips.

They climbed the steps, and Gary raised the heavy brass door knocker. The door opened to reveal a woman dressed in dark blue, her short gray hair neatly framing her face, gold-rimmed glasses perched on her nose.

She smiled. "I'm Eleanor, the senator's housekeeper. Mr. Lane, his personal assistant, will be down shortly. He'll take you to the senator."

Gary thanked her, and they stepped into the light hallway. A black antique chest of drawers, decorated with flowers painted on its sides and front, sat against the wall, two tall lamps on top. A cream-and-white polka-dot rug covered the wooden floor.

Eleanor gestured to the rear of the house. "I was about to take the senator some coffee. He's asked that you join him in the small sitting room. If you would just wait here...."

"Of course."

She gave them another smile, then walked sedately along the hallway. No sooner was she out of sight than a young man appeared, tall and slim, with long brown hair tied at the back in a ponytail.

"Gentlemen? I'm Curtis Lane, the senator's assistant. If you'd like to follow me?"

They joined him at the staircase that swept up in an elegant curve. Dan couldn't help but notice the abundance of art. There were paintings in the hallway, on the wall as they climbed the stairs.

On the second floor, Curtis paused at a wide oak door and knocked. "Senator?"

"Come in."

Curtis opened the door, and they entered a narrow, high-ceilinged room, its walls covered in a pale wood, in contrast to the dark varnished floorboards. Long floral curtains dropped from almost ceiling height, and a cream rug inset with red roses covered part of the floor. Bookcases filled the alcoves on either side of the huge fireplace, which was framed by two columns of warm marble. Two cream armchairs faced each other, one below the window, and against the wall sat a two-seater couch in red velvet. In the middle of them was a round wooden table, its shapely legs giving it a delicate appearance.

Senator Cain stood beside the fireplace, and Dan realized the image he'd seen online did not do the politician justice. In his dark suit, white shirt, and no hint of jewelry apart from his wedding ring and another ring on his right hand, the man exuded power.

"Detective Mitchell and Mr. Porter?" He greeted them with a polite nod. "Gentlemen, you're fortunate to have caught me. I'm only here today because I had a meeting that couldn't be rearranged."

They crossed the floor to join him, and Gary held out his hand.

The senator gave him an apologetic smile. "I'm sorry, but I'm afraid I can't shake hands at the moment." He revealed his palms, and Dan winced.

"You have my sympathies. My mother suffers from eczema too." Senator Cain's hands appeared red and painful.

"I don't suffer from it most of the time. Usually only when I'm stressed." He sighed. "Which happens to be my present state, unfortunately." His eyes sparkled. "Not that my stress levels have anything to do with a visit from detectives."

"It was good of you to see us, Senator," Gary said in a polite tone. "I know you must be extremely busy."

Senator Cain waved his hand. "Yes, but you said on the phone that you needed to see me. And to be frank, I was curious." He gestured to the couch. "Please, have a seat."

"We're part of a cold case team, and we're investigating the death of Cheryl Somers," Gary explained as they sat.

Senator Cain's breathing hitched. "The police are reopening the case? After all this time?" Dan arched his eyebrows, and the senator plunged ahead. "Please, don't take my words as a complaint. I couldn't be happier if the police are looking into this again. I simply thought her death had been swept under the carpet."

Dan didn't miss the tremor in his voice. "When did you see her last?"

"At the end of June 1992. I should explain that this is when the family decamps to the Fluke for the whole of July and August. It's a tradition."

Gary frowned. "The Fluke?"

Senator Cain smiled. "It's the name of our house on Cape Cod. Nantucket, to be exact. It's been in the family for decades. We usually stay there until after Labor Day. All the family comes: our children, grandchildren. In fact, that's where I should be now." He paused. "Okay, back to your question. I saw Cheryl before we left our house in Lenox for the coast, so yes, that would make it June. When we returned in early September, her father told me he hadn't seen her for a week. That was when I called the police." His brow furrowed. "So she's a cold case? Good. I was never happy about how this was left."

"Her father worked for your family for many years," Gary observed.

"Pete? Yes, I remember him from when I was a child." The senator smiled. "When I was younger, I worked one summer on a construction site. My father's idea. He wanted to give me a grounding, to see how most people lived. By the time summer was over, I'd become pretty handy with a saw and a hammer, and Pete put me to work around the house in Lenox." He chuckled. "My father loved that."

"When did you first meet Cheryl?" Dan asked.

Senator Cain tilted his head to one side. "I think that was when she was seven or eight years old and I was in my late teens. Of course that was before she transitioned." The word slipped easily from his lips.

Dan smiled. "Your attitude does you credit, Senator." He'd gone there with fixed views about politicians, having grown up with his dad's maxim playing in his head: "You can always tell when a politician is lying—his lips move."

Senator Cain was making a very favorable first impression.

The senator arched his eyebrows. "Do you refer to how I speak of transitioning as though it is a normal occurrence? It is for a great many people in this country. I count myself an LGBTQ+ ally, and sadly these days, there are too many people who would rather ignore the T. I am not one of them."

Yeah, the more the senator said, the more Dan liked him.

"But back to Cheryl. She had talent, even at that tender age. I think I was the one who first gave her a pencil and paper." His warm smile lit up his face. "And she improved by leaps and bounds as the years went by." He pointed to a portrait above the fireplace. "That's one of hers."

Dan gazed at the classically posed portrait of the senator and his wife. "She obviously favored photorealism." The attention to detail was meticulous, right down to the diamond brooch on Mrs. Cain's jacket and the gold ring on the senator's finger.

"Yes, she did." Senator Cain glanced at Dan. "Are you interested in art, Mr. Porter?"

"Yes." The house where he'd grown up had been full of paintings collected by his father and grandfather. Dan could remember spending rainy Sunday afternoons with his dad, going from painting to painting, listening as his dad told the story behind each work of art.

That had been before Dan had revealed his secret. His gift had erected an awkward barrier between him and his parents, and their relationship had been strained ever since.

There were days when Dan's gift felt more like a curse.

Gary expelled a breath. "I've seen some of her work online. It's even more impressive in real life."

Senator Cain nodded, his smile faltering. "She was an amazing artist." He indicated the wall behind them, where four paintings hung on long thin chains. "And that's another." It was a portrait of the senator, but this time he sat alone, and the style was more casual.

Dan stood and walked over to get a better look. "She really captured you." What he liked most was the senator's relaxed pose, the warmth in his eyes.

The same warmth Dan had seen when Senator Cain spoke of Cheryl.

"Yes, she did." The senator joined him. "She used to visit my art collection at the house in Lenox. She grew up there of course. And as she got older, her artistic talent developed, and I did my best to encourage her."

"Her father says you paid for her studies," Gary commented.

"I was glad he accepted my help. Someone as gifted as Cheryl…. It would have been a crime if she had not been able to study art."

That tremor was evident once more.

Dan turned to gaze at him, his heart aching for the senator's loss. "You cared for her."

Senator Cain stared at his portrait. "She was a beautiful human being." He scowled. "I cannot begin to tell you how angry I was when someone assaulted her. Cheryl never harmed a soul."

Gary stared. "You knew about that?"

"She confided in me. That lowlife—"

"And yet that 'lowlife' did work for you at the house in Lenox."

There was no mistaking the shock in his eyes. "What? As if I'd have let him set one *toe* on my property."

Gary nodded. "In 1992. You had a pool house constructed, didn't you?"

He frowned. "Yes, I remember that, but—"

"Aiden Reynolds was one of the laborers sent to work on it."

The senator's mouth fell open. "I had no idea. Not that I would have paid much attention to workmen. And Cheryl couldn't have seen him. She'd have mentioned it."

"You went to great lengths to find her when she disappeared," Dan remarked.

"Pete was distraught, and there was a limit to how much he could do. I simply gave more weight to his efforts."

"Which included applying a little pressure to the police department," Gary said with a twinkle in his eyes.

Senator Cain coughed. "Oh. You know about that. Not that it got us anywhere. I just felt they weren't doing all they could to find her." He glanced at Gary. "No disrespect intended to my present company. I even offered a reward, but nothing came of that either." He returned his gaze to the portrait. "I come in here often to look at her work. If she'd lived, who knows what she might have achieved? Her father had no idea where her talent came from." He smiled. "He certainly had no idea to what use she put it the last five years of her life before she disappeared." His smile faltered. "Cheryl didn't think he'd approve."

Gary frowned. "What do you mean?"

Senator Cain pointed to another painting. "That's also her work."

Dan stared at the painting of a young woman in a cream dress, seated at a musical instrument, a gold wrap around her shoulders. His brain would not compute. "But… that's a Vermeer."

The senator nodded. "Yes, it is. The original is in the vault at my bank. My grandfather bought it in 1947, and since then its value has increased tremendously. I didn't feel happy having it at the house, so I commissioned Cheryl to produce a copy." He held up one finger. "You will note she didn't sign it. She never intended such works to be forgeries, but clearly copies."

"'Works'?" Gary pulled his notepad from his pocket and peered at his scribbles. "Her father says she had a job as an art conservationist and that her portraits were a sideline."

Senator Cain nodded. "And so they were." He indicated the copy of the Vermeer. "This, however, became an even more lucrative sideline. I think she produced three, maybe four such copies before she… disappeared. But as I said, her father didn't know about those."

"She didn't paint them in Lenox?" Gary asked.

The senator blinked. "Now that you mention it, I have no idea where she painted them. I never saw her at work, apart from when my wife and I sat for her. That *was* in Lenox, at our house." He stared at Gary. "Why? Is it important?"

"Maybe." Gary smiled. "Thank you, Senator, for—"

The door opened, and a woman entered. Dan recognized her instantly. It was Mrs. Cain, as immaculate as if she'd just stepped down out of her portrait, not a hair out of place, the combination of high-waisted charcoal pants and a cream sweater with three-quarter sleeves making her look every inch a politician's wife.

Senator Cain frowned. "Della? You didn't mention you were coming to Boston today."

She gave a thin smile. "I didn't realize I had to keep you informed of my movements." Her eyes sparkled. "But if you insist, I'll let you know every time I intend to do a little shopping." She glanced at Gary and Dan, then back to the senator. "I'm sorry for interrupting. No one told me you were in a meeting."

"This is the detective who called me yesterday." Senator Cain gestured to Gary.

"Then I'll leave you to it." Her gaze flickered toward Dan.

"Actually, we're finished," Gary said politely.

The senator blinked. "That's it? No more questions?"

"I don't think so. If anything else occurs to me…."

Senator Cain nodded. "Then please, come see me. I wish you luck in your investigation. If there is anything I can do to help, I would be only too happy." He walked to the oak door and opened it. "Curtis?" The PA appeared, and the senator indicated them. "Please show my guests out."

"Thank you, Senator." Dan had to say something. "And… I'm sorry for your loss."

Senator Cain's eyes glistened, and he turned away quickly.

"Goodbye, gentlemen." Mrs. Cain's smile didn't reach her eyes.

Curtis escorted them to the front door, and they exited the house.

They strolled to the parking space Gary had found. "You know we keep talking about coincidences," Dan remarked. "Well, here's another. Both the Cains and the Brightmores have houses on Nantucket. For all we know, they could be neighbors."

"The same thought crossed my mind." Gary glanced back toward the square. "I'll be honest, he wasn't at all how I'd expected him to be."

Dan couldn't resist asking. "Well? Do you think he's our killer?"

Gary laughed. "You obviously don't."

"He grew up with her, encouraged her, supported her. But you know the one thing I took away from that conversation?" Dan's head was buzzing. "If she'd worked on the copies in Lenox, her father would have seen them. And the senator says she didn't tell him."

Gary had a gleam in his eye. "So that means…."

Dan nodded. "Somewhere there's a studio that may contain clues to her death."

A studio they knew nothing about.

Chapter Twelve

Saturday, July 21, 2018

WHEN THE after-dinner conversation morphed into Gary and Nina sharing their memories of Cory, Dan was glad. Nina's brother had been Gary's best friend since childhood, and it had been his murder that had eventually brought Gary and Dan together: Gary had confessed that needing to find Cory's killer had been the catalyst. He'd pushed aside his previous negativity toward psychics and demanded that Dan be brought into the investigation.

How does the saying go? "The rest is history."

Their history had a long way to go before it caught up with Gary and Cory's. And speaking of Cory…. Nina and Gary had been talking for maybe forty-five minutes before Dan decided he needed a little air.

He pushed his chair back from the table, murmured his thanks for the meal, stood, and headed for the hallway. He'd spied french doors that opened onto a small balcony. He stepped out onto the wooden surface surrounded by a dark brown railing. The sun had set maybe an hour ago, and the air was starting to cool. It was still too light to see stars. Below, he caught the hum of traffic from Main Street a few blocks away.

Dan drew in a deep breath, his nostrils filling with the scent of jasmine from the hedge that separated Nina and David's building from the property next door.

"You too, huh?"

Dan jumped as David joined him on the balcony. He clutched the railing, his heart hammering. "Warn a guy, okay?"

"Oh God, I'm sorry." David peered at the concrete path below. "Yeah, that could've been ugly." He straightened, then inclined his head toward the doors. "I don't think we're needed in there."

Dan had had pretty much the same feeling.

"I'm sure Gary doesn't mean to be rude," David added quickly. "They're both still raw from Cory's death. I mean, it's only been, what, eight weeks?"

"About that. I'm sure they must be. At least I know how Gary is feeling." When silence fell, Dan turned his head to find David staring at him. He attempted a smile. "Do I have something on my face?"

David studied him for a moment. "How on earth do you cope?"

Dan frowned. "I'm sorry?"

"No, it's me who should be apologizing. I've only met you twice: first at the funeral, and tonight. That doesn't give me carte blanche to fire such blunt questions at you. And it's none of my business."

Dan liked Nina's fiancé. David had an engineering background, and he reminded Dan a lot of his own brother. The invitation to dinner had been a pleasant surprise, and Dan had been happy when Gary said yes.

"I didn't understand the question," Dan confessed.

"I don't know how this… gift of yours works. Can you tell what he's thinking?"

Ah. Dan was suddenly on familiar ground. "No. But I pick up on his emotions." He gestured to the french doors. "This is our first social event as a couple."

"I had no idea." David smiled. "Then I'm glad you came."

Dan chuckled. "I'm still amazed to find myself in this situation."

"What do you mean?"

Dan went with honesty. Nina and David were part of Gary's life, and he wanted to lay a solid foundation for his friendship with them. "I avoided relationships. The thought of being close to someone and not being able to shut off the visions, of maybe seeing something that made me look at the guy in a different light, horrified me."

David's breathing caught. "Sounds as though it was a lonely existence."

"It was hard to bear at times." Except that was a gross understatement.

"But now you have Gary."

Dan smiled. "Yes. He's the man I was meant to be with."

"Oh wow."

He peered at David. "Wow?"

"The way you sounded just now… the warmth in your voice, the conviction." It was David's turn to smile. "That's how people should sound when they're in love."

Dan wasn't about to reveal the uniqueness of his and Gary's relationship. David knowing about Dan's gift was one thing—learning he'd had the same vision of Gary making love to him for the last thirteen years might prove a little *too* hard for David to swallow.

David peered through the glass toward the dining room where Gary and Nina sat. "Then it doesn't matter if he and Nina talk all night about Cory. When the night is over, you go home together."

Dan followed his gaze. "In a way I'm grateful to Cory. He opened Gary up to the idea of being with a guy. Cory paved the way for me."

David nodded, his eyes sparkling. "And you walked straight into his heart."

DAN SWITCHED off the bedside lamp, plunging the room into darkness. A heartbeat later Gary curled around him.

"I'm sorry," he whispered.

Dan stilled, then covered Gary's hand with his own. "For what?"

"I ignored you this evening. Once Nina started talking about Cory, I got sucked into the rabbit hole. And when I pulled myself up out of it, you weren't there."

Dan rolled over to face him, seeking his face in the inky blackness. "Now you listen to me. You have *nothing* to apologize for, okay?"

"But—"

"But nothing. Cory was important to you, and Nina helps you connect with memories of him."

"Now you're just being kind. We accepted an invitation to dinner, not a night of me getting so lost in a conversation that I forgot all about you."

Dan snuggled up to him. "Okay, if I'm being honest? Then yes, at first I did feel like a fifth wheel, but then David and I talked, and he made me realize something."

"What?"

Dan smiled in the darkness, his hand on Gary's neck. "My life is so much happier because I have you now." Then he rolled onto his back, bringing Gary with him to lie on top of him, Dan's legs wrapped around Gary's waist. "But right now? I need you."

"You've got me," Gary replied in a hoarse whisper.

Their lips met in a gentle kiss, but Dan knew from both experience and the heat building inside him, that their kisses wouldn't stay gentle for long.

DAN SAT upright in bed, shivering.

Tell me that was just a dream.

The apartment was quiet until a startled noise slipped out of the darkness. There was movement, and suddenly warm light flooded the room. Gary peered at him, his eyes heavy with sleep.

"You okay? What's wrong?"

Dan tried to breathe evenly. "A bad dream." Then he realized the details were still sharp, and that usually meant…. "Or maybe not."

"Can you tell me what it was about?"

Dan shuddered out a breath. "My mom. I-I dreamed she was in pain."

Gary stroked his back. "It probably wasn't a vision."

Dan grabbed his phone from the nightstand and stared at the screen as if willing it to burst into life.

"It's late, sweetheart."

Dan glanced at him. Despite his pounding heart and the perspiration that covered his chest and forehead, he managed a smile. "Have I ever told you how much I love it when you call me that? And yeah, I know it's late, but—"

"But you want to be sure." Gary leaned in and kissed his cheek. "Call them. I'll go make us some chamomile tea."

"Thank you." He waited until Gary had left the room and closed the door after him before hitting Speed Dial.

His dad answered on the second ring. "Hello?"

Dan's heart plummeted. *I knew it.* Something *was* wrong.

"Dad? This might sound funny, but… is Mom okay?"

There was silence for a moment, and that was all it took for Dan's imagination to go into overdrive.

"How did you…? Stupid question. Still gives me chills when you do stuff like this."

"Never mind your chills. What about Mom?"

Dad sighed. "She's okay… now. She woke up thinking she heard a noise downstairs. So instead of waking me, she went to investigate."

"What happened?"

"She tripped over the damn dog's toy rabbit, that's what. I keep telling her she needs to make sure all that stuff is in Casey's box before we go up to bed."

"Is she hurt?"

"Her ankle's swollen, and I think she's going to have a whopper of a bruise. I've given her Tylenol and wrapped it up. Got an ice pack on it too. Could've been a lot worse, though, given where Casey had left the damn bunny."

"And where was that?"

"Top of the stairs."

"Mom fell down the *stairs*?"

"I told you she's okay, didn't I? And it was only the top flight. Three or four steps. She grabbed hold of the handrail. She's more shook up than anything." He paused. "You okay?"

"I'm fine," Dan assured him.

"You still living in Boston with that detective you told us about?"

"Still here. No plans to go anywhere." It had taken him all these years to find the—literal—man of his dreams. Dan wanted just as many years to enjoy having Gary in his life.

"I-I meant to tell you—" Dad cleared his throat. "—I saw you in the papers last month. I read about that case you helped solve."

"Oh." Dan was too shocked to speak. *Since when do either of them talk about my gift? Maybe Mom's accident was more serious than Dad is making it out to be. Maybe it has upset the balance of his mind. Maybe—*

Maybe I should just stop blowing this up out of all proportion and listen.

"Dan? Are you still there?"

"Still here, Dad."

"Look, I know this is something we don't discuss, but… I was proud of you."

Oh my God.

"I even cut out the article and kept it."

Dan found his voice. "Just don't start keeping a scrapbook of all my press cuttings, okay? Especially the photos they use. I always look dreadful in them."

Dad laughed. "So what is it you're doing over there? Your last email didn't go into too much detail."

Heat bloomed in his cheeks, and his chest tightened. *When was the last time I saw them?* "You're going to love this. I have a job with the Boston Police Department."

"Seriously?"

"Uh-huh. I'm helping them solve cases that seemed to come to a dead end. They're hoping I can find another route to the truth of what happened."

"Like, cold cases? The kind you see on TV?"

"Yes, Dad, just like that." He waited for more reaction.

"That's great."

Dan blinked. "Really?"

"No, I mean it." He couldn't miss the earnestness in his dad's voice. "I think what you're doing is really important."

Dan's throat seized.

"I know there are plenty of people out there who'd give you a good argument for sticking with live cases—you know, present-day crimes—but cold cases are just as important. You're giving everyone involved what they really need."

"And what's that?"

"Closure. It doesn't matter whether the crime happened ten years ago, twenty, thirty…. That kind of pain doesn't go away, Dan."

The corners of Dan's eyes pricked.

"Does he make you happy?" his dad asked.

"God, yes." The words were out before he could stop them.

"Then I'm happy for you. I know this… thing you do hasn't made your life easy—quite the opposite. And when that guy knifed you…"

Dan did his best to forget that part.

"…I thought we'd lost you. But… you helped the police prevent more murders. And now you have someone who'll have your back too. He does, doesn't he?"

Dan smiled. "Dad, you really don't have to worry about me. Gary's a wonderful man, and I love him. He cares for me, supports me, and he also saved my life."

"What?"

Dan winced. *Me and my big mouth.* "That was the part that didn't make it into the papers."

"You mean this job of yours can get dangerous?"

"No, I don't think so. We're looking at cases that happened years ago. This summer was different." His heartbeat quickened. "I mean it, Dad. You mustn't worry about me. I'm fine."

Dad's sigh filled his ears. "It's late. You need to sleep. I'd put your mom on the phone to say hi, but those painkillers have knocked her out. You know what she's like when she takes them."

"Give her my love when she wakes up?"

"I will."

Gary came into the room carrying two steaming cups, and Dan's heartbeat slipped into a higher gear. "And Dad? How would it be if I came to stay with you one weekend, and I bring Gary so you can meet him?" He watched as Gary's eyes widened and his smile blossomed.

That was definitely a yes.

"That sounds great. Let me know when you're thinking of coming." Another pause. "Take care, son." Dad hung up.

Gary put the cups on the nightstand. "Looks as if I walked in at the right moment."

"I know I should've mentioned it before I told Dad, but—"

Gary held his hand up. "Stop right there. I'd love to meet your parents." He gave Dan an inquiring glance. "Well? Was it a vision?"

"Yup. Mom fell down the stairs, but she's only sprained her ankle."

"And is everything okay?"

Dan let out a happy sigh. "Actually? It couldn't be better."

Chapter Thirteen

Gary put his empty coffee cup down, opened the folder, and sought Pete Raskin's number.

"Why are you calling him?" Dan asked. "We don't have any new information for him."

"I'm hoping he'll have information for us." Gary dialed. "Mr. Raskin? Detective Mitchell here. I'm putting you on speaker." He clicked the icon.

"Good morning. Have you learned anything new?"

"Kind of. I'm calling about Cheryl's sideline."

"Her portraits, you mean?"

"No, her *other* sideline." Gary paused. "The one she didn't want you to know about, but the way I see it, that was a long time ago, and you might be able to help us."

"I think you'd better tell me what you've discovered."

Gary told him about the copy of the Vermeer, and how the senator had said she'd produced three or four such copies. "What we don't know is where she painted them. It obviously wasn't at the cottage in Lenox."

"I had no idea. So you mean she had another studio someplace?"

"We assume so, but we have no clue where it might be."

"Well, *I* certainly don't. At least she never mentioned one." He paused. "Wait a sec. One of her friends might know. Lori. I mentioned her, right? And I remembered her surname. Dettweiler. She'd be a good place to start."

"Thank you, Mr. Raskin." Gary glanced across to Dan's desk, pleased to see him making a note.

"No, thank *you*. You're the ones trying to find Cheryl's killer." He disconnected.

Gary gazed at Dan, who was peering at his monitor. "We could have this all wrong, you know. Maybe there *was* no second studio. She might have painted them in a friend's guest room."

Dan shook his head. "No, we're on the right track, I'm sure of it. She wanted privacy for this. There has to be a studio somewhere." Then he smiled. "Got her. Lori Dettweiler is the Collections Care Specialist at the Boston Museum of Fine Arts." He tapped his phone screen. "And now you have her number."

Gary retrieved it and hit Call.

"Lori Dettweiler."

"Ms. Dettweiler, I'm Detective Gary Mitchell. I'm investigating the death of Cheryl Somers, and I was hoping we could meet with you."

He didn't miss her gasp. "This isn't a joke, is it?"

"Why would you think that?"

"Why would the police be investigating Cheryl's death after all these years?"

"Because her father would like answers. And seeing as he says you were her friend, we thought *you* might want them too."

Lori sighed. "Okay. Then call me Lori. I hate all that Ms. crap. I'm sorry to disappoint you, but I have no new information about Cheryl that might be of any help."

"We're looking for her studio," Gary informed her.

"In Lenox at her dad's place? Surely he can't still be working there. He ought to be retired by now."

"He is, and no, not the Lenox one—the other one."

Beats of silence.

"You know about that?" Lori spoke in a hushed tone.

"It was a hunch, which you just confirmed. Well, can you help us?"

He caught her wry chuckle. "Seeing as I'm the one who rented it out to her—yes." There was a pause. "My lunch break is in two hours. Can you meet me here at the museum? In the Japanese garden, near the fountain?"

Gary scribbled a note. "We can do that. And thank you, Lori."

Another chuckle. "Thank you. With one phone call, you restored my belief in miracles."

GARY AND Dan strolled into the Japanese garden. Here and there, people sat on benches, eating or drinking from plastic bottles or insulated mugs. Gary followed the sound of trickling water, and they found a small fountain, a bench to one side of it. As they drew closer, a woman, approximately in her midfifties, rose to greet them.

"Detective Mitchell?" She smiled. "I'm Lori Dettweiler." Her shoulder-length blond hair was shot through with streaks of silver, and the contrast with her green eyes made her appearance striking.

Gary introduced Dan, and the three sat.

"Thanks for agreeing to meet with us," Gary began.

Lori waved her hand. "I come here every day." She gave Dan a frank stare. "You're the psychic who helped the police catch that serial killer this summer, aren't you?"

Dan nodded. "And now I'm working with the police to solve cold cases."

She arched her eyebrows. "And you're investigating Cheryl's death." She straightened. "What do you want to know?"

Gary removed his notepad from his pocket. "When did you first meet Cheryl?"

"In 1982. She'd have been eighteen years old at the time, about to go to college."

"So before she transitioned?" Dan asked.

"Yes. At that time, I worked as an art conservationist at the Boston Athenaeum, and Cheryl was a frequent visitor. She used to sit in front of the paintings for hours, studying the artist's brushwork, use of color. She'd bring an easel sometimes and paint from them. It was obvious from the start she had enormous talent." Lori frowned. "Then I didn't see her for a few years. I thought she'd left Boston." She bit her lip. "I have to admit I was shocked when she turned up one summer. It must have been… 1985, maybe? Yes, of course it was. That was the summer she started working at the Athenaeum. Anyway… gone was the gawky, awkward young man, and in his place?" Lori smiled. "She was growing her hair, and she wore a cream dress, a summery, flowing sort of garment. She wore a little makeup too, but to be honest, she could have gotten away without it. What a transformation." Lori's face glowed. "But it was the way she carried herself, the air of confidence that had been sadly lacking before, that made the biggest impression."

"Did she resume her painting sessions at the Athenaeum?" Gary inquired.

"No, because by then she'd started painting portraits, and my *God*, they were amazing. I was in awe of her talent. So young, so much promise…." She swallowed.

"Did you work together?" Dan asked.

Lori nodded. "We were in the same department. She was a joy to work with. Now and then we'd meet up during the lunch break, and she'd show me photos of what she was working on. She used to take Polaroids of all her paintings." She paused. "Then one day in 1987—it was the summer, June, I think—she met up with me during the lunch break as usual, but something was different." Lori smiled. "She was bubbling with excitement."

Saturday, June 20, 1987

LORI COULDN'T help but smile. Cheryl's effervescence was infectious. "What's gotten into you? Have you finished that portrait you showed me last week?"

"I need a place to paint," she blurted, her eyes sparkling, her cheeks flushed.

Lori frowned. "But… you *have* a place. Haven't you been working at your dad's cottage?"

Cheryl's eyes widened. "No. I can't do this there. Dad can't know about this."

"Know about what?" Lori placed her sandwich on the bench beside her and gave Cheryl her full attention. "Talk to me, please. You're not making any sense."

Cheryl took a deep breath, then fished a folded sheet out of her purse. She handed it to Lori, who opened it. It was a computer printout of a painting that she recognized instantly.

"Okay. It's a Vermeer. Why has this got you so excited?" It was of a young woman seated at a virginal, her gaze fixed on the artist painting her.

That sparkle hadn't left Cheryl's eyes. "This belongs to a friend of mine."

Lori blinked. "You have a friend who owns a *Vermeer*? Girl, you are clearly moving in more exalted circles than I'd ever imagined."

"That's not the best part." Cheryl's face glowed. "He's asked me to do a copy of it."

Lori frowned. "This friend of yours…. How good a friend can he be if he's asking you to do a forgery?"

She gaped. "Oh God, no. I wouldn't do that. This is legit. He's getting a little nervous about having something so valuable in his house, so he's decided to have a copy done—a *copy*, mind you, unsigned—and move the original to someplace safe. That way he can still enjoy looking at it."

"Cheryl, please. Breathe, honey."

She chuckled. "The thing is I want a place to paint where Dad won't see what I'm doing. This is going to take time, research. But I'd need a place with plenty of light, space"—she smiled—"and I thought of you."

"Me?"

Cheryl nodded. "You're selling your studio apartment, aren't you? The one in that restored Catholic school in Jamaica Plain? You were telling me all about it last month."

"Yes, I'm selling it." Lori had found a better apartment more centrally located.

"Well, can I see it? Because if I like it, you could… rent it out to me?"

Monday, July 23, 2018

"I take it she liked it," Gary remarked.

Lori nodded. "It was the perfect space for her, a five-hundred-square-foot studio with a wall comprised entirely of windows. She took one look at it, and that was that. So instead of selling it, I agreed to rent it to her."

"What did you do with the studio when she disappeared?"

"I did nothing for three months. I was convinced that any minute she would stroll into the museum, an easel under her arm. After that, I finally admitted something had to have happened to her. So…." She shrugged. "I rented it out."

Gary stared at her, aghast. "But what about all her work? Her materials? Her things? What happened to them?" He hated to think what they might have lost in the way of evidence.

Lori tilted her head. "You think they might have proved useful?"

"Possibly. It doesn't matter now. God knows where it all ended up."

Lori smiled. "I can tell you exactly where it ended up."

Dan grinned. "You kept it all."

She nodded. "I couldn't bear to throw any of it out. What if a miracle occurred and she turned up again? So I stored everything in the loft." Her face fell. "When she turned out to be the body in the tunnel, I should have gotten rid of her stuff, but I couldn't. All that talent thrown out with the trash? So it stayed in the loft. The tenants don't have access, just me." Then her smile returned. "And if it helps you find her killer, you're welcome to all of it."

"How much stuff are we talking about?" Gary had visions of renting a truck.

Lori counted off on her fingers. "There are canvases, paints, easels, a lot of books, camera equipment, lights, folders… oh, and a box of floppy disks."

Gary stilled. "You just said something interesting."

Judging by Dan's gleaming eyes, he'd had the same thought.

Floppy disks meant one thing—information.

Chapter Fourteen

Gary tasted the marinara sauce, added a little salt, and stirred it in. "You're very quiet in there. What are you up to?" He put the lid on the saucepan and went into the living room.

Dan was seated at the dining table, on which Gary had placed the boxes they'd brought from Lori Dettweiler's studio loft. Dan had already opened a couple of them. He glanced up as Gary approached.

"Are we allowed to have all this here? Aren't there rules about chain of custody? Because this is all evidence, right?"

Gary hadn't even considered that. "I'm not sure, with it being a cold case." He'd check with Travers in the morning.

"There has to be something here that will help us." Dan held up four floppy disks secured with an elastic band. "Like on these, maybe? Except where are we supposed to find a machine that can read them? In a museum?"

Gary laughed. "In the basement. I've got an old laptop with a floppy disk drive."

"What powers it—steam?"

He snorted. "It's only ten years old. I'll bring it up, and you can check them out—*after* we've eaten."

"Couldn't you go get it now? That way I could make a start."

It was the first time Dan had attempted puppy-dog eyes, and that was all it took for Gary to realize there was no way he'd ever win an argument again if Dan continued to employ such a powerful weapon.

Gary narrowed his gaze. "Okay, but I'm putting you in charge of the sauce."

Dan smirked. "What's it going to do—try and escape?"

Gary headed down to the communal basement. The landlord had constructed a series of lockable closets, one for each apartment, to be used for storage. It didn't take Gary long to locate the laptop.

You'd better still work, he thought as he climbed the stairs to the second floor.

Dan was in the kitchen. He grinned. "You were right. By the time I came in here, the sauce had already pushed the lid off and was slurping its way across the countertop, heading for the window. I had to beat it into submission with a spoon." His gaze alighted on Gary's empty hands. "Couldn't you find it?"

"Relax. It's firing itself up as we speak. Except that might take a little time."

"I'll leave you to the sauce." Dan dashed past him into the living room.

Gary shook his head and went back to following Nina's recipe for meatballs in marinara. He'd never made them before, and the addition of parmesan to the mixture of ground beef, herbs, and crushed garlic had been a surprise. They'd tasted delicious when she cooked them, however, which was why he'd asked for the recipe.

They'd better taste as good as hers. He'd made sixty-four meatballs.

"Hey, it works," Dan hollered from the dining table.

"Good." Gary poured a little olive oil into the frying pan, then added ten meatballs, shaking the pan to coat them in the hot fat.

"Cheryl must have been a very organized person," Dan called out after five minutes of silence.

"What makes you say that?" Gary inquired, pushing the meatballs around the pan to seal them before he dropped them into the saucepan.

"Each disk is for one work. It contains notes, photos of the original, close-up photos…. Plus there's a folder with a photo of the finished piece, and a document containing the title of the original, the artist, date of completion of the copy, name of the purchaser, and the price charged." He whistled. "Wow. The senator wasn't kidding when he said it was a more lucrative sideline than portraits."

When he fell silent, the hairs stood up on the back of Gary's neck. "What have you found?"

"One of the buyers. It's a name I'm starting to recognize."

Gary put the lid back on and turned the heat down, then joined Dan at the table. "DiFanetti?" Dan nodded. "Which one? Gianni? Bruno?"

"Neither. This is a Paul DiFanetti." Dan stared at him. "Just how big is this family?"

"We'll look him up." Dan grabbed his phone, and Gary gave him a hard stare. "I didn't mean *now*. Dinnertime, remember?"

Dan peered at the phone. "I'm not looking for him. Just a hunch." His thumbs slid over the screen. After a minute he looked up with a triumphant smile. "A painting of the same title sold in 1992 for thirty-six thousand dollars."

"So?"

Dan bit his lip. "Look, it's only a theory, but… what if he kept the original and sold the copy, claiming it was the real thing?"

"Didn't Senator Cain say all her copies were unsigned?"

Dan nodded. "So let's say he gets someone to forge the artist's signature, then passes off the copy as the real thing."

"Surely the buyer would have had the painting checked by experts before he bought it."

Dan's eyes glittered. "And of course no art expert would *ever* accept a bribe to declare something to be the genuine article. There's another theory. What if the expert got to see the original, and once the sale had gone through, it was swapped for the copy?"

He had a point. "Okay, fine, it's a theory, but where does it take us?"

"What if Cheryl discovered what Paul DiFanetti had done? What if she confronted him about it? I checked the date of the sale. It wasn't long after that Cheryl went missing. And listening to Lori Dettweiler, I got the impression Cheryl wouldn't have been happy if she thought something fraudulent was going on."

Gary was sold. "We'll go see Paul DiFanetti ASAP." He went back to his saucepan and stirred its contents. "Can you move those boxes off the table, please? Dinner's almost ready." The pasta was *al dente*—any more cooking and it would coalesce into a lump.

Then he realized Dan had fallen silent again.

"You've found something else, haven't you?"

"One of these copies was for Senator Cain."

Gary frowned. "We saw it. The Vermeer, remember?"

"No, not that one." A moment later Dan appeared in the doorway. "This was a painting of John the Baptist, by Caravaggio." He held his phone up to show Gary the image. "Which was *also* sold at auction after completion."

Gary turned the heat off under both pans. "I think we need to pay the Senator another visit."

"And Paul DiFanetti?"

Gary knew which visit took priority. "He's at the top of the list. The Senator can wait. First thing tomorrow, I'll see if I can find an address."

"No, look now. I'll put the dinner out."

Gary rolled his eyes. "It's seven thirty. This is not something I can do from home, okay? I'd need to check public records, the county clerk's office, local assessors, to make sure we have every known address for him. *Then* we'd have to call and make an appointment to see him—*if* he'll see us."

The prospect of visiting a member of the DiFanetti family filled him with a small amount of trepidation.

What are we walking into?

Wednesday, July 25, 2018

GARY STARED at the house on Cliff Road. "I'm starting to get a weird feeling about this." Finding out Paul DiFanetti lived in Nantucket was one thing—Gary was getting used to all the coincidences involved with this case—but discovering he lived next door to the Brightmore family was one coincidence too many.

"I can't really see Mr. Brightmore conversing over the fence with a guy who moves in DiFanetti's circles, can you?" Dan offered. "My parents have never spoken once to one set of their neighbors, and they've lived in that house since before I was born."

"Even if Roland Brightmore and Paul DiFanetti are a similar age?" Paul was seventy-four years old, and Bruno's younger brother.

"It still doesn't mean they're best buddies." He peered at Gary. "What are you thinking?"

"That Paul DiFanetti could possibly be the avenging angel Brightmore spoke of. Who better to bump off Cheryl than someone with DiFanetti's connections?"

"Okay, maybe." Dan touched his arm. "But we're not going to learn anything standing out here on the street, are we? And he *has* agreed to see us." He stilled. "You're nervous."

"You bet I'm nervous. Because if even a quarter of the stuff I've heard about this family is true, this is someone I really don't want to cross swords with."

"Which is why you made sure Travers knew we were coming here." Dan inclined his head toward the front door. "So let's see what he can tell us."

Gary took a deep breath and opened the white gate, only to be stopped by Dan's hand on his arm.

"I don't care who this man is," Dan murmured. "He isn't above the law, and *you* are the law. So stir him up if you have to. We might learn more that way."

Gary chuckled. "The first time I met you, I thought you were a nondescript kind of guy. I'm only now learning what remarkable camouflage you have."

Dan smiled. "I've lived through two murder suspects trying to kill me. It does tend to make you think 'Fuck it.'"

Gary liked this new Dan more and more.

They walked along the path to the house. The housekeeper welcomed them and then led them to the yard where Mr. DiFanetti sat on a couch on a deck, an open book in his lap, a Panama hat perched on his head, its brim providing shade. He seemed relaxed, an elderly man enjoying the sun, retirement. Someone's grandfather or great-grandfather.

Then he raised his head to look in their direction, and all such thoughts fled at the sight of narrowed gray eyes—cold eyes—thin lips pressed together in a firm line, heavy jowls.

It was not a kind face.

"You're the detective who phoned yesterday?" His voice was husky, as rough as a blunt saw driving its way through wood.

"Yes, sir. Detective Gary Mitchell. This is Mr. Dan Porter."

Mr. DiFanetti picked up the bookmark that lay on the table beside him, marked his place, closed the book, and set it aside. He waved his hand toward the two patio chairs facing the couch.

Gary figured that was all the invitation they'd get.

He walked over to the chairs and sat, Dan taking the other. Before Gary could get to the purpose of their visit, Mr. DiFanetti cleared his throat.

"I agreed to see you out of sheer curiosity. You said on the phone this was something to do with a cold case. I'm familiar with the term—I do watch television—but I fail to see how such a case could have anything to do with me."

"We're investigating the death of Cheryl Somers," Gary began, keeping his voice low, even, and respectful.

"Who?" His shaggy eyebrows scrunched up.

"The artist you commissioned to copy *Young Woman in a White Turban*, by Frederick Arthur Bridgman." Gary smiled. "The painting hanging in the room we passed through to join you out here." Dan had spotted it instantly and pointed it out.

"The same painting you sold in 1992," Dan added.

"I have no idea what you're talking about." Mr. DiFanetti's eyes gleamed. "I think you'd better leave."

"The sale is a matter of public record," Dan continued. "What *we'd* like to know is which one you sold—the original or the copy."

"And I still have no idea what you're talking about," Mr. DiFanetti ground out through gritted teeth.

Gary held up a folder. "Cheryl kept records of everything, including the photos she took of the original. Photos clearly taken in this house."

The air became frigid.

"That fucking…."

"Can I take a closer look?" Dan asked. Before Mr. DiFanetti could respond, he headed back indoors, Gary following.

"No, you may *not*." For an elderly man, DiFanetti moved fast. He hurried over to where Dan stood in front of the painting. "I asked you to leave." His hands were at his sides, clenched into fists.

"And we will, in a moment." Dan turned to look at Gary. "It's signed." He touched the frame. "This is the Bridgman." Then he gazed at DiFanetti, and Gary was awed by his boldness. "You sold her copy, didn't you? How did you do that? Auction the original, then swap it for the copy? Or maybe you went with a little bribery."

"That's a very serious accusation."

Dan nodded. "Which is why I said maybe. It was just a suggestion. So what happened? Did Cheryl find out? Did she threaten to report the fraud?"

"How dare you come into my house and accuse me of such… nonsense?"

Except DiFanetti was pale.

"It isn't nonsense if we have the painting checked out and discover we were right all along," Gary said quietly.

"And what makes you think I would give you access? But I *can* promise you this." DiFanetti's eyes were like steel. "If you pursue this line of inquiry, you'll regret it."

Gary arched his eyebrows. "That sounds like a threat."

Stirred up indeed.

DiFanetti regarded them with wide eyes. "Now, would I threaten a police detective? I'm a law-abiding citizen who happens to have friends in high places. I believe I've asked you twice to vacate these premises."

"We'll leave," Gary told him. "But this won't be our last visit. And that's *my* promise."

Something smelled rotten in Nantucket, and Gary aimed to discover what lay beneath that foul odor.

"If you have any more questions, feel free to pass them on… to my lawyer." DiFanetti turned his head toward the front of the house. "Mrs. King? These gentlemen are leaving."

The housekeeper showed them to the door, and they stepped into warmth and sunlight.

Dan shuddered. "Okay, *that* was scary." They headed for the gate.

Gary's mind was working nonstop. "Now we've met him? I like your theory that Cheryl discovered the fraud and confronted him. I wouldn't be surprised to learn someone in this family had her killed to silence her. I wouldn't put anything past *this* family."

"We need to examine the painting he sold. It belongs to a private collector now."

Gary had been thinking about that too. "Maybe… maybe she left a visual clue. Something in the painting. Or maybe something on the back of the painting, under the lining." When Dan stared at him, Gary sighed. "I'm making this up as I go along."

Dan looked up and down Cliff Street. "The Fluke must be around here somewhere. You know, Senator Cain's summer home."

Gary stared at him. "Whatever you're thinking, the answer is no."

"But we know Senator Cain is here now. The whole family is staying until Labor Day, remember? So why can't we pay him a visit while we're here?"

Gary shook his head.

"Give me one good reason why not."

"I'll give you two," Gary replied dryly. "One, you nailed it when you said the whole family is here. I am *not* walking into a houseful of people to question a senator. *When* we speak to him, we do it without an audience. Let's wait until we know he's in Lenox."

"Why?"

"That's the second reason." Gary smiled. "I want to get a look at his art collection."

Dan frowned. "You're surely not going to wait until September to speak to him there."

"We won't have to wait that long," Gary said confidently. "If we tell him it will help us find Cheryl's killer, he'll agree to meet us at the Lenox house."

Dan tilted his head. "How far is Lenox from Hyannis?"

"It has to be at least a six-hour drive, there and back."

"And you think he'll agree to drive all that way just to see us?" Before Gary could reply, Dan continued, "You might be right. He really did care for Cheryl. He looked after her and her dad. And he wants her killer found." He glanced at Gary. "What's his background?"

"Why do you ask?"

"Because I'm sure you ran a background check on him. I mean, he struck *me* as an honest kind of guy, but just because he's a senator doesn't mean he's squeaky clean, not in these corrupt times. That's like saying just because someone's a detective, he won't commit a crime—as we both know all too well."

Gary grimaced. "Don't bring Lewis up, okay? I still have a hard time believing what he did. And as to your question, the Cains are an old Boston family. Politics seem to run in the blood. His father was a senator. His grandfather too."

"You said he's popular with the voters," Dan observed. "So if he supports gun control, he's not the kind of politician who'd accept large donations from the NRA?"

Gary had to agree. "From what I've read, he seems to be clean."

Dan chuckled. "You sound disappointed."

Gary snorted. "Day ain't over yet. Let me make some calls, see if I can get us another interview."

"Why do you want to see the senator's art collection?"

"Well, don't *you* want a look at his Caravaggio? What if he pulled the same trick we're accusing Paul DiFanetti of? And Cheryl found out?" Gary smiled. "What did you say to me a moment ago? 'Just because he's a senator doesn't mean he's squeaky clean, not in these corrupt times.'"

And a corrupt senator had more to lose than most.

Chapter Fifteen

Thursday, July 26, 2018

DAN CHUCKLED as Gary walked into the office. "I thought you went to get coffee. You've been gone a while." He stared at the cardboard tray containing two large cups, and the bag clutched in Gary's hand. "And now I see why. That didn't come from the precinct cafeteria."

"You'll thank me when you try these." Gary held up the bag. "Probably the best cinnamon rolls you'll ever taste. And the best coffee too." He set them down on his desk. "What have you managed to find out?"

Dan peered at his monitor. "I've tracked down the private collector who bought the Bridgman from Paul DiFanetti." He inclined his head toward Gary's desk. "I've emailed you the contact details."

"Excellent." Gary sat. "I've been thinking about the painting too. If we're going to follow this through, we need to ascertain whether the collector bought the original or the copy." He glanced at Dan. "I know you said DiFanetti has the original, but—"

"But you need proof that'll stand up in court if required," Dan concluded. "I understand. So is that the plan? We contact the collector, share our suspicions…."

Gary smiled. "And then we suggest having the painting verified by an expert."

Dan saw where he was going. "Lori Dettweiler."

He nodded. "If she thinks she isn't up to the task, she'll know an expert who is."

"Call her before you talk to the collector," Dan suggested.

"I was going to do that right after we had our coffee."

Dan sniffed. "And after I've tried one of those rolls. They smell amazing." He got up and went over to Gary's desk.

"No time like the present." Gary got his phone out and dialed. "Lori? Detective Mitchell here. … Yes, we're making progress, but it's slow. I'm calling because you might be able to help us."

Dan tuned him out and opened the deliciously scented bag. One bite assured him Gary hadn't been wrong. He had to stifle a moan of pleasure to prevent Lori from hearing him. He took a cautious sip of the coffee and found it to be hot and delicious too.

"Thanks, Lori. I'll call you back when I have more information." Gary finished the call. "She says she's only too willing to help."

"Great. Then what are you waiting for?"

Gary rolled his eyes. "Can't I at least have my coffee first, boss?"

Dan laughed. He loved this: the easy banter, the way they worked together. When Travers had first proposed the idea of Dan joining forces with Boston PD to solve cold cases, Dan had imagined there wouldn't be much he could do apart from using his gift where appropriate. Being Gary's research assistant was fun, however. It gladdened his heart to be useful.

Gary picked up his cup of coffee. "The collector isn't going to be happy, not if we're right."

"If he's had the painting verified, and then *we* come along and tell him he's been involved in a fraud, then no, I don't suppose he *will* be happy." Dan cocked his head. "But that's not going to stop you calling him, is it?"

Gary chuckled. "No. Because if our theory is correct and Cheryl did threaten to expose DiFanetti's fraud, that's one hell of a motive."

GARY LACED his fingers and stretched his arms high over his head. "I'm done. And seeing as we're driving to Lenox tomorrow morning, let's call it a day." He peered at Dan. "Has Lori called yet?" He'd contacted the collector, Mr. Webster, that morning, and it had been an uncomfortable call. At first Webster had refused to entertain the possibility his favorite painting could be a copy. He'd been there when the art expert had examined it.

Then Gary asked if the painting had been out of his sight even once between its verification and its delivery.

The line had gone very quiet.

When Gary offered Lori's services to verify the painting's authenticity, along with her credentials, Webster had told them he'd be in touch.

All they could do was wait.

Dan nodded. "She called while you were meeting with Travers. Webster got in touch. She's going to examine the painting next week." He bit his lip. "She also said he sounded pissed."

"Now there's a surprise."

The door opened, and an officer stuck his head around. "Detective Mitchell? You have a visitor, Interview Room Three." He held out a card. "He said to give you this."

Gary took it and stilled. "Thanks." He waited until the door closed before glancing at Dan. "Aaron Stillwater."

"Who's he?"

"An attorney, according to this." And Gary had a pretty good idea who had hired him. "I wonder if we've rattled someone." He grabbed his jacket and notepad. "Let's go find out."

They walked briskly to the interview rooms, and Gary paused at the door. "Let me do all the talking, okay?"

"Absolutely."

Gary entered the small room. Aaron Stillwater was a short man whose thick dark hair didn't match his wrinkled face. His Ted Baker suit was a good fit, and Gary had a feeling the flash of gold from the heavy, expensive-looking watch on Stillwater's wrist was the real thing.

"Detective Mitchell?" Stillwater didn't crack a smile. "I'm here at the behest of my client, Paul DiFanetti. It seems you've been investigating him."

"That's my job." Gary looked him in the eye. "And if your client truly sold the original Bridgman painting, then he has nothing to worry about."

"I believe he told you to pass on any questions you may have to me. Except you didn't. I only found out about the inquiries you're pursuing when my client received a phone call today." He narrowed his gaze. "You told Mr. Webster his painting is a forgery. I could sue you for—"

Gary held his hand up. "Excuse me, but I didn't say that." He'd been very careful *not* to say that. "I simply told Mr. Webster there was some doubt about the authenticity of his purchase, and that perhaps he should have it verified—again."

Stillwater frowned. "I am here to ask you to desist in your investigation."

"And if we don't?"

The cold glint in Stillwater's eyes sent a shiver through him. "Do not pursue this, Detective Mitchell. Because if you insist on trying to implicate Mr. DiFanetti in this matter, you may not like the consequences."

Gary arched his eyebrows. "I'll say the same thing to you that I said to your boss yesterday—that sounds suspiciously like a threat." He pointed to the door. "And if that's all, *Mr.* Stillwater, you'll find the exit that way."

Stillwater drew himself up to his full height—which had to be about five feet five—and leveled one final malevolent stare. "The next time we meet will probably be in court, Detective." And with that he strode past them, flung the door open, and closed it with a bang.

Dan expelled a breath. "You like living dangerously, don't you?"

Gary glanced at him. "You think he's dangerous?"

"Er, yes? Just listening to him made me shiver." Then he smiled. "It also made me think we're onto something."

"Then let's hope Lori can prove DiFanetti sold Webster the copy. Because if she does that, DiFanetti won't have a leg to stand on."

"And if she doesn't, you just made an enemy."

Gary didn't want to think about that.

GARY SWITCHED off the engine. "I am *so* ready to kick back this evening." He got out of the car. "How about pizza, a couple of beers, and a movie?" Not to mention a comfortable couch.

Dan raised his eyes heavenward. "You had me at pizza." They walked along the path that led to the main door of the apartment building. "What time do we need to be out of here tomorrow morning?"

"It'll take us over two hours to get to Lenox." Beside him, Dan came to a halt, and Gary glanced at him. "What's wrong? Did you forget something?"

Dan gave a shudder. "There's someone at the door."

Gary jerked his head in that direction. A tall slim figure emerged from beneath the porch, wearing jeans, boots, and a black leather jacket.

"Detective Mitchell?"

Gary took a step toward him, and Dan grabbed his arm.

"Careful."

The urgency in Dan's voice caused an eruption of goose bumps.

Gary took in the man's cool smile, the dark eyes that glittered, the heavy jaw. "Who are you?"

"My name isn't important." His smile broadened, though still devoid of warmth. "Let's just say I'm a messenger."

Cold spread through him. "Who sent you? And what's the message?"

As if he didn't know the answers to both questions.

"I think you know who sent me, Detective. And the message is very short. Stop."

Gary played dumb. "Stop what?" He was aware of Dan, as still as a statue at his side.

The man stared at him. "You're not stupid. This is only the first message. You keep this up and there'll be more."

Cold gave way to ice in Gary's veins. "Okay, you've delivered it. You can go now."

"I'm going anyway." He glanced at the apartment building. "You've got a pad on the second floor, right? Nice place to live." He surveyed the street. "I'll bet it's a nice safe neighborhood too. You can't be too careful these days." The man swaggered past them, smirking. "Have a good evening." He whistled as he walked away, his hands thrust into the pockets of his jacket.

Dan hadn't moved from Gary's side. "Do we need to be worried about this?"

Gary hoped not.

"A one-word message isn't anything to concern us." The fact that he knew where they lived was another matter, however.

Dan stared at him. "And if the messages get longer and more frequent?"

"Then we'll deal with them," Gary stated with more confidence than he felt.

"Just bear in mind you've had two such encounters today. I think you've rattled Paul DiFanetti." Dan gripped his arm. "And that's not a good thing."

Gary had a feeling he'd need to watch his back—especially if Lori confirmed their suspicions.

Chapter Sixteen

Friday, July 27, 2018

"Are you sure we're on the right road?" Gary demanded.

Dan laughed. "You're just saying that because I made you turn off GPS. I'll get us there, okay? Trust me, I can follow a map."

"But all I can see is trees. There isn't a house for miles, and you said we were almost there."

Dan glanced at his phone. "If it makes you feel better, we're coming up on the turnoff for the house."

"What turnoff?"

He pointed ahead to the left. "There's a house. See that? There's a road immediately after it."

They turned off Under Mountain Road, substituting its smooth surface for a narrower gravel-covered lane that wound through pine trees in a long curve.

"We're going to get eaten by bears, aren't we?" Gary murmured as they drove deeper into the woods.

Dan snorted. "The bears should be more worried. You've got a gun."

They reached a fork in the road, and Dan directed them to the left. Ahead of them, they glimpsed a white building.

"How many acres did you say this place is set in?" Gary asked.

"Two hundred eighteen, mostly forest." Dan had googled the house once they'd received confirmation that the senator would meet them there that day. From the air, the place looked pretty impressive.

Google Maps had not prepared him for that first view.

The driveway ended in a circle in front of the horseshoe-shaped house, its two wings coming forward, the main door set back beneath a rustic portico, and to the right, a long arched window with a balcony.

Gary pulled up in front of the door and switched off the engine. "How the other half lives," he muttered.

Dan wanted to see what it was like on the inside.

The front door opened, and Mrs. Cain stood there, as elegantly dressed as she'd been in the senator's office.

They got out of the car and walked toward her. The tightness of her expression and the stiff way she held herself led Dan to believe their presence was not welcome. When they came to a halt, she gave them a slight smile that seemed forced.

"My apologies, gentlemen. Normally the housekeeper would greet you, but all the staff are on vacation." She indicated the door. "Please, come in."

They followed her into a spacious entrance hall, its walls covered in dark wood panels, the hardwood floor pale with intricately patterned rugs here and there. There were two staircases leading in opposite directions, the walls adorned with mounted stags' heads and paintings in varying styles.

Mrs. Cain paused in the middle of the hallway, frowning. "You visited my husband a week ago. Didn't I hear you tell him you had no further questions?"

"Yes, I did, but something has come up since then."

She gazed at Dan. "We haven't been introduced. Are you also a detective?" Gary performed the introductions, and she blinked at the mention of Dan's name. "I recognize that name. Weren't you the psychic who was involved in that famous case earlier this summer? The serial killer?"

"Yes, ma'am."

"And what case are you working on now? My husband neglected to mention that part."

"We're investigating the death of Cheryl Somers," Gary told her in a polite voice.

Mrs. Cain stilled for a moment, then squared her shoulders. "Ah. What brought about the resurrection of *her* case, I wonder?" That thin smile returned. "Anyway, my husband is in his office in the middle of a phone call. If you would kindly wait here, he'll be with you shortly." A faint line creased her forehead. "I don't appreciate having to come back here during the summer." And with that, she turned on her heel and walked away, heading for a door beneath the right-hand staircase.

When it closed, Dan glanced at Gary. "Is it me, or did she stress the word *her*?"

Gary chuckled. "I think you're reading too much into it." He gazed at their surroundings. "I wonder when this was built."

"In 1903, Detective Mitchell." Senator Cain stood on the left-hand staircase, dressed in jeans and a sweater. "My great-grandparents bought it not long after it was built." He smiled. "Gentlemen. Welcome to my home." He didn't offer to shake their hands, and Dan noted the white gloves that covered them.

"And such an amazing home," Dan commented.

"I'd give you a guided tour, but I believe you wanted to see my art collection? So maybe later. Follow me, please."

They joined him on the stairs. "I don't think Mrs. Cain is happy about our visit," Dan commented in a low voice.

"She insisted on accompanying me." The senator sighed. "To be honest, I'm not sure why, not when all the family is at the Fluke. She said something about wanting to check out the state of the house." He paused at a wide door on the second floor. "Although I'm uncertain as to what concerns her about it."

Dan frowned. The senator's explanation and Mrs. Cain's obvious reluctance to be there didn't match up.

"How many bedrooms does this place have?" Gary asked.

"Originally? Seven, and six baths." Senator Cain pointed to the door. "This is my office."

They entered a decent-sized room, furnished with a desk, chair, and several bookcases. The windows faced the front of the house. What drew Dan's eye, however, was a pair of doors facing the window, each one an impressive five feet across. A chaise lounge sat in front of the left-hand door.

"This was originally a bedroom, the largest of the seven," the senator informed them. He pointed to the doors. "Then I had that wall constructed and the pocket doors installed. When I go in there, I can shut out the world." He walked over to them and touched the right-hand door. "Al did me proud." He gave it a light push, and it slid effortlessly into the wall. "Gentlemen?" He beckoned them with a crooked finger. "My collection."

They walked into a darkened room where no daylight penetrated. The windows were hidden behind thick curtains. Then the senator flicked a switch, and spotlights burst into life, aimed at the paintings.

A great many paintings.

Dan couldn't stop smiling.

"My father would love to see this," he said in a low voice. "These are stunning." He could see paintings in various styles: Neoclassicist, Romantic, Art Nouveau, Realist, Impressionist, Expressionist, and Surrealist, and those were just the ones that stood out. Dan pointed to a long canvas depicting a couple in twenties' formal wear descending a staircase. "That's beautiful."

Senator Cain smiled. "That's by Joseph Christian Leyendecker. I love his work." He gestured to the paintings. "Most of these were collected by my father and grandfather, but I've added a couple. The Leyendecker was one of them."

Gary nodded. "A very impressive collection. And yet I don't see Caravaggio's *John the Baptist*, another of Cheryl Somers's copies. I didn't see it in Boston either. So unless you've hung it in the pool house…."

The senator's eyes gleamed in the spotlights. "And *that* is what's brought you here? Well, Detective Mitchell, you don't see it because it was sold."

"We know."

Senator Cain frowned. "Then why—"

"What we were wondering," Dan interjected, "was if you sold the original or your copy."

The senator's brow smoothed. "Ah, I see. I sold both."

Gary stared at him. "Excuse me?"

"The purchaser bought both. The original was sold at a public auction, and the copy was a private sale. Since the Caravaggio had come into my family's possession, it had become incredibly valuable."

"And yet you sold it?" Gary appeared confused.

Senator Cain smiled. "Ah. No, I didn't sell it for some nefarious purpose. A family friend was starting up a charity for the homeless. I donated the difference between what my grandfather had paid for the painting and what it sold for. And my donation helped provide accommodations, food, staff, jobs…. I am listed as one of the charity's main benefactors." He looked Gary in the eye. "I have scruples, Detective Mitchell. But I *am* curious as to why this sale should interest the police."

"Yours isn't the only such sale we're looking into," Gary explained. "And in the case of the other copy, her client definitely *didn't* have scruples."

The senator expelled a long breath. "So is your theory that Cheryl learned her client had sold her work as original and confronted them about it, and they got rid of the evidence—namely, her?"

"That's one of our theories."

Senator Cain nodded. "Then I wish you luck. I do understand that you have to check every lead, but where Cheryl is concerned, I can assure you, she was an honest person who simply provided a service. You cannot blame her if someone took advantage of her talent to line their pockets." He gestured to the art room. "Have you seen everything here that you wished to see?"

"Yes, thank you."

"Then perhaps I might give you a tour of the house, followed by tea out on the patio. It's such a beautiful day."

"I would like that," Dan said with a smile.

They followed the senator down the stairs.

"This house was built in the Arts and Crafts style," he told them as they stepped once more into the entrance hall. "When I was a child, my favorite activity was to sleep under one of the porches on summer nights. If I was fortunate, deer would come quite close to the house."

Dark wood panels gave way to strips of pale pine as they walked through the many lounges and sitting rooms. The furniture reflected the house's era, with antique desks and tables, even a butler's pantry. Loggias beckoned visitors to step outside, where the southern views were stunning to behold. There were many windows, allowing natural light to spill into the interior, each one framed by floral curtains.

The senator took them into one of the living rooms situated at the front of the house. "I've changed my mind. We'll stay indoors, I think." He pointed to the couches. "Take a seat, and I'll organize some tea." His eyes twinkled. "Which means I'll be making it. No one else is around."

A cough had them all turn their heads toward the door.

Mrs. Cain smiled. "I'll see to tea if you want to stay with your guests."

Senator Cain frowned. "I'll help." He left them and followed her out of the room.

Dan turned to Gary. "Well?"

"Well what?"

"Do you think he's clean?"

Gary scowled. "Yes, dammit."

Dan chuckled. "Mrs. Cain is something of a ninja, isn't she? I didn't even hear her come in." He gazed at the room. "This place is amazing."

Gary agreed. "There must be a pool somewhere on the grounds too."

"I glimpsed that when we were in the summer dining room. The pool house too."

The door opened and Senator Cain entered, carrying a tray. He set it down on the coffee table. "Help yourselves. I was trying to locate some of Mrs. Kent's cookies, but I think my wife took them with her when we left here last month." He sat in the winged armchair by the window.

"Thank you again for coming back to meet us," Gary said as he poured tea into the cups.

"It was no bother, not if it helps you with your case."

Dan couldn't help thinking that was not Mrs. Cain's view. He heard what sounded like a creaking floorboard. "Is this place haunted?"

Senator Cain laughed. "No, but it does have its share of noises, like any old house."

"I can't get over the size of this place," Gary commented.

"And yet you haven't seen all of it," the senator remarked. "At the end of the driveway is the guest residence. I used to play there. For a child, it was a wonderful place, comprising quirky ceilings, curved windows, and so many nooks and crannies to hide in." He chuckled. "I once offered it to Cheryl as a place to paint, but she took one look and told me it was too dark."

Dan could understand that reaction. "We saw the studio in Jamaica Plain where she worked on the copies. So much light."

"Then you found it." Senator Cain's face glowed. "I'm so glad. Did you learn anything useful?"

"We haven't gone through all her stuff yet, but we did find information about the paintings."

"Which is what led you back to me. I understand." Senator Cain's brow furrowed. "However… there is another lead you might want to investigate." He waved his hand. "Except you've probably already gone down that route if you've studied the case notes."

"And what route would that be?" Gary asked.

Dan leaned forward, intrigued.

"Before she transitioned, Cheryl was involved in a car accident. 1983, I think."

Gary nodded. "We know about that. Connor Brightmore. And we also know about the death threats that stopped when she transitioned."

Senator Cain relaxed into the chair. "Of course. You've seen her father. He would have told you."

"We went to talk to Connor's father," Gary continued. "I don't think he knew about Cheryl, but he did know Benjamin Raskin was dead. He said no one in his family had had anything to do with that, and that the death was the work of an 'avenging angel.'"

The senator sipped his tea. "And in the course of this conversation, did he happen to mention the angel's name?"

"No, he did not." Dan blinked. "You know who it was?"

Senator Cain nodded. "I can think of one person who might want Cheryl dead—and who is *not* one of the family."

"Who?" Gary reached into his pocket for his notepad.

The senator set his cup down on the table. "Connor Brightmore may have been young—twenty, I believe, when he died—but he was in a relationship. It might be reasonable to assume the surviving partner would want revenge. If the family blamed Cheryl, then why not Connor's partner too?"

Gary stared at him. "How do you know all this?"

Senator Cain shrugged. "I did some digging when Cheryl disappeared. I wasn't going to leave any stone unturned."

"Did you share your findings with Cheryl's father?" Dan inquired.

"No. But I did inform Boston PD. Not that my theory was given a lot of credence by the detective I spoke with. He thought the length of time between Connor's death and Cheryl's disappearance was too long for the theory to be credible."

"What was her name? Connor's partner, I mean."

The senator smiled. "*His* name was Ian Gordon. They met in college. And I believe it was serious."

Dan let out a breath. "*Now* I understand that cryptic remark Connor's father made."

Gary gave him a puzzled glance. "What remark?"

"Don't you remember? He said that with Connor's death, the family line had come to an end, but then he added that had Connor lived, the result would have been the same. If Connor was gay…. Someone from his father's generation might believe that meant no children. Not that it does nowadays, of course."

"Senator, why didn't you mention this Ian Gordon the last time we saw you?" Gary asked.

"Because I assumed you'd already looked into him, just as I *assumed* there was a record of my findings in the notes. This is apparently not the case."

Gary glanced at Dan. "We'll take a look tomorrow." Dan nodded. Gary returned his attention to the senator. "Thank you, sir. And regardless of what one of my former colleagues might or might not have done with the information you uncovered, rest assured, we *will* look into it."

Senator Cain smiled. "Then I'm glad I brought it up."

They finished their tea, and Dan asked questions about some of the paintings he'd seen upstairs.

Mrs. Cain reappeared. "I'll just take all this away." She loaded all the cups onto the tray, then carried it from the room.

The senator watched her leave with a shake of his head. "Della clearly likes you, gentlemen. She isn't usually so attentive to my guests." He smiled. "Of course, she's eager to get back to Nantucket."

"Thank you again, Senator. We must be going too," Gary informed him.

He showed them to the door, and they headed for the car.

As Gary drove away from the house, Dan twisted in his seat to glance back at the senator standing at the front door, waving.

"So… what were your impressions?" Gary inquired.

"He cared a great deal for Cheryl, and he's a man of integrity. He's also capable of strong emotions, but I sensed he was keeping a lid on them."

"You might have learned more if you'd shaken his hand," Gary suggested.

"True, but asking to take his hand would have seemed strange, especially now we know what those hands look like under the gloves. Eczema can be really painful."

"I've been thinking about what he told us. Either I missed it completely, or there was no record of him giving Ian Gordon's name to the department."

"Is it possible the detective he spoke with back then didn't make a note because he or she didn't think it was worth following up?"

"It's possible, sure."

Dan gave an emphatic nod. "Then we add Gordon's name to the list of suspects." He reached into his pocket, withdrew his phone, and pulled up Google Maps. "We pass close by Springfield, don't we?"

"Fairly close, yes."

Dan's heartbeat raced. "Then I have a request."

There was silence for a moment. "Please don't ask me to take you back to the park where Brad died. I don't think I could face that."

Dan's gut clenched. "No. I wouldn't ask that of you. But I did think you might... take me to meet your parents."

Panic rolled off Gary and crashed over Dan, and he instantly regretted the request.

"I'm not talking about you coming out to them, okay? But... I'm a psychic, remember? I'm just another avenue to try. After all, they've consulted psychics before, you said."

Gary glanced at him. "You just want to get a feel for Brad?"

"Yes," Dan assured him. "Tell them you've brought me to meet them to see if I can help." He cocked his head. "Will there be enough of his belongings there for me to use?"

Gary's shudder was all the answer Dan needed.

"Then call your mom. We can't turn up unexpectedly."

It was about time he did something to fulfill the promise he'd made to Gary.

Please, let me find something.

Chapter Seventeen

Gary switched off the engine but didn't make a move to get out. Dan reached over and covered Gary's hand with his.

"I know, okay?"

Gary jerked his head to look at him. "Is it that obvious?"

"No, but we've talked about this. I know the way these visits make you feel. Well, that's why I'm here. Maybe we can turn them around."

Oh Lord. Gary yearned for that.

Dan inclined his head toward the house. "Don't look now but we're being watched. I assume that's your dad."

Gary turned. Dad stood at the front door, staring at the car. He appeared a little older than the last time Gary had seen him in May. That was also the last time he'd seen Cory. They'd met at a gay bar on Gary's way home from Springfield, mainly so he could decompress.

The recollection didn't help his present mood.

There was nothing to do but get out of the car.

Gary led the way along the path, and Dad frowned as they drew closer.

"This is a surprise. It's not Sunday."

Before Gary could respond, Dan surged ahead. "When Gary told me about… your loss, I'm afraid I pretty much strong-armed him into bringing me here, Mr. Mitchell."

"Mr. Porter, isn't it?" Dad's frown deepened. "Gary said on the phone that you're a psychic?" He stared at Gary with obvious incredulity. "You've changed your tune."

"Maybe I have, but don't you think it would be more polite to invite us in rather than discuss this on the doorstep?"

His dad huffed but stood aside to let them enter. Once they were inside, he closed the door. "My wife's in the kitchen. I'll go get her. Gary, take your guest into the dining room."

When Dad was out of sight, Dan leaned in and whispered, "Why the dining room?"

Gary's chest tightened. "You'll see." The familiar chill he always experienced on entering the house stole over his skin, stroking it with icy fingers.

It doesn't feel like a home anymore.

If anything, it felt more like a mausoleum.

As soon as Dan stepped into the room cluttered with photos of Brad, Gary saw the change in him. His breathing slowed, and he went from frame to frame, touching them lightly.

What does he feel?

Ever since he'd moved to Boston, Gary had tried to shut off his emotions when he visited, but he'd never succeeded. And as he watched Dan attempt to connect with whatever memories of Brad still lingered, Gary knew he wanted more than for Dan to lead him to Brad's murderer.

He wanted Dan to bring light into his former home—and into his parents' hearts and lives.

They've lived too long in the shadows cast by Brad's horrific death.

Mom came into the room with more hesitation than Gary had anticipated.

"Mr. Porter?"

"Dan, please." He indicated the photos. "Brad was a handsome young man."

"So how do you work?"

Gary blinked. His mom wasn't usually so abrupt. Then he reconsidered. *She's been through this so many times, and it's always been without success. She's steeling herself for failure.*

"I thought I'd take Dan to Brad's old room," he offered.

"Do you want us there too?" *Dad seems as ambivalent as Mom.*

"If you don't mind, I'd rather see it on my own. Gary can stay with me, however, if that's okay. I'm used to working with him around," Dan explained.

"Whatever you want."

Gary winced internally to hear the resignation in Mom's voice. He recalled her past enthusiasm, even desperation, when she'd told him of yet another visit by yet another psychic, and each time no new information materialized, it seemed to him that something fractured inside her, splintering, shattering, taking off another piece of her soul.

He wasn't sure Dan's gift could do anything to repair that.

DAN PAUSED at the door to Brad's former bedroom, his heart pounding. There was no way he could anticipate what awaited him on the other side of that door. Each time he opened himself up fully, each time he allowed his gift to reveal where it would lead him, it always ended the same way—in sheer exhaustion. Heightened emotions sapped his energy, and he needed a day or two to recharge his batteries.

This was different.

This was Gary's brother, ripped from the world in the same manner some… monster had ripped Brad's heart from his body before laying it in his hands.

Gary touched his back. "He might not have been in there for the past twenty-three years, but this is still Brad's room. Nothing has been touched. It's more like a shrine."

Dan nodded. He sucked air into his lungs. "I'm ready. Open the door."

Gary did as he asked, and Dan took another deep breath before stepping into the room.

At first glance, it appeared to be a simply furnished bedroom. A colorful quilt covered the bed, and an oak chest of drawers stood against the wall. On top of it were models of fighter jets, planes. Books, posters, ornaments… they all told a story. Dan walked around the room, touching, soaking up what emotions remained.

There were so many of them.

Dan glanced at Gary. "He was a happy child, wasn't he?"

Gary smiled. "Yes, he was."

Dan went over to the drawers and pulled the top one open. Gary joined him.

"This was where he kept what he called his treasures."

Dan dipped his fingers into the clutter. "So many memories," he murmured. The room was full of them.

Maybe it was time to see where those memories might lead.

Dan picked up the first thing that came to hand. It was a plastic ring, the kind that used to come in cereal boxes. He held it, unable to repress the shiver that trickled through him.

A pleasurable shiver.

"You're picking up on something, aren't you?"

Dan had to smile. "Whoever gave him this? Brad was in love with them."

Gary stared at him. "I never thought Brad might have been in love. Put it this way—he never said anything about there being anyone in his life."

Dan regarded him with arched eyebrows. "You were fifteen when he died. Was that the kind of relationship you had with him? Would he have shared something so intimate?"

Gary stilled. "No, I don't think he would. We were always close, but…." He gazed at Dan, and the hope Dan saw there made his heart ache. "I don't suppose you know who they were?"

"I don't have a name, if that's what you're asking. But I do know one thing about them." He smiled. "They were male."

Gary's jaw dropped. "Brad was gay?"

"Ah, I thought that might be news to you. It isn't something I've ever heard you mention." He nodded. "Brad was most definitely gay." He replaced the ring in the drawer, then wandered over to the bookshelf, peering at the titles on the spines. "He liked to read."

Gary chuckled. "Brad always had his nose in a book. He loved horrors and thrillers, and Mom used to say she couldn't understand why anyone would read those kinds of books."

One title caught his eye. "Why does this one ring a bell?" he murmured. Dan brushed his fingers down the spine, and a jolt of… something lanced through him.

Don't pick it up.

He'd gotten this far, and far louder voices in his head were telling him to do exactly that. He plucked it from the shelf, then dropped it almost instantly to the rug, where it bounced, landing cover side down. Dan nursed his hand against his chest, wincing at the sensation.

It was as if the book's surface had burned him.

"What's wrong?" Gary's hand was at his back in a heartbeat.

"I'm sensing really strong emotions, only they're not Brad's." He shivered again, but this time there was no pleasure connected to the reaction.

Far from it.

Gary bent down and picked the book up. He turned it over to reveal the cover. "John D. MacDonald. *The Executioners.*" His eyes widened. "Have you seen this before? Was it in a dream? Or a vision?"

Dan was asking himself the same question.

"You told me Brad knew his killer." Gary held the book up. "Did this belong to them?"

Dan steeled himself and took it from him with a shudder. He peered inside. "I was hoping for a name at least." Just as quickly, he closed it and handed it back to Gary.

"I could have it dusted for fingerprints," Gary suggested.

Dan shook his head. "Who knows how many people have handled it?"

"It might have belonged to someone at college. Or high school."

"Possibly." Dan didn't want to think any more about the book. His senses recoiled at the prospect of touching it again. "But we *have* learned something important. Your brother was gay." He gazed at his surroundings. "There is so much love in this room: Brad's love for you, for your parents." He couldn't hold back the sigh that escaped him. He'd picked up on something else as well—Gary's mom's despair, her sorrow, her hope.

"After so long, you've given *me* hope too," Gary murmured.

It was only then that Dan realized he'd spoken out loud. He held his arms wide. "Come here." Gary walked into them without a second's hesitation, and Dan held him, feeling the pounding of Gary's heart.

So much emotion barely contained below the surface….

He cupped Gary's bearded chin and looked him in the eye. "This could be a marathon, not a sprint. You know that, right?"

Gary nodded. "And I can deal with that, as long as I have you."

Dan pulled him in closer, and their lips met in a gentle kiss, only to break the embrace with a start when he heard a gasp.

Gary's mom gaped at them.

"I think you two have got some explaining to do."

Chapter Eighteen

Gary and Dan sat at the dining table, facing Gary's parents. Gary took one look at his dad's furrowed brow and his mom's blank expression and realized what would follow would not be a conversation.

More like an interrogation.

Dad cleared his throat. "So… want to start at the beginning?"

It was as good a place to start as any, and there seemed little point in hiding the truth, not now the cat was well and truly out of the bag.

Gary glanced at Dan's hand on the table, reached over, and covered it with his own. Dan stilled, and the warmth in his eyes as he gazed at their joined hands nearly unraveled Gary.

He raised his chin and met his dad's stare. "Dan is my partner. He's living with me."

Dad said nothing for a moment, his eyes fixed on their hands. Finally he spoke. "So how long has this been going on?"

"Not long."

Mom huffed. "Can't say I'm all that surprised. I always thought you and Cory…."

Gary smiled. "Yeah, his sister Nina had the same thought. But Cory and me, we were just friends, maybe more like brothers at times."

Mom cocked her head. "How long have you known you were gay?"

"But I'm not gay," he protested. "I think bisexual is a better description. And as for how long? Maybe I've always known. I just chose not to do anything about it." He glanced at Dan. "Until I met Dan and I couldn't ignore the truth anymore."

They didn't need to know what Gary knew—that he believed he and Dan were meant to be together.

"And is he really a psychic?" Mom's arched eyebrows betrayed her skepticism.

"I can answer that for myself." Dan smiled. "Google me."

Dad snorted. "I did that when Gary called to say he was bringing you, but we didn't pay much attention, to be honest. We've met a lot of your kind. None of them ever found anything."

His eyes told a different story. That hopeful light, the same one Gary observed in his mom's eyes, kindled an even greater hope in Gary's chest.

Dan exuded a calm that Gary envied. He held out his hand to Mom. "Give me your hand."

She hesitated, then did as he asked in a tentative manner. Dan held her hand between his and closed his eyes. His breathing deepened, and Gary found himself holding his breath, praying for something to reveal itself, anything that would open their hearts and minds. The clock on the sideboard ticked the minutes away, yet no one spoke, and Gary realized his parents were just as focused.

They want this to work. They need to know.

Dan's breathing caught, and he opened his eyes. "You knew." He relaxed his shoulders, and a wave of relief crashed over Gary.

Thank you, Lord.

Mom swallowed, stiffening. "Knew what?"

Dan smiled. "Brad was sitting where I am now. He told you he'd found someone. He didn't tell you their name, but he did reveal he was gay." He squeezed her hand. "And then you cried and told him you were happy for him."

She widened her eyes. "How could you know that?" Dan gazed at her, his smile still evident, and all of a sudden she was smiling too. "Oh my God. You're for real." Then all words ceased when tears welled up and trickled down her face. She grabbed Dad's hand, her chest heaving. Dad nodded, unable to speak, his eyes glistening too.

Dan gently released Mom's hand. "I'm here to help you, all right? I'm going to find out what happened to Brad, if I can. Just… don't expect me to tell you next week, okay?"

Dad wiped his eyes. "We don't care how long it takes. We just need to know you're trying to find the monster who did this so they can be brought to justice."

"I want that too," Dan assured him. He glanced at Gary. "All three of you need to heal."

Gary's throat tightened. "We should be going now." He felt drained of energy.

Is this how Dan feels when he does this? For the first time, Gary understood how deeply Dan's gift affected him.

Mom regarded them with a pained expression. "Can't you stay for dinner?"

"Please stay," Dad added. "We've got a lot to talk about."

"I'll make your favorite—mac and cheese." Mom's beseeching gaze tugged at his heart.

He peered at Dan, who nodded. His lips twitched. "Mac and cheese beats your leftover meatballs."

Gary gaped in mock anger. "I thought you liked them."

"I did! I mean, I do." Dan's eyes twinkled. "I happen to like mac and cheese more, that's all."

Mom laughed. "Are you sure you haven't been together long?"

"And you haven't said yes yet," Dad remarked.

"You wouldn't have to leave right after dinner." Mom beamed. "You could stay the night. I'll make up the bed in your old room, and Dan can—" She blinked, her mouth snapping shut.

Gary coughed. "Dan can stay in my room too. *If* we stay." But he already knew he was fighting a losing battle. The enthusiasm in Mom's voice, Dad's eagerness…. It had been so long since he'd encountered either of those things, and he didn't want to dampen them with an abrupt departure. There was finally a crack in the wall his parents had built between themselves and Gary, and Gary wanted to see if he and Dan could widen it a little more.

Mom frowned. "Oh. I'm not sure about that."

Gary let out a chuckle. "Mom, I'm thirty-eight, not eighteen. You're not *really* going to make my boyfriend sleep in another room, are you? Because the only room left is Brad's." The word boyfriend still tasted strange on his tongue, but it was a taste he was growing to like more and more.

Dad nodded. "And besides, they'll only creep around the house when they think we're asleep and end up in the same bed." Gary gaped at him, and Dad stared back. "What? You should've seen what *we* got up to when I stayed for a weekend at your grandparents' place."

"Hey!" Mom smacked his arm. "They do *not* need to hear that, okay?"

Gary choked back the tears that threatened to overwhelm him. His parents weren't back, but they were on the right track, and it was all down to Dan.

I don't think I could ever put into words how much this means to me.

That didn't mean he wouldn't have a damn good try.

Gary smiled. "Of course we'll stay."

His parents' smiles told him he'd made the right decision. But as he went into the kitchen in search of Mom's cookies while she made coffee, what went through his head was Dan's reaction to the book in Brad's room.

Whatever he'd felt, it wasn't good.

Chapter Nineteen

Saturday, July 28, 2018

Dan opened his eyes. Gary lay beside him, facing the door, his breathing regular. Sunlight poured through the thin curtains at the window, and he became aware of noise elsewhere in the house. He grabbed his phone and peered at the screen.

Seriously?

He gave Gary's shoulder a shake. "Hey. Hey."

"Mm?" Gary rolled over to face him. "Morning." His tousled hair made Dan yearn to tease it straight with his fingers.

Dan chuckled. "But not for much longer." When Gary frowned, Dan held the phone in front of his face. "It's almost ten."

It took a second or two for his words to sink in. Then Gary sat upright. "Why didn't you wake me?"

"Wake *you*? I've only just opened my eyes." He threw back the comforter. "We'd better get dressed and get down there before they wonder what on earth we're doing."

To his surprise, Gary grabbed him and pulled him into his arms. "I'm pretty sure they've got a good idea."

Damn, Gary felt good. He smelled good too.

Then Dan remembered where they were. He stared at Gary. "If you think we're going to get up to anything under your parents' roof, then think again."

Gary laughed quietly. "Relax. I'm not *that* bold. But I'm not moving until I get my morning cuddle."

That was all it took to have Dan melting into his arms.

"You don't need to do this," Dan protested as Gary's mom pressed a plastic container full of leftover mac and cheese into his hands.

"You said how much you liked it. I made plenty. And don't worry about the box. You can bring it back next month when you come to

Sunday lunch." Her gaze met his, and he knew without a word what she was asking.

He smiled. "I'll make sure to bring it."

She beamed. "Oh, great." Then his heart soared when she threw her arms around him. "I'm so glad we got to meet you," she whispered against his cheek.

"Even if it was something of a surprise?"

She chuckled. "Yes, well, I won't deny that." She drew back. "And please, don't feel my wish to see you again is simply because of your... gift."

He squeezed her hand. "I knew that." The previous evening, the four of them had talked long into the night. In fact, Gary had shown extreme reluctance to go up to their room. And when Dan had finally closed the bedroom door behind them, Gary had been in his arms in a heartbeat. They'd lain with Gary curled up around him, talking quietly, until at last they'd both fallen asleep.

Brunch had been a cheerful meal, and Dan had helped in the preparation while Gary had gone out into the yard with his dad to discuss the recent changes he'd made. It had been Dan who'd suggested that they really did need to make a move, and Gary had finally agreed.

Gary emerged from the house, accompanied by his dad. He took one look at the box in Dan's hands and laughed. "My cooking isn't that bad, you know."

After another round of hugs, they were in the car and on their way back to Boston. Dan kept quiet. Gary had been in a contemplative mood all morning, and while Dan was loath to mention the idea that had come to him as they'd drunk coffee and chatted, he knew he'd have to bring it up sooner or later.

When they were about forty minutes from home, Dan summoned up his courage.

"Can we talk about Brad?"

"We did nothing *but* talk about Brad most of last night and this morning." Gary glanced at him. "Something particular you want to discuss?"

"What if Brad's killer didn't stop at Brad?"

Gary stilled. "Go on."

"What if there were more victims? What if Brad wasn't his first?"

Silence fell for a moment. Gary sighed. "Those are good questions."

"I've been thinking about where we could start looking. Brad's a cold case, right? Okay, so he's not one of ours, but he *is* a cold case."

"Yes, I agree."

"Well, if there were more victims, maybe they're unexplained too."

Gary pursed his lips. "This assumes Brad's killer hasn't already been incarcerated for another murder, like Frank Wyler."

"That's a possibility. What we need to do is investigate other violent deaths around the same time as Brad's." He peered at Gary. "Unless you've already done that?"

Gary shook his head.

In that moment, Dan saw the truth. "You haven't investigated Brad's death at all, have you?"

Gary gave a start, jerking his head in Dan's direction. "Is this going to be a recurring part of our lives from now on? You see so much."

"Too much?" The last thing Dan wanted was to make Gary feel awkward or uncomfortable.

Gary smiled. "No, it's okay. And you're right. I haven't looked all that much into Brad's death. Which is strange seeing as I joined the police to do just that."

Dan laid his hand on Gary's knee. "It's not strange. At least, not to me. You have a strict sense of duty." He tilted his head. "You felt torn, didn't you? Torn between spending time on Brad when you had cases of your own to investigate, and feeling as if you'd failed him if you didn't find his killer. And in that situation of being pulled in two directions, you didn't move forward. You stayed stuck in the same place."

Gary's Adam's apple bobbed. "And with each new year, I promised myself I'd find the person responsible. I'd do something."

"And now you *are*," Dan assured him. "And something else occurred to me. You know how we're tracking down Cheryl's friends from college? Maybe we should do the same with Brad's. College, high school…. Maybe some of them know something." He squeezed Gary's thigh. "But like I said, we'll find a way to do it on our own time."

Gary covered Dan's hand with his own. "Seeing how much you've already discovered, I have no doubt we will do it."

What Dan noticed immediately was the change in Gary's breathing, the way he relaxed into the driver's seat.

I did the right thing, telling him.

Sunday, July 29, 2018

GARY REACHED across the bed, seeking Dan's warm body, and encountered nothing but the smooth cotton sheet. He snapped on the light and peered at his alarm clock. Two in the morning. Gary sat up, threw back the sheet, and got out of bed. He padded into the living room to find Dan sitting naked on the rug, boxes of Cheryl's stuff around him. He'd emptied a couple of them, and various objects were spread out in front of him.

Dan was lost in a world of his own.

Gary cleared his throat, and Dan jerked his head up. "Hey. Why aren't you asleep?"

"I could ask you the same question." He crouched beside him.

Dan gestured to the piles surrounding him. "The answers must be here. She handled all this." He frowned. "I should be able to get a sense of her." He picked up a scarf and held it to his face.

"What this situation requires is hot chocolate," Gary said decisively. He stood and went into the kitchen. As he heated the milk, he glanced at his naked body.

He's getting me into new and strange habits. Gary was used to wearing *something* around the place, but he had to admit, he liked the idea of letting it all hang out.

He carried the two cups into the living room and set them down on the coffee table. "You're going to put all this back in the boxes, drink this, and then we're both going back to bed." He gestured to the scarf. "Anything?"

"I think this was a gift, and a romantic one at that."

Gary arched his eyebrows. "Interesting. We must ask her father if she had a partner."

Dan opened one of the folders. He removed a sheaf of photos and spread them out on the rug. "She worked from these." He pointed. "Look, there are smears of paint on them." Dan leaned back on his hands. "I'm getting a sense of her routine. And I think she developed all the photos herself." He held up a sheet of negatives. "See? The ones she didn't intend using, she put a line through them." Then he stilled.

"What is it?"

Dan stared at the sheet. "The emotions linked to the negatives. The main one is curiosity. Intense curiosity."

Gary frowned. "About photos *she* took? That doesn't make sense."

Dan nodded, his eyes wide. "I know! But this was important to her." He put the sheet of negatives down and pulled another box toward him. He peered into it. "So many books. Mainly biographies of artists, art in general." He reached into the box and removed one with a smile. "I don't think this one was for reference, however."

Gary peered at the hard-backed book's cover. "The *Kama Sutra*?"

Dan chuckled. "A well-thumbed copy of the *Kama Sutra*."

Gary took it from him and flicked through it. "I'm not going to ask what you feel when you hold this."

Dan's eyes glittered. "Good. Because I'm a gentleman, and some things should remain secret." His cock rose, diverting Gary's attention.

"Pity there isn't a gay version," Gary remarked, unable to tear his gaze away from Dan's crotch.

Then Dan coughed loudly, and Gary blinked. Dan grinned. "There is. And I have a copy. Actually, it's in one of my boxes in your closet."

Gary stood. "Bring the hot chocolate. This can wait." He held out his hand to Dan.

Dan got to his feet. "We're not going back to bed to sleep, are we?"

"Not even close."

CHAPTER TWENTY

Monday, July 30, 2018

GARY'S PHONE rang, and he peered at the screen. "It's Pete Raskin." He clicked Answer, then put him on speaker. "Good morning."

"I know I shouldn't be doing this, but I just wanted to know if you'd made any progress. Have you learned anything new?"

Gary could hear the barely concealed anxiety in his voice. "We do have a few leads to look into," he admitted. Aiden Reynolds wasn't off the hook yet, and *someone* had told Connor Brightmore's family that Cheryl was dead. And then there was Paul DiFanetti. "We met with Aiden Reynolds."

Pete huffed. "I bet you felt as if you needed a bath after that."

At his desk, Dan frowned. "You've seen his posts on social media."

"I'm not on any of that, but my buddy Francis is. I got him to do a search. Didn't much like what he found."

Neither did I.

"We still have some inquiries to make about him." Then Gary remembered the scarf Dan had found. "Mr. Raskin, did Cheryl have a partner? I know you haven't mentioned one, but did she date much?"

"Not really. She was either working or painting. But…."

His hesitation pricked Gary's interest. "What did you just think of?"

There was a pause. "Do you have children, Detective Mitchell?"

"No."

"Well… one of the things about being a parent is sometimes you get a kind of sixth sense. I'll share something with you. I think Cheryl was keeping a secret."

Gary thought it was probably the copies.

"I think there might have been someone she never told me about. I do know it wasn't that Rayne."

Gary frowned. "Who?"

"Rayne Wilcox. They met at college, right about the time she was starting to go by the name of Cheryl. Anyway, Rayne came home with

Cheryl two, three times. She stayed with us. Tried her luck too, not that she got anywhere."

"What do you mean?" Dan called out.

"She had a thing for Cheryl." Pete chuckled. "Not that she was subtle about it. She might just as well have worn a neon sign on her head that said Date Me, Cheryl? And then one night while she was staying with us, I got up to go to the bathroom, and I caught Rayne coming out of Cheryl's room. Judging by the look on her face, she'd struck out. They were okay the following morning, though, so I guess Rayne didn't take rejection too badly. But they were close. Yeah, you should talk to Rayne. She might know if Cheryl was interested in anyone." His voice took on a decisive edge.

Gary watched Dan scribble on a notepad. "We'll do that. And Mr. Raskin? I know you're anxious for news, but—"

"But I should wait for you to call me," he interjected. "Yeah, I can see how me calling all the time might get to be a nuisance. Okay. I'll let you get on with it."

There was something in Pete's voice that told Gary he wouldn't be happy about waiting, however.

Dan got up and walked over to Gary's desk. "Mr. Raskin, we want to find the person responsible too."

"I know. And I thank God you've taken this case on. So I guess I should let you do your job." He said goodbye and hung up.

Dan sighed. "We've brought back all the pain again." He returned to his own desk.

"Then let's see what we can learn from this Rayne character. Maybe that'll bring us closer to the truth." Gary tapped on the keyboard, peering at the monitor. "Aha."

"That was fast. Have you found her already?"

He nodded. "Rayne Wilcox. Works at the Institute of Contemporary Art." He grabbed the phone and dialed. It wasn't long before he was connected to the right department.

"Hello?"

"Rayne Wilcox? This is Detective Gary Mitchell. I'm part of Boston PD's cold case department, and we're investigating the death of Cheryl Somers."

"Oh, that's great. Do you need background info on her? Is that why you're calling? Because I knew her pretty well."

"That's exactly why I'm calling."

"I don't work Tuesdays. I could come to the police precinct tomorrow if that would be okay."

Gary made a note. "That would be great. Morning or afternoon?"

"Afternoon would be better. I've got some things I need to see to in the morning."

They agreed on an approximate time, and Gary thanked her before disconnecting.

Dan smiled. "A positive result. Let's hope she can help us."

Gary went back to the keyboard. "What was the name of Connor Brightmore's boyfriend?" He scanned the surface of his desk. "Where's my notepad?"

"I've got it here." Dan grabbed it and hunted through its pages. "Ian Gordon, the senator said."

Gary did a search. "Okay, there are three Ian Gordons in Boston. That's assuming he still lives in Boston." If none of those checked out, they'd widen the field.

"He'd be in his midfifties by now. That might help narrow down the search." Dan went back to his desk. "I'll take a look on social media."

The first Ian Gordon turned out to be in his thirties. The second was in college.

"Hey, I might have found him." Dan stared at his phone. "This guy is the right age. He's a software designer here in Boston." Dan smiled. "According to his Facebook page, he works from home. Perfect."

"Then let's find an address for him. We'll pay him a visit."

"Don't you want to call him first?"

Gary shook his head. "I want you to see him, hear him… get a feel for him. And if I call first, he might refuse to see us."

"You're hoping he's our man, aren't you?"

"He has one of the strongest motives so far, don't you think?"

Dan leaned back in his chair, his fingers laced.

Gary cocked his head. "But you don't think that, do you?"

"Did you check the case notes? Is there any mention of the senator supplying his name to the detectives at the time?"

Gary had given the notes a cursory glance. "None at all." When Dan fell silent, Gary studied him. "What's on your mind?"

"It just strikes me that we're only going to see this Ian Gordon because of what Senator Cain told us. But what if the senator is lying?"

Gary cocked his head. "I thought you liked him."

"I do. But that doesn't mean we should trust him implicitly."

"But why would he lie?" The only reason Gary could think of would be to deflect attention away from himself, except that made no sense. The senator wasn't under suspicion.

Dan's gaze grew thoughtful. "No one is above suspicion, except for Cheryl's dad."

Gary chuckled. "You really need to stop doing that."

"Doing what?" Dan appeared confused.

"Coming out with stuff that I'd been thinking only a second or two before." He liked that they seemed to be on the same wavelength, but all the same, it still felt as though Dan was in his head.

Concern flickered in Dan's eyes. "I'm not sure I can turn it off. Is that going to be a problem?"

If they weren't in the office, Gary would have taken Dan in his arms and reassured him with a kiss. "I don't think so. Now, back to the senator…."

Dan bit his lip. "All I'm saying is… check out his statement before we make a move. Who were the detectives on the case back then? I'm talking about when she first disappeared."

Gary picked up the folder and opened it. "Detectives Owen Williams and Phil Harris." He stilled. "Wait a sec. I know that name." He smiled. "Got it. I'm sure that's the same Phil who runs the coffee shop on Massachusetts Avenue. I think he opened it when he retired."

"Isn't that where you stop for coffee some mornings? The one that does those amazing cinnamon rolls?"

"The same." Gary grinned. "You know what? I think we need a coffee break."

Dan was already reaching for his jacket.

THE SMELL inside the coffeehouse was as fragrant and delicious as always. Gary inhaled deeply, breathing in the aromas of freshly brewed coffee, sugar, spice. He'd been coming to Phil's Place for about three years. It was popular with his coworkers, and Phil brewed a great cup of coffee.

"I'll grab a table." Dan headed for the corner.

Gary went to the counter to order coffee. Phil was chatting with the young woman who often served Gary first thing in the morning. He broke off their conversation when he caught sight of Gary and flashed him a broad smile.

"Don't normally see you twice in one day, Detective. Not that I'm complaining." He inclined his head toward Dan. "Does he want his americano as usual?"

"Please, and a coffee with cream, no sugar, for me. A couple of danishes too." Gary paused. "And a few minutes of your time if you can spare them. This isn't exactly a social visit."

Phil arched his eyebrows. "I see." He removed his black apron. "Dee? Take over for me for a minute, would you? And I'll have a coffee with cream, two sugars."

"Sure, Grandpa."

Phil walked out from behind the counter and accompanied Gary to their table. Gary sat beside Dan. Phil pulled out the chair facing them and sat. He regarded Dan with interest. "I recognized you when you came in last month. You're that psychic who's been helping out my former coworkers."

Dan gave a nod. "And we're here because we need *your* help."

"Color me intrigued." Phil clammed up when Dee came over with the coffees and pastries. "Thanks, honey." He waited until she was back behind the counter. "Okay, guys, what do you need from me?"

"In 1992, you investigated the disappearance of Cheryl Somers."

"Ninety-two? Wow. Talk about ancient history. The name's familiar." Phil froze. "Wasn't she the one who turned out to be the body in the tunnel? Yeah, I remember." He frowned. "But I wasn't one of the detectives investigating how she came to *be* in that tunnel. She was only a missing person when I got involved."

"We know," Gary said. "But that's the part *we're* interested in, the initial investigation."

"Specifically, if you recall speaking with Senator William Cain," Dan added.

Phil sipped his coffee. "He and her dad reported her missing, I recall that much. Is that what you're talking about?"

Gary shook his head. "The senator claims he came to you with an idea about who could have been responsible for her disappearance."

Phil's brow furrowed. "Claims?"

"Yeah. There's no record of him doing that in your case notes." Gary waited.

"Then why would he—" Phil's eyes widened. "Wait a minute. Yeah. He had this theory that some guy was out for revenge. Something to do with a car accident?" He frowned. "I don't recall the exact details, but yeah, I vaguely remember the conversation."

"But you didn't make a record of it."

Phil sighed. "Give me a minute, all right?" He sipped his coffee, the furrows in his brow deepening. "If memory serves—and it's not as sharp as it used to be—I thought it was a little far-fetched, if I'm honest. I mean, she'd been missing a week at that point. And the accident he said she'd been involved in was *how* many years before that? Nine, ten? Something like that at any rate. And all that part about death threats." He shook his head. "I think I told him he had an overactive imagination." He looked Gary in the eye. "So what you're telling me is he might have been right all along?"

"Let's just say it's a theory. We wanted to check with you that the senator had actually suggested it."

Phil nodded. "Yeah, he did. And I'll tell you something else. That was one distraught guy. Apparently this Cheryl had grown up on the Cain estate, was that right?"

"Yes. He pulled out all the stops trying to find her," Dan told him.

Phil's face fell. "If this guy he spoke about turns out to be her killer, I'm gonna feel like a total shit for ignoring him, you know that, right?"

"Do you want to know what we discover?" Gary could do that if it meant they put Phil out of his obvious misery.

Phil nodded once more. "Although if it *is* him, I'm not sure I'll ever forgive myself." He pointed to the plate containing the danishes. "Those are on me, guys. And be sure to come back when you solve this case." Then he pushed back his chair, stood, and returned to his usual spot behind the counter, taking his coffee with him.

Dan watched him with a solemn expression. "I think we've just ruined his day."

Gary had the feeling Dan was right. "Let's finish our coffee, and then we'll pay Ian Gordon a visit."

IAN GORDON was in his midfifties, his dark hair showing little evidence of gray. He was casually dressed in jeans and a button-down shirt. He greeted them politely, then showed them into his living room. "Have I got a parking ticket I know nothing about? Although I hardly think that would warrant a visit from a detective." He indicated the couch. "Can I get you some coffee, tea, juice?"

Gary held his hand up. "We're fine, thank you. And just to clarify… you *are* the Ian Gordon who was in a relationship with Connor Brightmore?"

Ian stilled. "Now that's a name I haven't heard for a long time." A faint frown creased his forehead. "Yes, I was in a relationship with Connor back in college, but I'm puzzled. Why would you be here about something that ended—tragically—over thirty years ago?"

"We're investigating the death of Cheryl Somers."

He frowned. "I don't believe I've ever known someone of that name. I think you might have the wrong person."

"Before she transitioned, her name was Benjamin Raskin."

Ian's back became rigid. "I see."

Dan didn't take his eyes off Ian. "You *were* dating Connor Brightmore at the time of his accident, weren't you?"

"I was, yes." He managed a shrug. "It was a long time ago. And I *was* very young." His frown was back. "But I don't understand why you're here."

"Cheryl received anonymous letters and death-threat phone calls for a couple of years after Connor's death," Gary told him. "We wondered if there was anything you could tell us about those."

Dan focused on Ian, opening himself to whatever emotions were coming his way.

Ian stared at Gary. "I have no idea what you're talking about."

And just like that, the shutters came down and no one was home.

"Connor's father told us whoever killed Cheryl informed him of her death." Dan spoke quietly. "He called this person an avenging angel."

Ian's expression was neutral. "And you think that person was me?"

Neutral my ass. Something was going on inside Ian Gordon. Dan could feel it.

Now all he needed was to prove it.

"Are you saying it wasn't?" Gary's tone told Dan he wasn't convinced by Ian's lack of emotion either.

"When we spoke with Mr. Brightmore, we didn't know about you." Dan straightened. "Maybe we should go back to him and ask if his 'angel' was called Ian."

He was pushing, but it was all he could think of until he had more to work on than just his feelings.

Ian paled. "No. Don't do that."

"Why not?" Gary demanded.

Dan couldn't speak. Every sense he possessed told him something was coming.

"Because…." Ian launched himself across the living room to the sideboard, where he picked up a cigarette pack. He opened it and groaned. "Christ." He tossed the empty packet aside.

Dan's heart hammered. "Wait a sec. You can have one of mine." He reached into his jacket pocket and pulled out the pack he'd taken to FMC Devens. He held it out and waited, his heartbeat racing.

"Thanks." Ian's hand shook as he took it. He removed a cigarette, then grabbed his lighter from the sideboard. He lit it and took a long, shuddering drag on it before glancing at a nearby framed photo. "My husband keeps telling me to quit, but I just can't." He handed Dan the packet.

Dan took it, his breathing catching as their fingers brushed. *Here we go.* He focused all his energy and concentrated.

Ian gave him a quizzical glance. "Are you all right?"

Dan ignored him, aware of the first trickles of knowledge crawling over him, making him shiver. And when realization hit, it floored him.

Gotcha.

He stared at Ian. "You told Mr. Brightmore *you'd* killed her."

Ian's face was like milk.

Gary studied him. "Mr. Gordon?"

"How… how could you know that?" Ian's eyes were impossibly large. "And how much *more* do you know?"

"That doesn't matter now."

"Are you for real? What the hell did you do, read my mind or something?"

"Suppose you tell us what happened." Dan regarded him with a speculative glance. "Don't you think it's time for that?" He softened his voice. "I already know the truth," he lied.

He knew most of it, including one item that had him scanning the room, his heartbeat racing.

Where is it?

"Then you don't need to hear it from me," Ian croaked.

"Tell us, please." Gary spoke in a coaxing tone.

Ian sank onto the couch, his fingers trembling as they clutched his cigarette. "When... when we lost all trace of Benjamin Raskin, I was devastated."

Yet more knowledge washed over Dan. "You did send those letters, didn't you?"

Ian nodded, swallowing. "But I didn't make any threatening phone calls, I swear." Another hard swallow. "I-I really thought the letters would do the trick, but... nothing. Then he just vanished. I-I was starting out in business as a software designer, and I needed capital. So...."

Dan expelled a long breath. "So you went to Connor's father—Connor's very wealthy father—and told him *you'd* gotten rid of Raskin."

"Not in so many words, but—"

"But you hinted," Dan continued. "You hoped he'd read between the lines and help you out with a little investment."

"Did he?" Gary asked.

Ian nodded once again. "As far as he's concerned, I'd killed the man responsible for his son's death. But I didn't, honest." He gaped at Dan. "You have to believe me."

"But you did threaten him," Dan countered.

Ian set his jaw. "I was twenty-one years old, and Raskin had robbed me of the man I loved, the man I envisaged spending the rest of my life with. And don't tell me I was way too young to feel that depth of emotion. You know nothing about me. I was willing to bide my time until Connor knew what *I'd* known the moment we met—that we were meant to be together." He grabbed an ashtray from the coffee table and stubbed his cigarette out. "I thought my letters would pay off, that Raskin would suffer, but then he up and disappeared. I mean, there was no trace of him whatsoever." Ian locked gazes with Dan. "He'd escaped it all, and Connor's family and I, we were left to grieve." He shuddered. "Please, don't tell Roland I lied."

"He'll have to know eventually." Gary's voice was gentle.

"Why will he?"

"Because we're going to discover who the real murderer is," Dan told him. "And once we do that, the media will be full of it. How will you explain that?"

The horror in Ian's unwavering stare almost made Dan feel sorry for him.

Almost.

Then he realized both Ian Gordon and Mr. Brightmore were alike in one important respect.

"The hate in your voice when you speak of Cheryl—Benjamin—and your actions would make a lot more sense if Benjamin had actually been the one at fault in the accident." Dan didn't break eye contact. "But he wasn't."

"Wasn't he?"

"According to both the witnesses and the police, no, he wasn't."

"And no one's ever bribed witnesses? Or police officers?" Ian retorted.

At last it made sense.

"You think they all lied. You think someone paid them to exonerate Benjamin."

"It makes more—"

The sound of the back door opening made all three of them jump.

"That's my husband," Ian said, his voice cracking. "I don't want him to know about this."

"Then we'll be on our way." Gary gave Dan a nod, and they headed for the front of the house, leaving Ian standing in the living room, looking lost.

Dan was shaking as they walked toward the car.

"You need to rest, don't you?" Gary gave him a sympathetic glance.

Resting could wait.

"What if he really did kill her? And what he hinted to Connor's father was the truth?"

"You didn't get a clear picture, did you?"

Dan had gotten a few images, but not enough to point to Ian Gordon's absolute guilt or innocence.

"At least we know now that the senator was telling the truth."

"Yeah, I guess."

Dan glanced at Gary. "You want him to be dirty, and he keeps coming up clean."

Gary rolled his eyes. "Can you blame me? Whoever heard of an honest politician?"

Dan chuckled, but then his mind went back to the conversation with Ian. "One thing puzzles me," he murmured. "Gordon owned up to the letters, but not the calls."

"Who's to say he's telling the truth?"

"But why lie? One act isn't worse than the other. But that leaves us with a conundrum. Who made the calls? Because *someone* did." Dan shivered. "And if he didn't intend harming Cheryl, why did he buy a gun?"

Gary came to a halt in the middle of the sidewalk. "He did what? How do you know?"

"I saw it when we touched hands. But he didn't buy it from a gun shop. That would leave a trace. I'd be willing to bet if you check, there'll be no record of him owning one, but he got hold of it from somewhere— and he still has it." Dan met Gary's gaze. "He says he didn't kill Cheryl. We don't know that for certain."

"He also says he didn't know about the transition."

Dan shrugged. "Sure, he *says* that. Doesn't make it true. And here's something else to think about. Maybe Cheryl's head was removed not to impede identification, but to get rid of the evidence."

"Evidence of what?"

Dan arched his eyebrows. "The bullet hole, what else?" He sighed. "I wish I'd seen more."

Sometimes his visions sucked.

Chapter Twenty-One

Tuesday, July 31, 2018

THE DIFANETTI Construction Company occupied an unimposing building on Dorchester Avenue, stuck in the middle of a lot that comprised a couple of gyms, a glass factory, a paint shop, and the home of Building Restoration Services.

"Do you think they'll have kept time sheets going back that far?" Dan asked as they got out of the car.

"If they've evolved along with the rest of the modern world, everything will be digital now." At least that was Gary's hope. They knew Aiden Reynolds had been employed by the construction company in August of 1992—all they wanted to do was pin it down.

They strolled over to the wood-and-glass door that bore the DFF logo, and Gary pressed the intercom.

"Can I help you?" The voice came from the tiny speaker.

Gary peered up at the camera above the door and flashed his badge. "Police. We'd like some information about a former employee."

A second later the door buzzed open, and they pushed inside. The office front was nothing but a desk, filing cabinets, and a couple of chairs, with another door at the rear marked Private. In one of the chairs, a man sat reading a newspaper, his jeans and boots smeared with dust. He glanced at them with the merest hint of interest before resuming his reading.

Behind the desk was a middle-aged woman, tapping at a keyboard. She stopped as they approached, and Gary held his badge up once more.

"Detective Mitchell, Boston PD."

She gave him a polite smile. "Good morning. What kind of information are you looking for? I'm afraid I can't divulge personal details."

"We're after time sheets," Gary told her. "We're trying to ascertain where one of your former employees was working on a particular day. Are you able to give out that information?"

She glanced toward the rear door. "Normally I'd ask the office manager, Mr. Abrahams, but he's not in today." She bit her lip. "I'm sure it'll be okay." She picked up a pen. "What's the name? And what was the date?"

"Aiden Reynolds. And we need details for August twenty-eighth, 1992."

She blinked. "I see. I don't recognize the name, but I've only worked here for six years. And I'm not sure if I can look back that far, but I'll try. If it's not on the system, I'll check in the paper records. We do still have some of those." Her eyes glinted. "Let's hope he's in here." She patted the monitor. "Because if he isn't, that'll mean a lot more work to track him down."

Gary got the sinking feeling Reynolds was going to be problematical.

Behind him a newspaper rustled. "Why are you interested in Aiden?"

Gary turned to find a pair of brown eyes focused on him. The man was in his mid to late forties, his dark brows scrunched up.

"Do you know him?" Dan asked.

"I used to work with him. What's he done to have the police checking up on him? Aiden's a great guy."

"All we're doing is verifying some details he gave us." Gary held up his notepad. "And believe it or not, he'd want us to verify them."

The man sneered. "Yeah, right."

The receptionist cleared her throat. "Detective? Our digital records only go back to 2000."

"But you mentioned paper records. How long do you keep them for?"

She got up from her chair with a grumble. "I'll take a look." She disappeared behind the rear door.

Dan turned back to the man in the chair. "How long did you work with Mr. Reynolds?"

The man stroked his stubble-covered chin. "I started with this company when I was twenty-three. That was in '95. Aiden was my foreman. We worked together till he left us in 2009."

Damn. That meant they hadn't worked together on the tunnel—it had been finished in 1994.

"Was he a good foreman?" Dan asked.

The man shrugged. "He was okay. Better than some. You could have a laugh with him at least. You didn't have to watch your mouth, not like some of the guys I work with nowadays." The sneer was back. "Working on a construction site isn't like it used to be. When I first started, if you saw a nice bit of skirt walking past, you'd whistle at her or call out to her. Times have changed, though. These days you gotta be careful. Either she'll report you, or you find out she isn't a she in the first place."

"Some people might argue those changes are for the better," Dan murmured.

The man's eyes narrowed, but before he could say a word, the rear door opened.

"Detective?" The receptionist held up two index cards. "I have the details you're looking for."

They walked over to her desk, and Gary plucked his pen from his pocket.

"In August 1992, Aiden Reynolds was working on the Ames Building. They were renovating it at the time."

Gary arched his eyebrows. "Getting that contract must have been quite a feat." He made a note. "So he was in Boston on the twenty-eighth."

And miles from Lenox.

"Yes, he was. Well, only at the end of the day. For the rest of it, he was finishing up a job he'd been working on the previous month."

Gary held his breath.

"And where was that?" Dan inquired.

"He'd been building a pool house in Lenox."

Gotcha.

Gary made a note. "Thank you for your help." He glanced at Dan. "We'd better go. We're interviewing Rayne Wilcox in an hour." He thanked the receptionist once more, and they hurried from the office.

"So he *was* there," Dan muttered as they got into the car.

"Before you get *too* excited, something just occurred to me." Gary frowned. "We don't know if Cheryl was there. We only know her father saw her that morning at the house. We have no idea how long she was there, or if she even stayed there. For all we know, she came back to Boston."

"If she did, even better." Dan's eyes gleamed. "We can place Reynolds in both locations."

GARY ENTERED Interview Room One, and Rayne Wilcox stood to greet him. She was in her midfifties, with short red hair, a glorious shade that had to come from a bottle. The frames of her glasses were red too, as were her lips. She wore black pants and a long white blouse, open at the neck, beneath an equally long black jacket. Gary's first impression was one of height, until he noticed her shiny red high-heeled shoes.

Rayne held out her hand, and Gary took it. She gripped his hand firmly as they shook, looking him in the eye before she greeted Dan with a confident air.

"Thank you for coming in today." Dan gestured to her chair, and she sat once more. They joined her at the table, and Gary prepared to take notes.

They'd agreed Dan would take the lead on this one.

"Gentlemen." Rayne leaned back, relaxed. "You're looking into Cheryl's death? You're about twenty-six years too late, but I guess better late than never."

"You met in college, we've been told," Dan began.

Rayne nodded. "Of course when we first met, she was still Ben. And a *very* different person. But once she made the decision to listen to what her heart and body told her, she was so much happier." She smiled. "I liked her before, but after…." She sighed. "We were close."

Dan leaned forward, his hands clasped. "Just not as close as you would have liked."

Rayne's cheeks flushed, and her eyes widened. "How did you…?"

Dan gave a modest shrug. "Let's just say I'm good at picking up on things."

"I'd hazard a guess that might be the understatement of the year." Rayne cleared her throat. "Well, seeing as you already know that part… it was nothing heavy." She gave a half smile. "I asked, she said no, and we left it at that. I hoped I hadn't ruined what we shared, and thankfully we stayed friends for years after college. We'd meet for coffee, catch up, go see a movie, stuff like that." Another smile, only this one was more relaxed. "We shared a common interest, and that formed the basis of our relationship."

"That would have been art, considering your job and hers," Dan proffered.

She nodded. "Art was our life, so we always had plenty to talk about." Rayne tilted her head to one side. "You know what I loved most about Cheryl? You always knew where you were with her. No subterfuge, no hidden agendas…. If she had an opinion, she shared it." She bit her lip. "At least, she did."

"What changed?"

Rayne stared at the tabletop. "She'd have been twenty-five, I think, when I first got the feeling she was holding out on me. It was a few months after that scumbag assaulted her." She grimaced. "I'd never seen her in such a mess. Come to think of it, that was the longest we ever went without meeting up. It must have been about five months before I saw her again. And what a transformation."

"What do you mean?"

Gary was curious too.

"She turned up at our usual coffee shop, and… wow." Rayne's cheeks pinked. "She'd had a boob job, and she looked amazing. But it wasn't just the boost it gave to her confidence. It was more than that."

"Did she ever talk about her personal life?" Gary inquired.

"Nope. It was always her latest portrait, how her dad was doing, her work at the museum. But that light in her eyes, the spring in her step. She couldn't fool me." Rayne smiled. "She'd met someone. It was written all over her."

Saturday, November 25, 1989

RAYNE WAS certain she was doing a great impression of the Cheshire Cat from *Alice in Wonderland*: she hadn't stopped smiling since Cheryl walked into the coffee shop and joined her at her table.

"Sweetheart, you look like a million dollars."

Cheryl's face flushed. "I do not." She removed her heavy coat and soft-looking scarf and placed them carefully over the back of the chair before pulling it out to sit facing Rayne. "Oh, thanks. You already ordered for me."

Then Rayne got a better look at her, and *damn*, her face felt as if it were on fire.

"You've had a little work done since I last saw you." Cheryl's usual attire of high-necked blouse or top was no longer in evidence, and in its place was a low V-necked sweater that revealed new curves, not to mention a stunning cleavage.

Cheryl's eyes sparkled. "I'm still getting used to it. Sometimes I catch sight of my reflection in a store window and I don't recognize myself." She peered at Rayne through long lashes. "Do they look okay?"

Rayne snorted. "You *are* kidding, right? Honey, they look fabulous."

Cheryl's cheeks went from pink to red.

They chatted about their work and the portrait Cheryl was working on. Cheryl shared photos of it, and as usual Rayne was in awe of her talent. What was different, however, was Cheryl. It wasn't just the implants or the glow about her.

She was practically buzzing.

Rayne leaned forward, lowering her voice. "So what gives?"

Cheryl blinked. "Excuse me?"

Rayne smiled. "You can't fool me, sugar. It's written all over you."

"What is?"

She laughed. "Oh my God, Cheryl, never decide to start playing poker."

"I don't know what you're talking about."

Rayne rolled her eyes. "Talk about blood out of a stone. Okay, let's cut the bullshit. Who is he? Or she? And don't give me that *I don't know what you're talking about* line again, because I didn't swallow it the first time." She grinned. "Cheryl's in lo-ove," she said in a singsong voice.

"Will you hush?" Cheryl glanced at the coffee shop's occupants, but no one was paying them any mind. "And who says I'm in love?"

"Your face. Your voice. The way you floated in here on a cloud of happiness."

Cheryl picked up her cup and took a drink, her face glowing.

"Just tell me one thing. Is it serious?"

For a moment, it looked as if Cheryl was going to deny everything again, but then a sigh rolled out of her. "I don't know. It's early days, all right?"

A pang sliced into Rayne's heart, but she was a big enough person that she could forget all she'd hoped for and be happy for Cheryl. It was difficult to be anything *but* happy when faced with the joy that radiated from her.

"You still haven't told me their name," she said with a smile.

Cheryl's eyes were sparkling again. "No, I haven't, have I?"

Tuesday, July 31, 2018

"And that was all I ever got out of her," Rayne concluded.

"So you have no idea who she might have been seeing? And whether they were male or female?" Gary paused in his note writing.

Rayne shook her head. "I'd always thought Cheryl was crap at keeping secrets, but that was one she kept until the last time I saw her. And while she never came right out and said it, she was in love."

"When was the last time you saw her?" Dan asked.

Rayne frowned. "That would have been my birthday, August twenty-sixth, 1992. We met for dinner at a sushi restaurant. I'd organized a party for the weekend, the twenty-ninth, just a few friends, and I invited Cheryl. But she said she couldn't make it." She sighed. "She was polite about it, but I wasn't stupid. It was obvious she was going to meet whoever it was she was seeing."

"The last person to see her—that we know about—was her father," Dan remarked. "And that was the morning of August twenty-eighth."

Rayne stared at him. "You don't think…. But she was so happy. She wouldn't have been so relaxed and radiant if whoever she was dating was dangerous. She wasn't stupid. The episode with that Reynolds guy had taught her to be careful."

"Is there anything else you can tell us?" Gary closed his notepad.

Rayne shook her head. "Just promise me you'll find the person responsible, okay?"

"That's what we're here for," Dan said with a smile.

They'd learned something new at least.

Dan showed Rayne out of the building, and he and Gary returned to their office. Gary sat at his desk, reading the notes he'd taken. Dan came in and closed the door.

"Rayne did get one thing wrong," he observed.

"And what was that?"

"Cheryl wasn't as bad at keeping secrets as Rayne supposed. Her dad had no clue about her copies, for one thing." He stroked his chin. "That stuff we got from Cheryl's studio… I haven't finished going through it all. Maybe there's something there." His gaze met Gary's. "There'd better be. We need all the help we can get."

"We're further along than you realize." Dan arched his eyebrows, and Gary counted off on his fingers. "We're not done with Aiden Reynolds. Or Paul DiFanetti. Or Ian Gordon, if it comes to that. And we won't let one of them off the hook until we know for certain they had nothing to do with her death."

The more he learned about Cheryl, the more determined he became to catch the person who had snuffed out what promised to be an awesome life.

DAN HARDLY noticed as Gary removed the dishes from the dining table. He was leafing through one of Cheryl's books, unable to account for the way it made him feel. The illustrations were erotic, but more often than not, he focused on the male, noting the way the artist had drawn his clenched buttocks, the strong line of his muscular thighs, the arch of his back.

"Found something interesting?" Gary stood by the table, a book in his hand.

Dan jumped. "Sorry. I must've zoned out for a moment."

Gary grinned. "The *Kama Sutra*—again?" Then Dan stilled, and Gary stared at him. "What is it?"

Dan wished he knew.

"This book… I get the feeling it's important. As if the answer is right here at my fingertips." He put it aside with a sigh. "This is going to bug me till I work out what it is that keeps pulling me to it. I've got enough weird stuff going on, thank you very much."

"What kind of weird stuff?"

"You know how sometimes you wake up with a song in your head?"

Gary pulled a face. "Earworms. I hate them."

"Well… the last couple of nights, I keep seeing flashes of a movie. The same movie. And what's more, it stays with me when I wake up."

Gary blinked. "Which one?"

"*Cape Fear*. I've seen it maybe two, three times. It's not even one of my favorites."

"You mentioned it a while back. You're still seeing it?"

"Yeah, except when I told you about it, I was only seeing it as a DVD cover or a movie poster. Now it's scenes from the movie." He shrugged. "Maybe it's just a persistent dream."

The silence hit him, and he jerked his head in Gary's direction.

"And maybe it's not," Gary said slowly. "Maybe… it's a vision."

"One that keeps coming back." Dan shivered. "The last recurring vision stuck around for thirteen years. I hope this one isn't the same."

"But that vision has stopped now, right?"

Dan assured him it had.

Gary smiled. "That's because you're where you belong."

Warmth seeped into every part of Dan's body. "I know that look. We're having an early night, aren't we?"

Gary's eyes gleamed. "Yes, we are."

"We've been having a lot of those. Late mornings too." Not that he was complaining.

"I'm making up for lost time. Plus, don't they say practice makes perfect?"

Dan bit back a smile. "Trust me, you're doing pretty good." Gary's eagerness in bed was a delight, and if Dan was getting less sleep than he was used to, it was *so* worth it.

Then he took a closer look at the book in Gary's hand. "What's that you've got?"

"Brad's address-and-phone book. I found it when we were at my parents' place. I was looking for a journal, but either he didn't keep one, or it's hidden someplace I don't know about."

"Any useful names in it?"

"A few possibles to look at. I'll make a list." He smiled. "In the morning." He held out his hand, and Dan took it, allowing Gary to tug him toward the bedroom and a night of making love.

One without *Cape Fear*—he hoped.

Chapter Twenty-Two

Wednesday, August 1, 2018

Gary had barely sat at his desk when his phone rang.

"Detective? You have visitors. I've put them in Interview Room Two."

"Do these visitors have names?"

"Only one of them gave their name. It's Aiden Reynolds."

Gary thanked him and finished the call. He glanced across to where Dan peered at his monitor. "You're not going to believe this." He stood and grabbed his jacket. "Mr. Reynolds wants to see *us*."

Dan blinked. "Then let's not waste time. Let's go see what he wants." He pointed to the notepad on Gary's desk. "Don't forget that."

They hurried through the hallways to the interview rooms, and when Gary stepped into Room Two, he came to a halt. Reynolds leaned against the table, talking to a woman Gary had never seen before. She wore a white apron over jeans and a blouse, and a black baseball cap that covered her hair, brown interspersed with strands of gray. She wasn't smiling.

Reynolds scowled at Gary. "You've been checking up on me."

"I said I would, didn't I? How did you get to hear about it anyhow?" The light dawned. "You got a call, didn't you?" It had to be the guy at the DFF office, the one who'd worked with Reynolds.

Reynolds grinned. "You bet I did. Marty rang to tell me *all* about it, and it was a good thing he did."

"Aren't you going to introduce us to your friend?" Dan asked.

The woman snorted. "I'm not his friend. I wasn't even that when we worked for the same company. I should be cooking breakfasts right now, but this asshole turned up and told me I had to give him an alibi."

"Hey, don't say that," Reynolds retorted. "Just tell him where I was."

"Okay, okay." She rolled her eyes. "Keep your hair on—what you have left of it, at any rate."

"Who are you?" Gary demanded.

"I'm Sonia Klopek. And on August twenty-eighth, 1992, I was on a date with this jerk."

"Hey!" Reynolds glared at her.

Gary pulled out a chair and sat. "How convenient. I thought you had no idea what you were doing that day."

"I didn't." Reynolds's smug smile made Gary yearn to wipe it off his face. "But you know what jogged my memory? You getting them to check where I was working that day. As soon as Marty told me what he'd heard, I remembered."

Gary gestured to the chairs. "Take a seat."

"We're not stopping. I'm here to tell you what you want to know, and then I'm outta here, and you're gonna stop harassing me."

"No one has harassed you," Gary assured him.

"That's what *you* say. Now, about that day… I went back to Lenox. We'd left a shitload of materials there when we finished the pool house. No one from the house had complained because they were all off on vacation someplace, and truth be told, I'd forgotten all about it." He frowned. "The boss hadn't, though. He told me to get my ass back there, then bring it all to the material store. So I did as I was told."

"That was Friday morning?" Gary checked his notes.

Reynolds nodded.

"Did you see Cheryl?" Dan asked.

That scowl was back. "I didn't see *anybody*. I packed up my truck, then drove to Boston, to the office so I could hand over the list of materials. Didn't want the boss on my back."

"What time did you arrive at the office?"

Reynolds arched his eyebrows. "It was late afternoon. That's all I can remember. And while I was there, I got talking to Sonia."

"I was the receptionist back then," Sonia explained. "And like I said, he asked me out on a date."

"How can you be sure it was that date?" Dan appeared incredulous.

"Because August twenty-eighth is my birthday. What's more, that particular birthday was my thirtieth, and up until the time *this* guy walked into the office, it had been a really crap day. Even the boss forgot, and he *always* remembered."

"I took pity on her," Reynolds said. "I hung around until the office closed and then took her to dinner." His eyes gleamed. "Hey, how about that? I guess I *do* know what time this was after all. Office closed at six."

That smug expression was starting to piss Gary off.

"So where was this date?"

Sonia cackled. "Applebee's Grill. Totally forgettable. Then he made it worse by inviting me back to his place." She glared at Reynolds. "Come have a drink," she mimicked. "Except a drink wasn't all he wanted, which is why he got a smack in the mouth. And that's also why I wasn't keen to do him any favors by coming here, except he gave me this sob story about how the police were trying to frame him for murder."

"Thank you for coming, Ms. Klopek." Dan extended his hand, and Gary knew exactly what he was doing.

Sonia gave him a startled smile as they shook. "You're welcome."

"Is that it?" Reynolds stared at Gary. "Are we done?"

Gary glanced at Dan, who nodded. "Apparently we are. Thanks for clearing this up."

Reynolds gaped. "Seriously? No more questions? You don't want me to hunt through bank statements to prove we actually went to Applebee's?"

"That won't be necessary," Dan said in a pleasant tone.

"Great. Then we'll get outta here."

Sonia smacked his arm. "You mean you'll take me back to the diner before the boss gets in and I lose my job."

"Sure thing." Reynolds gazed at Gary, his eyes twinkling. "So long, Detective. Good luck with the case." He strutted out of the interview room, Sonia following him.

When the door closed behind them, Gary glanced at Dan. "She was telling the truth?"

He nodded. "No doubt about it."

"Then I guess we have to cross Reynolds off our list." Gary sighed. "If ever there was a suspect that I really wanted to be guilty, it was him."

"We still have Ian Gordon and Paul DiFanetti. Especially Paul."

"True. Now all we have to do is prove it was him before he has us bumped off."

Gary took a bite of his sandwich, followed by a mouthful of coffee. "I'm going to call some of the numbers from Brad's address book, starting with a Sean Nichols."

"Why start with him?" Dan gave him a pointed look. "And should you be doing that at work?"

Gary gestured to his half-eaten sandwich. "I'm not working. I'm on my lunch break. And if Riley can call his girlfriend every break he gets, I can make a few calls. As for why I'm starting with Sean, I don't have a reason. I just opened the book at random and stuck a pin in there."

Okay, it hadn't been *that* random a choice. Gary was certain he recalled Brad mentioning someone of that name a few times when he came home during his breaks.

He peered at the entry and dialed.

"Sean Nichols."

"Mr. Nichols, you don't know me, but—"

"Whatever it is you're selling, I'm not interested."

"Well, that's good, because I'm not selling anything."

"Then what can I do for you?"

"My name is Gary Mitchell, and I'm calling because you knew my—"

"You're not Brad's little brother, are you?"

Gary was impressed. "Wow. You have a good memory."

"He was always talking about you. Mostly about how glad he was you ended up with the ginger gene, not him."

Gary laughed. "That sounds like something Brad would say. And the reason I'm calling is… I'm trying to track down his friends from college."

"Sounds intriguing. Why?"

Gary decided to come clean. "I'm a detective with Boston PD, and I'm trying to find his killer."

Silence.

"Mr. Nichols?"

"You get to call me Sean." He paused. "The police interviewed me at the time of his death. I wasn't able to help them. And I know they questioned all his college friends too. No one knew a thing."

"I've only just learned some… facts about my brother, and I need to discuss them with someone who knew him."

Another pause. "Then we should meet. I work in Boston, at the Fairmont Copley Plaza."

"Would you be able to get away from work to talk to me?"

Sean chuckled. "Oh, I think so. I'm the manager. I can see you this afternoon about four if that works for you? Just ask for me at reception. And Detective Mitchell? I'm looking forward to meeting Brad's little brother." He hung up.

Gary glanced across to where Dan sat. "He knew who I was."

"Brad was obviously pretty memorable. Will he see you?"

Gary nodded. "At four o'clock at the Fairmont Copley Plaza."

Dan gave him a hopeful glance. "Can I come too?"

Gary chuckled. "I think that's a foregone conclusion. Now let me finish my lunch. Then we'd better get some work done."

That was if he could work with all the butterflies flapping around in his stomach.

THEY ARRIVED at the hotel, and a neatly dressed valet showed them to Sean's office.

Sean Nichols rose from his chair to greet them, tall, slim, and elegant in his gray suit. His light brown hair was flecked with silver at the temples, as was his neat beard at the chin. Gary wasn't given to noticing guys, but Sean was very easy on the eye.

Beside him, Dan cleared his throat, and Gary knew he'd been busted. There was an amused expression in Dan's eyes that told Gary they'd be discussing this later.

"Gentlemen, please, take a seat. Coffee is on the way." They did as asked, and Sean looked Gary up and down. "You've changed quite a bit since I last saw you in Brad's photos."

Gary shrugged. "I get that a lot. It's the beard." They both chuckled before Sean gave Dan an inquiring glance. "This is Dan Porter. We're working on a cold case, but—"

"But you thought you'd investigate Brad's death on the side." Sean leaned back. "What do you want to know?"

"You and Brad were good friends?"

Sean's smile reached his eyes. "Oh yes. We met the first semester, and that was it, we were inseparable." His face took on a faraway expression. "God, the things we got up to…."

"I can imagine." Brad had always been the prankster of the family.

Sean laughed. "Oh Lord, I hope not."

The time for small talk was over. "What we want to know is… did Brad have any boyfriends?" Gary's heartbeat quickened.

Sean fell silent, his mouth open. Finally he spoke. "You know he was gay?"

"I do now." He indicated Dan.

Sean frowned. "I don't understand." He stared at Dan for a moment. "I remember you. Didn't you stay here pretty recently?" He widened his eyes. "Oh God. You're that psychic. The one who helped the police—"

"Yes, yes he is. Now, about—"

The door opened, and a young man dressed in black brought in a tray containing a coffeepot, milk jug, sugar bowl, and three cups and saucers. He placed them on Sean's desk, then left the room.

"About Brad's boyfriends," Gary continued. "Did he have any?" Then his chest tightened when Sean's eyes glistened.

"Yes, he did." Sean grabbed a tissue from the box of Kleenex and wiped his eyes.

Gary stared at him as realization dawned. "Oh my God. You. You and Brad…."

Sean blew his nose and dropped the wad of tissue into the trash. "We started dating during our final year. It didn't last longer than that—he died the year after. And no, I can't think of anyone we knew who'd want to harm Brad. Because whoever killed him had to be a psychopath."

Gary's gut clenched. "I hate to tell you, but to misquote Wednesday Addams, psychopaths look just like everyone else."

"You gave him a plastic ring, didn't you?" Dan interjected.

Sean gaped at him. "How did you—" He held up his hand. "Forget I asked. Stupid question. Yes. I can't remember where I got it, but I do remember slipping it onto his ring finger as a joke." He swallowed. "Only I wasn't joking. I'd have married him in a heartbeat."

"He loved you." Dan's voice cracked.

Sean's breathing hitched. "You… you learned that from the ring?" Dan nodded, and Sean teared up. "Thank you for that."

"We're going through Brad's address book," Gary told him, "contacting as many of his classmates as we can, hoping for a breakthrough."

Sean froze. "Then stop what you're doing. I can save you a lot of time. How would you like to meet all of them under one roof?"

Gary blinked. "Seriously?"

"Every six years, we have a class reunion. I have no idea who decided on six, but there you are. We like keeping track of each other, finding out who's doing what, who's doing *who*. And there's one coming up soon. It'll be here, too, at the hotel." He smiled. "I drew the short straw to organize it. And I think *you* should be here."

"We'd have no right to attend it," Gary protested.

Sean arched his eyebrows. "Yes, you would. You'll be there representing Brad."

Dan stared at him. "You think we might learn something."

Sean's smile lit up his face. "I think *you* might learn something. Like I said, I don't think for a minute one of them will turn out to be Brad's killer, but yes, you might learn more about Brad. If you leave me an address, I'll send you an invitation. After all—" He gave Gary a sad smile. "—we could've been family."

Dan had lost all track of time. He'd been staring at the negatives and the photos relating to the Caravaggio since before dinner. Not that he'd learned anything. He couldn't shake the feeling of curiosity that accompanied each touch of the negatives.

What aroused your curiosity, Cheryl?

And then there was the *Kama Sutra*. Time after time, he found himself drawn to the book, and he had no idea why.

Gary joined him on the couch. "Hey, it's late."

Dan glanced at his phone. "Good Lord, where did the evening go?"

"Have you found something?"

God, he was weary. "Maybe? But it doesn't make a lot of sense."

Gary took the negatives and photos from him, tucked them into their folder, and placed it on the coffee table. "Bed, now. You're tired. And you're trying too hard."

"But I—"

"But nothing." Gary's voice was firm. "I know your gift can be a pain—it doesn't exactly work to order, does it?—but don't try to force it. It'll come."

Dan couldn't suppress his smile. "You sound more certain than I feel." Then something tugged at his consciousness, a trickle of instinct, an awareness of conflict within Gary. "What is it?"

Gary heaved a sigh. "Dan, I… I need you."

"What's wrong?" He grabbed Gary's hands and held them tight. He gave himself several mental kicks for not noticing Gary's emotional turmoil earlier. He'd allowed Cheryl's case to take over.

Gary gazed at their joined hands. "I think it was meeting Sean, the prospect of meeting Brad's friends. The possibility that maybe one of them knows more about Brad's death." He raised his chin, and Dan's heart quaked at the pain he saw in Gary's eyes. "I need you to take me away from this. I need to stop thinking about it."

Without a word, Dan rose, still holding Gary's hand, and led him to the bedroom. He undressed Gary in silence, sinking to his knees to worship Gary's cock with lips and tongue. And when Gary began to thrust deep, his hands keeping Dan's head steady as he pumped, Dan knew he was ready for more.

Then Gary came to a halt, gazing at him, his chest heaving. "Make love to me?"

Dan's breathing quickened. "Are you saying…?"

Gary nodded. "I want you inside me. I think we've waited long enough."

They'd talked about Gary becoming more versatile, but in the two months since they'd first initiated a physical relationship, Dan had been more than happy to be on the receiving end. Not that he hadn't imagined sliding into Gary's warm body, feeling it tighten around him. He wasn't a greedy man. He loved every intimate moment they shared, and even if it took Gary years to decide he was ready to bottom, that was fine by him.

It seemed Gary was ready.

They explored each other with fingers and tongues, taking their time, until both were moaning, Dan's need at fever pitch. After what seemed like hours of licking, sucking, stroking, and fondling, they lay naked together on the bed, Dan spooned around Gary, slowly rubbing his rigid dick through Gary's crack, listening to Gary's staccato breaths, hearing the need in his voice when he begged Dan to take him.

"We go slow," Dan whispered.

"Slow is good." Gary's soft exhale when Dan finally entered him was like music to Dan's soul, and he stilled inside him, waiting for a sign, his arms around Gary, his hand over Gary's heart, feeling each beat.

They had all night, and they made it last, their soft sighs and moans mingling, an erotic accompaniment to Dan's sensual rocking in and out, their bodies joined, moving as one. And when Gary came at last, Dan held him and kissed him until he couldn't hold his orgasm back a second longer.

Gary widened his eyes. "I can feel you," he whispered.

Dan kissed him on the lips. "I love you." The words didn't come close to conveying the depth of his emotions. Their kisses grew languid as they lay connected, Dan's cock locked in the warm prison of Gary's body.

"I think we need to practice more," Gary said when Dan finally eased out of him. "At least three or four times a week."

Dan chuckled, his head on Gary's damp chest. "I like the way you think."

Gary turned his head toward the nightstand, where Dan's copy of the *Gay Kama Sutra* sat. "Who would think such delights lie within the covers of a book?"

Covers....

Something in Dan's mind clicked into place, and he sat bolt upright. "That's it!" He lurched off the bed and hurried into the living room.

"What's it?" Gary called after him.

"One of Cheryl's secrets."

Chapter Twenty-Three

DAN SAT on the couch, picked up the copy of the *Kama Sutra* from where he'd left it, and held it, his eyes closed.

"I take it you know something."

Dan brought a finger to his lips. "Give me a minute, please." He could hear Gary's breathing, as erratic as his own, and he forced himself to calm down, concentrating on the beat of his heart, his focus locked on the book.

"It's here, I know it is," he murmured. That surge of knowledge he'd felt in the bedroom was dissipating as the seconds ticked by, and Dan strove to cling to it.

Show me. You've got me this far, now show me.

His body ached in the most pleasurable way, and Gary's musky scent insinuated itself into his nostrils, distracting him, tugging him back to the bed.

That will have to wait.

"*What's* here?" Gary demanded.

Dan opened his eyes. He lifted the front cover and turned every page. When he reached the back, he paused, his hand on the inside back cover.

Wait....

He looked closer, stroking the cover with the tips of his fingers, his heart thumping. He gazed at Gary. "This lining paper.... It's not the same as it is at the front of the book." He ran his finger down the spine, and his heart went into overdrive. "Have you got a pair of tweezers?"

Without a word, Gary dashed to the bathroom. When he returned, he knelt on the rug beside the couch, holding out the delicate metal tool. "Why do you need tweezers?"

Dan showed him the inside back cover. "Look. Someone glued paper over the original back lining." His senses told him that someone was Cheryl.

"But why?"

Dan pointed to the edge of the paper closest to the spine. "This is open. I felt it when I ran my fingers over it." He slid the ends of the tweezers into the slit and caught his breath. "There's something inside." With great care he eased the object from its hiding place, and—

And there you are.

Dan held up the color photo for Gary to see.

Cheryl Somers lay in a bed, naked from the waist up, and she wasn't alone.

Gary gazed at it. "She looks so beautiful. So happy."

Dan examined it once more. Cheryl's long hair flowed over her pillow, and a white sheet lay over her, below her navel. Judging by the angle of the photo, the camera had to have been on a nightstand. A man's arm was draped over her, his hand cupping her left breast, his face buried in a pillow, hidden from sight.

Dan stared at him. "This has to be the person she was keeping secret. The mystery lover." Then he looked closer, and his pulse sped up. "Do you have a magnifying glass?"

"Somewhere." Gary was off again, only to return a moment later. "Here." He thrust it at Dan, who peered at the photo.

His heart sank.

Hasn't there always been a part of me that knew?

He sagged into the couch. "She probably took the photo on a timer. Maybe the camera was on her nightstand. But I don't think he knew she took it."

In fact, Dan was certain of it.

"Why do you say that?"

Dan sighed. "Because I don't think he would have let her." He pointed to the man's hand, where there was a heavy-looking ring. "I've seen that before."

Gary frowned. "Which one of them was wearing it? Aiden Reynolds, Paul DiFanetti?"

"Neither." Dan looked him in the eye. "Senator William Cain."

Gary gaped at him. "How can you be sure?"

"He wore that ring in Cheryl's portraits of him, and he was wearing it the day we met him in Boston."

"The senator… and Cheryl?"

He set his jaw. "We need to talk to him. And not in Boston. Or in Nantucket. It has to be at the house in Lenox."

Gary's brow furrowed. "You can't tell if they're in a bedroom at the senator's house. Not that we saw any of them."

Dan shook his head. "This has nothing to do with a bedroom. We need to see his art room again."

"Why?"

Dan picked up the folder containing the Caravaggio photos and negatives. "Because there's a mystery here, and I need to solve it. So call him first thing in the morning. If you can't reach him, then leave a message, email him, whatever…. But insist he comes to Lenox tomorrow, or Friday at the latest." As an afterthought, he added, "Maybe this time he should leave Mrs. Cain behind."

And as suddenly as illumination had overtaken him, it fled, leaving him bereft of energy. He put his head back on the seat cushion.

"I don't think I can move," he said, half joking.

Gary grabbed his hands and tugged, pulling him to his feet. "That's probably a combination of all the gymnastics you got up to—mental *and* physical. So let's go back to bed." He gave a rueful smile. "I don't think we're going to be getting up to much now. Well, I know *I'm* not."

Dan stilled. "Are you okay?" He remembered his first time.

Gary bit his lip. "I'm fine. And very thankful."

Warmth rushed through him. "I didn't do all that much."

Amusement danced in Gary's eyes. "I wasn't referring to you—though you *were* awesome, don't get me wrong."

"Then what are you thankful for?"

That twinkle in his eyes was so attractive.

"Lube."

Dan laughed, and they headed back to their bed. Despite the sated feeling that stole over him, he couldn't shake off his discovery.

"He lied to us," he murmured as they climbed into bed and Gary covered them with the sheet.

"Not so much a lie as an omission."

Dan shook his head. "It amounts to the same thing. And it also tells us something important about the senator, something we should have realized."

"What's that?"

"He's a damn good actor. Isn't that a basic requirement for a politician? And if he could hide their relationship so convincingly, what else is he hiding?"

He didn't want to believe the senator capable of murder, not after sensing all the emotion inside him when he spoke of Cheryl.

He couldn't fake that—could he?

Chapter Twenty-Four

Friday, August 3, 2018
10:00 a.m.

Gary turned right off West Street and drove along Under Mountain Road. "I think this is a reasonable enough hour, don't you?" He'd called Senator Cain first thing Thursday, insisting that he meet them at the house in Lenox the following day. That hadn't gone down well, not when he'd only seen them there a week ago, but Gary had stressed the importance of their visit.

Dan said nothing. He'd said little while Gary made breakfast and poured coffee, and he'd been quiet for most of the two-and-a-half-hour trip. Gary had a good idea of what lay at the heart of his silence.

He doesn't want to believe the senator was involved in Cheryl's death.

Gary was having a hard time believing it himself.

"Maybe he did love her," Dan murmured. Gary glanced at him, and Dan shrugged. "And if he did, there's no way he could have done that to her."

Gary was inclined to agree. "But he didn't tell us the truth. We need to know what else he might be hiding."

"If I touch his hand, I'll know." Dan stared through the windshield. "I'd rather he told us, instead of having to resort to my gift, but that's the only way we'll be sure that he's leveled with us." His chin dropped to his chest. "I can't believe he killed her."

Gary took a left onto the long, winding driveway. "We'll have more answers soon enough."

As they pulled up in front of the portico, the door opened.

"Oh God," Gary muttered.

Mrs. Cain stood there, her eyes like flint.

"I told him there was no need for her to come too, not when they have all the family staying with them," Gary muttered.

"Maybe she insisted again," Dan suggested. "All I know is, I'm going to feel awkward as hell bringing up his infidelity with her under the same roof."

Gary switched off the engine, and they got out of the car. Mrs. Cain's lips were a thin line as they approached. She didn't move, and they were forced to come to a halt in front of her.

Lord, she looked pissed.

"My husband is waiting for you in his office," she said tersely. "And I don't care how important this visit is. As far as I'm concerned? This is starting to feel like harassment." She pointed up the staircase to the left. "I believe you know the way."

And with that, she left them standing in the hallway and walked stiffly toward the kitchen.

They climbed the stairs, the strains of classical piano music growing louder as they reached the top step. Gary paused at the door.

"It doesn't matter that he's a senator," Dan said in a low voice. "That doesn't put him above the law."

"We don't know if he even *broke* the law," Gary remonstrated.

They were about to find out.

Senator Cain sat at his desk, writing. He glanced up as they entered, and reached over to hit a button on the music system, plunging the room into silence. He stared at them, his forehead creased.

"Another visit, gentlemen. I really don't appreciate being asked to break my vacation yet again to meet with you." His frown deepened. "The only reason I agreed to do so is because you made it sound almost… urgent. And also in the hope that this would be the last of such visits." He closed his notebook. "Although I don't see what more help I can be to you. I've already told you everything I know." He grabbed a small jar and opened it, and a faintly medicinal smell filled the air. He rubbed white cream into his palms.

Gary couldn't help but notice the senator didn't offer them a seat.

He walked over to the desk and stood in front of it, his back straight. "There was something you forgot to tell us when we were last here, Senator."

Dan joined him, reaching into the leather bag slung over his shoulder.

The senator arched his eyebrows. "Really? And what was that?" He put the lid back on the jar.

Gary looked him in the eye. "You left out the fact you were having an affair with Cheryl Somers."

Senator Cain blinked. Blinked again. "What are you talking about?"

Dan held up the photo of them in bed. "This *is* you, isn't it?"

The senator stared at it, his mouth opening and closing. Then he sat straight in his chair, his chin held high. "No, it isn't. And frankly, I'm shocked you could even think such a thing."

Dan took a step closer. "Look again, Senator. Because that's definitely your ring in this photo." He pointed to the senator's right hand. "*That* ring. The same one you're wearing in your portraits." His breathing caught. "Did you care so little for her that you feel comfortable lying about what you shared?"

Silence fell, broken only by the creak of a floorboard beyond the office door.

Senator Cain swallowed, and suddenly it was as if something broke inside him. He crumpled before their eyes, sagging into his high-backed chair. "Where did you find that?"

"Cheryl hid it in a book." Dan tilted his head. "You didn't know of its existence, did you?"

Senator Cain shook his head.

"And you're not going to deny your feelings for her, are you? Because that would be an insult to her memory."

Another shake of his head, his Adam's apple bobbing sharply.

Gary looked around and went over to where two chairs stood against the wall. He drew them closer to the desk, and they sat.

"Lord, I need a drink." The senator got up, went to the bookcase, grabbed the bottle of whiskey sitting there, and poured a couple of fingers of it into a squat chunky glass. He took a long drink from it, his throat working as he swallowed.

He returned to his chair and sat heavily, placing the glass on the varnished surface. For a moment he said nothing but simply stared at it. Finally he raised his head and gazed at them. "What do you want to know?"

He sounded exhausted.

Gary removed his notepad from his pocket, then sat back, his pen poised. "When did the affair begin?"

Senator Cain rested his head against the back of the chair. "In 1989, shortly after that bastard assaulted her. She came to me." He sighed. "She was such a mess. And I'm not just talking physically. I got her to calm down and made her tell me the whole story. It wasn't until later that I learned she'd kept something back." He paused to take a drink. "Cheryl said her father wanted her to go to the police, but she couldn't face them. I persuaded her. In fact, I took the two of them to the police precinct. I was determined Reynolds should *not* get away with it."

"This was someone you'd known since her birth," Dan observed.

The senator nodded. "And somehow, the assault brought us closer." He met Dan's gaze. "We… we'd always shared a bond. We'd talked about art ever since she was old enough to pick up a pencil. But suddenly she was twenty-five, and I was seeing her in a whole new light." His face glowed. "I watched her blossom, watched her confidence grow, saw how beautiful she was inside *and* out…. She blossomed as an artist too, and the more time I spent around her, the more certain I became that she was something special."

"And you fell in love with her." Dan's voice was soft.

Senator Cain nodded. "I encouraged her, supported her, and I loved her with all my heart. What seemed so incredible to me was that she loved me back. She didn't want her father to know—I was a married man, after all, and she knew he would disapprove—so we did our best to keep it a secret from him. And when we'd been together about four months, she finally broke down and told me the whole story of the assault."

"What hadn't she told you?" Gary asked.

The senator's face tightened. "How Reynolds had worked out she was trans. I saw a solution, but I hesitated to suggest it." He sighed. "I didn't want her to think I was trying to fix her—not that she needed fixing, you understand. And because she knew me so well, she saw through me and demanded to know what was wrong. So…." He lifted his chin. "I asked if she'd ever considered breast implants and offered to pay for the surgery."

Gary remembered the silicone pouches found with her body. "I'm guessing she liked the idea."

"Liked it? She couldn't contain her excitement. I told her I'd been reluctant to suggest it because I said I didn't want her to think I was… building my own girlfriend."

"How did she react to that?" Dan asked.

Senator Cain's expression softened. "She looked at me and said, 'Don't you think I know the man I love by now? You want to do this because you want me to be happy, because you love me too.'" He stared into his whiskey glass. "What we had…. Yes, it was intensely physical, but it was *more* than sex. She….” He closed his eyes. “She *shone* when we were together.” Pain contorted his face. “When her father came to me with the news she’d been identified as the body in the tunnel, I wept.”

Gary’s heart went out to him. “At least now we know why you pushed the police so hard to find out what had happened to her.”

“I had to do something. I felt so useless.”

“You’d lost someone you loved, and you couldn’t tell a soul about it.” Dan frowned. “But what about your wife? Did she know?”

Gary had a feeling that would explain the hostility Dan had noticed when they first met Mrs. Cain at the house. Maybe that wasn’t so much due to her opinion of Cheryl as a trans woman, but as a love rival.

The light died in the senator’s eyes. “Yes, she knew.”

“And how did she react?” Gary asked.

Senator Cain took a sip of whiskey. “She tolerated it.” He bit his lip. “Maybe this is where I should tell you ours is not a… regular marriage.” He expelled a long breath. “The way I felt about Cheryl? I’d *never* felt like that about Della. And yes, I know that makes me a bad husband, but I couldn’t help it. I had no idea where our love would take us, Cheryl and me. Both of us grabbed every moment we could to be together—and then she was snatched from me.” His voice quavered.

Gary glanced at the framed photos on the senator’s desk. “You said you have children?”

He nodded. “Two, but they’re adopted.” Then he froze at the sound of a knock on the door.

Mrs. Cain came into the office, carrying a tray of coffee. She raised her eyebrows at the sight of the whiskey glass but said nothing as she placed the tray on the desk. She straightened and gave her husband an inquiring glance. “Are you all right?”

“Della…. They know about Cheryl and me.”

Mrs. Cain’s back became rigid. “I see.” She narrowed her gaze. “You *swore* to me no one knew about it.”

“And no one did.”

“Then who told them?”

Dan cleared his throat. “Cheryl did.”

Her mouth fell open.

“You stayed with your husband,” Gary remarked.

Mrs. Cain gave a casual shrug. “I didn’t want a divorce. Why should I? I *like* being the wife of a senator.” She straightened. “And now I’ll leave you to your questions. Doubtless you have more of them." Then her shoulders slumped a little. "I thought we'd heard the last of her when she turned up in that tunnel." She walked out of the door.

Senator Cain stared at the closed door. "You'll have to forgive Della. I was thirty-five when Cheryl and I first… got together, and Della was convinced it was nothing more than an early midlife crisis. She let me have what she thought would be a momentary dalliance, except it wasn't. Cheryl captivated me. She went to a place in my heart I hadn't even known existed." He blinked, then coughed. "I don't see why anyone has to know. It was a long time ago. And it has nothing to do with her death."

Gary had to agree. He didn't doubt for a second the senator loved Cheryl—Gary could hear it in his voice, see it in his face. He turned to Dan to see if Senator Cain's words had made the same impression.

Dan was staring at the pocket doors, which were closed.

"Dan?"

No reaction.

"Is something wrong, Mr. Porter?" the senator asked.

Dan blinked, and he looked for all the world as if he was coming out of a dreamlike state. "When we were here last week, you said Al did you proud."

Senator Cain nodded. "Yes. He was the carpenter who made those doors."

"How did you find him?"

"I didn't. A friend did."

Gary stilled. "James Sebring."

The senator frowned. "Who?"

"James Sebring. He was a carpenter whose coworkers called him Al as a joke, only it stuck. He died two years ago."

Senator Cain's breathing hitched. "Seriously? He couldn't have been that old."

"His death was declared an accident," Gary informed him. "But we have our suspicions it was murder."

The senator's jaw dropped. "But why would anyone want to murder a carpenter?" He swallowed.

Dan was still staring at the doors.

"What is it that so fascinates you about them?"

Gary was starting to get the feeling something was going on, something he needed to know about.

Then Dan shivered. "Sorry. I must have zoned out." He gave the senator his full attention. "You should have told us the truth, Senator."

"I know, but surely you can understand why I didn't."

"Yes, I can." He smiled. "And we'll continue working to discover *more* of the truth." Dan paused, casting one more glance toward the pocket doors.

WHAT THE hell is bugging me?

"Senator, would it be okay if I took another look at your art collection?"

Senator Cain frowned. "I don't see how that would help you in your investigation."

"At this moment, neither do I, but I've learned never to ignore my… hunches." After all, getting inside that room again was the main reason for their visit—or it *had* been the previous evening.

The senator shrugged. He walked over to the right-hand door and pushed it open. "Then be my guest."

Dan entered the darkened room. Senator Cain flicked the lights on, and Dan scanned the works of art.

Come on, you've got me this far. Show me why I'm here.

Gary joined him but said nothing. Dan stood in the middle of the room, opening himself up to whatever awaited him. When nothing occurred he walked slowly around the room, pausing at each work of art.

Nothing. Except….

A shiver trickled through him when he reached the fireplace. He froze, his breathing quickening, waiting for more.

Nothing.

Dan headed for the doorway, and as he reached the threshold, another shiver coursed through him, stronger than the first. He stilled, desperate to find whatever was causing such a reaction.

And then the feelings abated, leaving him calm again.

"You sensed something, didn't you?" Gary murmured.

"Yes, but…."

This was getting them nowhere.

HE GLANCED at Gary. "I think we've taken up enough of Senator Cain's time." He left the art room, Gary with him.

"You *will* let me know what you find out, won't you?" the senator asked as he walked them to the door of the office.

Gary assured him they would. They thanked him and went downstairs. He glanced at Dan as they crossed the floor, heading for the main door.

"Something *is* wrong, isn't it?"

"Not wrong, exactly. Just a feeling I can't shake."

"About the senator?"

Dan frowned. "I'm not sure."

"Is that it? Are you finished?" Mrs. Cain emerged from a door to the left.

Gary wanted to tell her yes, but based on how the case had twisted and turned so far, he knew better. "For now."

She opened the door. "Then I'll bid you good day." As soon as they stepped into the warm summer air, the door closed behind them.

They crunched across the gravel to the car, Dan still in a world of his own. Gary got behind the wheel.

"Okay, what's this feeling you can't shake?" He switched on the engine.

"I wish I knew." Dan pulled his bag onto his lap and reached into it. When he removed one of Cheryl's folders, Gary stared at it.

"Why did you bring that along?" he asked as they drove toward the road.

"Because they're part of the mystery." Dan opened the folder and removed a photo. "Especially this one." He lapsed into silence, studying it.

When nothing else was forthcoming, Gary chuckled. "Well? Are you going to let me in on it too?" He took a right onto the road.

"Not yet," Dan murmured. "There's something I need to check on first."

Gary's phone rang, and he peered at the screen. "It's Lori Dettweiler. Put it on hands free, will you?" When Dan did as instructed, Gary spoke loudly. "Lori, what can we do for you? You're on speaker."

"I don't know if this will help, but I've remembered something." There was an edge to her voice, an undercurrent of what sounded like excitement.

"Tell us."

"The thing is… I had a phone call from Cheryl, August twenty-eighth, which must have been right around the time she disappeared."

"How can you remember the date so exactly?" Dan asked.

"Okay, this will sound weird, but… I've been on a real decluttering jag lately. So last night I was going through my books, trying to decide which ones to keep, like you do. I have *way* too many books. Anyhow, I came across a children's book I'd kept. *The Borrowers*. It's by an English writer, Mary Norton. Anyway, she died August twenty-ninth, 1992, and that was the day after Cheryl called. It was only seeing the book again that made me connect the two events."

"What did she say?" Gary's skin prickled into goose bumps.

"I think it was something like… 'I've found it. It's been in plain sight all the time. I'm looking at it right now.' Then the call ended. I tried to call her back, but there was no answer."

"Do you have any idea what she was talking about?"

There was a pause. "Maybe? I wondered if she'd stumbled across something related to one of the stolen paintings."

Gary and Dan glanced at each other. "What stolen paintings?" Gary was lost.

Lori gave a wry chuckle. "Are you *sure* you're from Boston? I thought everyone knew about it. That heist rocked the art world."

"From the Museum of Fine Arts?" Dan looked as confused as Gary felt.

"No. Okay, I'm not being clear, am I? Cheryl and I both worked at the Athenaeum. Remember I told you that?"

"Yeah, I remember," Gary assured her.

"All right, then. After that, but before I came to work for the Museum of Fine Arts, both Cheryl and I were art conservationists at the Isabella Stewart Gardner Museum in Boston. I was there from 1991 to 1997. That was *after* the event."

Something stirred in the deep recesses of Gary's memory.

"Like I said, I don't know if that will help you. But you know, thinking about that phone call, it was strange, the way it ended so abruptly…."

Beside him, Dan grabbed his phone, his thumbs flying over the screen, his breathing erratic.

Gary was beyond curious.

"Thanks, Lori. I'll make a note of it. One last thing. Can you remember approximately what time she called?"

"It was early evening, that's all I can say. I'd finished work at five, and I was home when she called."

"Thanks." They said goodbye, and she disconnected. "Well, that confirms Reynolds's story. He was out on his date with Sonia at that time." He glanced at Dan's phone. "What are you googling?"

"Let's call it a hunch." Then he froze. "Stop the car. We need to go back." His voice rang out.

"What?" Ice crawled over Gary's skin.

"You heard me. Turn this car around. We have to go back to the house."

"But why?"

Dan stared at him, his eyes huge. "Because he's hiding something."

CHAPTER TWENTY-FIVE

DAN LIFTED the heavy door knocker and brought it down with a dull *clang*. His heart pounded; his skin tingled. He was dimly aware of Gary behind him.

Mrs. Cain opened the door, glaring at him. "I shall be reporting this to your superiors."

"You do that," Dan murmured, brushing past her and hurrying to the staircase. He climbed it two steps at a time, not bothering to knock at the office door before he barged inside.

Senator Cain was seated at his desk. "What is the meaning of this?" He stared over Dan's shoulder. "Detective Mitchell?"

Before Gary could utter a word, Dan blurted out, "It's time to solve this puzzle, Senator."

"What are you talking about? What puzzle?"

"I was about to ask the same thing." Mrs. Cain seemed a little breathless, as though she'd run up the stairs.

"Senator, if we might have a word with you—alone." Dan stared at him.

The senator gave his wife an apologetic glance. "Della, give us a minute, please?"

"But this is—"

"Della."

She glared at him but said nothing as she withdrew, closing the door behind her.

Senator Cain turned to Dan. "Okay. What's this puzzle you're talking about?"

Dan made an effort to breathe evenly. "Have you ever seen a Chinese puzzle box? You know the kind of box I'm talking about, right? The pretty veneered ones where you have to work out in what order to slide the panels to reveal a hidden drawer." He smiled. "Only it wasn't a drawer in your case—it was a door."

Senator Cain stared at him, his brow furrowed. "You're not making any sense."

"You know how to open a puzzle box? You need to look for the join in the veneers. It isn't always obvious, but once you do, the whole puzzle opens up." He met the senator's stare. "Everything you've told us…. You fed us a packet of disinformation. Just enough truth that we couldn't see what lay beneath."

"But you *know* what lies beneath," Senator Cain protested. "You know about the affair. I told you everything."

Dan shook his head. "Not everything. Yes, I believe you loved Cheryl. But there's still something hidden from view, something you don't want us to know." He walked over to the doors that led to the art room. He touched one of them. "This is what it's all about."

Senator Cain blinked. "My art collection? But… you just looked at it again."

Dan stared at him. "I'm not referring to your collection, Senator." He touched the door again. "I'm talking about this door."

"If this is the result of one of your… visions, Mr. Porter, then I'm sorry to tell you, it's led you astray. And I fail to see what bearing a door has on Cheryl's death."

"All the same, we're going to hear him out," Gary announced. "Unlike you, Senator, I have faith in Dan's visions."

Dan fired him a grateful glance before giving the senator his attention.

"I couldn't understand why someone would have such beautiful doors created—doors you could open to reveal that wonderful collection—and then put furniture in front of them."

The senator frowned. "The pair are ten feet across. That takes up a lot of room. And the furniture has to go somewhere."

Dan held up a finger. "There you go again. Disinformation. A grain of truth intended to placate us." He slid the right-hand door open with a fingertip, then peered into the art room. "No furniture in front of them in here." Dan walked back to the senator's desk, slipping his hand into his bag. He held up the folder. "Do you know what this is? It's the join in the veneer. The first clue how to open this puzzle box you've created." He opened the folder and withdrew a clear plastic sheet filled with strips of negatives. "I knew the answer was somewhere in Cheryl's files. I kept turning it over and over in my mind, trying to find it, but I couldn't see it—until just now." He glanced at Gary. "Lori gave us the answer when she told us what Cheryl said the day she disappeared. '*It's been in plain sight all the time.*'" Dan held up the sheet. "And she was right."

"What are those?" Senator Cain's voice was quiet.

Dan walked over to the antique desk lamp and tilted its green shade. "These are negatives of the photos Cheryl took when she was doing her prep work for the Caravaggio. The ones she wasn't going to use for reference, she crossed through with a Sharpie." He held them up to the light. "You're in here too."

The senator frowned. "I am?" Then he nodded, his brow smoothing. "I remember. She turned and said, 'Smile.'"

Dan pointed to the negative. "There you are. And then there's this one." He indicated another negative.

The senator peered at it. "What is it supposed to be? It doesn't look like anything."

Dan pointed to another. "See there? That's the line I was telling you about, the one she drew through all the photos she wasn't going to print. Now let's go back to our mystery negative. Can you see? She started to draw a line through it, then stopped."

"She obviously changed her mind," Senator Cain said with a shrug.

"But *why* did she change it? And more importantly, what made her draw a question mark on the sheet under this one?"

The senator gave him a look of exasperation. "But what is it a photo *of*?"

"I'll show you." Dan pulled a photo from the folder and placed it on the desk.

Gary leaned in to get a better look. "That looks like the archway between the office and the art room. See? That's your desk and chair in the background." He frowned. "It was taken at an odd angle, though, from inside the art room."

"Ah." Senator Cain's eyes gleamed. "I remember now. She'd just taken the one of me. She lowered the camera and then clicked the shutter by accident."

"That doesn't explain why she started to cross it out and then changed her mind. Or why she wrote the question mark. And why print it?" Dan tapped the folder. "And suddenly the puzzle box starts to open." He removed another photo and placed it in front of the senator, who stared at it with a frown. "Don't you recognize it?"

"Why should I?"

"Because it's a photo of *your* floor. This is a blowup of part of this one." He placed the previous photo beside it.

"But that still doesn't explain why she printed the photo in the first place," Gary remonstrated.

Dan smiled. "I think *I* know why." He picked up the sheet of negatives once more, and pointed to one. "I don't know if you can see it from there, but there's a faint white line across part of the threshold." He tapped the blowup. "It's clearer here."

"A lens anomaly?" the senator suggested.

Gary shook his head. "If that were the case, it would be on every photo."

Senator Cain made an impatient noise at the back of his throat. "I fail to understand why you've done a blowup of a photo that was taken by accident."

Dan stared. "Oh, but *we* didn't blow it up—she did. This is Cheryl's photo."

The senator bent over to peer at it. "I know what this is. Al— James—installed the doors shortly after the floor had been waxed. The bottom rollers on the door left a mark on the floor."

Dan went over to the right-hand door and crouched, examining the floor. "But these are pocket doors. That means they're top hung."

"Then something must have gotten caught or trapped under it," Senator Cain persisted.

Dan stood. He slid the left-hand door open and walked into the art room. Gary and the senator followed him. Dan peered at the floor. "No marks." Then he reached out and placed his hand on the protruding edge of the door. "And why is *this* door so much heavier than its counterpart? I can open that one with a fingertip."

Gary stared at him. "You *know* why, don't you?"

Dan nodded. He inclined his head toward the left-hand door. "This? This is the final panel. That means it's time to reveal the secret it's been hiding."

He didn't miss the senator's sharp intake of breath. "Mr. Porter...."

Dan ignored him. He drew the door back to the center until it reached the doorstop set into the arch. He peered up at it.

"Don't."

Dan stretched up and pressed the catch, which disappeared into the doorframe with a *click clack....*

"No!"

Dan turned to look at him. "You know I'm not going to stop. Not now." He touched the door again, and a shiver trickled through him, the same shiver as before, only more intense.

"What do you sense?" Gary asked.

Dan stroked the smooth wood surface. "Strong, positive emotions. Exhilaration, joy…." He grabbed the door edge and dragged it over toward the other side, and another panel slid into view.

Shock thrummed through him. He'd suspected, but he hadn't been prepared for the reality of his discovery. Dan took several steps back, until he was almost at the opposite wall, to fully take in the panel attached to the doorframe. Secured to it was a painting, maybe sixty inches high and fifty across. It depicted a stormy scene at sea, a dark, dramatic painting.

It took Dan's breath away.

Gary expelled a breath. "That's beautiful. Why would you want to hide it away?"

Dan didn't wait to hear the senator's response. "Because it's *Christ in the Storm on the Sea of Galilee*, by Rembrandt. It was stolen from the Isabella Stewart Gardner Museum in March 1990, one of thirteen works of art stolen in one night. The FBI valued the stolen works at hundreds of millions of dollars. None of them have ever been recovered, and there's a reward of ten million dollars for information leading to their recovery."

"How do you know all this?" Gary demanded.

"What do you think I was googling on the way back here? Lori gave me the idea." He glanced at the senator. "Care to explain what *you're* doing with it?"

Senator Cain swallowed. "It's a copy. Cheryl painted it."

Dan approached the canvas with reverence, then touched it lightly. "No, it isn't a copy." Another glance. "Want to try that again?"

The senator swallowed. "It was… loaned to me."

Gary gaped at him. "By whom? The Isabella Stewart Gardner Museum? I sincerely doubt that."

Dan took another step back and almost stumbled over the marble hearth in front of the fireplace. He put his hand out to stop his fall—and froze.

Senator Cain stood in front of the painting. "So *that's* how she knew. She never told me. Six months after she disappeared, I changed the rollers on the picture panel."

Dan sighed. "It's too late, Senator."

The senator became so still. "What do you mean?"

"There are no sliding panels left. It's time to reveal what else you've been hiding." He locked gazes with him.

Senator Cain's breathing hitched. "You know, don't you?"

"Know what?" Gary looked from the senator to Dan with a bewildered expression.

Dan said nothing, waiting.

Senator Cain shuddered out a breath. "That I killed her."

Chapter Twenty-Six

Gary prided himself on being prepared for most eventualities, but he hadn't seen that coming.

"*You* killed Cheryl?"

Senator Cain nodded. "But—"

Gary held his hand up. "Stop right there, Senator." This was one conversation that needed to take place at the precinct. He thought fast. The nearest police department was in Lenox, but…. "We're taking you back to Boston. We'll continue this when we get there." And before the senator could utter another word, Gary Mirandized him, arresting him for receiving stolen property and the suspected murder of Cheryl Somers. One glance at Dan's expression told him Dan was as shocked as he was.

He didn't see this coming either.

Maybe it was more the case that neither of them had wanted to believe the senator capable of such a crime.

All three of them jumped when the door opened, the painting disappearing from view as it slid into the recess.

Mrs. Cain walked into the art room, frowning. "What is going on? Have they offered an explanation for barging into our home?" She glared at Gary. "The police commissioner's wife is a friend. You can be sure I'll be speaking about—"

"Della." The senator gave her a sad smile. "I'm going to the Boston police department with these gentlemen, 'to help with their inquiries,' I believe the phrase is. I suspect there will be officers here shortly. Let them take whatever they want." He fixed her with a hard stare. "*Whatever* they want." Then he turned to Gary. "Make sure they don't damage it?"

Gary gave a nod. "I'll make a call. I know someone who'll assist in its removal." Lori would take great care with it.

Senator Cain glanced at the door. "There are no permanent fixings through the stretcher. It's held in place with turn buttons." He squared his shoulders. "Let's go." Another glance at Gary. "Will I have to wear…?"

Gary saw where he was headed. He shook his head. "Cuffs won't be necessary in the circumstances."

The senator flashed him a look of gratitude. "Thank you." And with that, they escorted him through the house and out to the car. Mrs. Cain followed them, aghast, calling out that she'd contact the family lawyer and have him go to the precinct.

Senator Cain said nothing.

Gary got behind the wheel.

We're about to learn the truth behind Cheryl's death, and I'm not sure I want to hear it.

A truth he felt sure would break Pete Raskin.

2:00 p.m.

GARY WAS about to go to the interview room where Senator Cain awaited them when his phone rang. It was Travers.

"Sergeant Michaels informs me we have Senator William Cain in custody. *Custody?* What on earth have you dug up?"

"I'll tell you when we've spoken to the senator. Am I okay to let Dan sit in on the interview?"

"Seeing as he's probably been instrumental in getting you to this point, I would say yes. And Gary? Come to my office as soon as you're done with the senator."

Gary told him he would, then hung up.

Dan's grim expression mirrored Gary's own internal turmoil.

"Let's get down there." No sooner had the words left Gary's lips than his phone buzzed. He fished it out of his pocket and peered at the screen. "It's from Sean Nichols. The class reunion is in September. It's being run as a charity dinner, and there will be a raffle to raise more funds. Tuxedos to be worn."

"Tell him we'll be there." Dan cocked his head. "Do you own a tux?"

"I'll rent one." Gary composed a quick reply, then stared at the door.

"I know how you feel." Dan's voice was low. "I can't believe it either."

"Then let's go hear his story."

They headed down to the interview rooms to find an officer standing outside.

"Senator Cain's lawyer just arrived. He's in there now."

Gary glanced at his badge. "Thanks, Lomax." He opened the door and they went inside.

Senator Cain sat at the table, in quiet conversation with a smartly dressed man. A jug of water and two glasses were in front of them. Both men fell silent as Gary and Dan took their seats facing them. Gary checked the recording apparatus was functioning properly and went through the routine of assuring the senator was aware of his rights.

Gary opened his folder. "Let's start with what happened the day Cheryl died. Do you remember everything?"

"Senator, I—"

Senator Cain patted his lawyer's arm. "You're here because Della sent for you, but I'm afraid all you're going to do is sit there and listen. I've kept quiet for long enough." He regarded Gary, his face drawn. "Believe me, that day has haunted me for the past twenty-six years."

"You weren't in Nantucket as you previously claimed."

The senator shook his head, and his lawyer pointed to the mic. "No. We'd closed up the house in Lenox for the summer as usual. The staff were due to come back from vacation just before Labor Day, to clean, make beds, etcetera. I came back to the house alone that day."

"But it wasn't *just* that day, was it?" Dan interjected. "You and Cheryl were there at other times over the summer."

Senator Cain stared at him. "How did you know that? There was never anyone around."

"Aiden Reynolds was building your pool house, remember? He saw you in the gardens."

The senator sighed. "Of course. I'd forgotten they were there." He clasped his hands on the table. "Those last three summers, Cheryl and I got into a routine. One day a week, I'd drive back to the house under the pretext of having some work to do. There was no one around—all the staff were on vacation too. We'd spend most of those days in bed."

"And the day she died?" Gary inquired.

Senator Cain took a drink from the glass of water. "We'd agreed to meet on Friday evening. I was going to stay until Sunday morning, then drive back to Nantucket. It would be the last time before Della and I came back to the house. But when I got there...." He regarded Gary with a pained expression. "She wasn't where I expected to find her."

Friday August 28, 1992

SENATOR CAIN closed the front door behind him. It never ceased to amuse him that despite him knowing for certain there were no staff in the house, he always closed the door quietly so as not to be detected. Cheryl's car wasn't out front, but then again it never was. She usually left it at the cottage where Pete and his wife lived and walked over to the house. The chances of anyone seeing it were slim, but the senator wasn't about to risk it.

He climbed the stairs, his heartbeat racing at the thought of seeing her again. It had only been a week since their last meeting, but *Lord*, he'd missed her. Granted, his days had been full of time spent on the beach with the children, his evenings full of dinners outdoors, the smell of the sea carried on the breeze, the heat of the day gradually receding.

He longed to hear her voice, to lie in bed with her, talking about her painting, her job. Everything about her fascinated him. One day a week was all they got, and he knew once September arrived, their meetings would have to be severely curtailed.

That only made him more determined to wring every ounce of joy possible out of those precious minutes they got to share.

When he reached the second floor, he headed for the guest room they always used.

I'm such a hypocrite. I talk about the importance of family, the sanctity of marriage, but I'm happy to commit adultery. However, his moral compass wouldn't allow him to make love to Cheryl in the bedroom he shared with Della. That felt like a step too far.

He heard her voice, but it didn't come from the guest room—Cheryl was in his office, and from the sound of it she was making a phone call. Intrigued, he walked into the room, and his heart stuttered when he saw the left-hand door.

It was pulled all the way across.

Oh dear Lord.

He crossed the floor, reaching out to draw it back, and then he caught her words.

"I've found it. It's been in plain sight all the time. I'm looking at it right now."

His heart hammering, Senator Cain pushed the door back, and there she was, staring at him, mouth open, her phone in her hand.

He didn't hesitate. He snatched the phone from her, ended the call, then dropped it to the floor with a clatter.

Cheryl looked at him as if he'd grown another head. "What… what are *you* doing with *this*?"

Her horrified expression cut him to the bone.

He said the first thing that came into his head.

"Copy it for me? Then… then I'll give it back. I-I only have it on loan."

For a moment there, he could have sworn she wavered.

Not for long.

"I won't do it. But you're right about one thing—you *are* going to give it back." She swallowed. "Will, I thought I knew you."

"You do. *No one* knows me the way you do."

She shook her head, and his throat seized to see the disgust written all over her face. "The fact that you have this in your possession? I would never have believed this of you. It… it calls into question your whole character."

That was when Senator Cain's world came crashing down, and he knew they were through.

"Please…. You can't tell anyone," he pleaded. "Just give me a chance to send it back to where it came from."

"And where's that? The Isabella Stewart Gardner Museum? Because I'm pretty sure that was *not* where you got it from." She glanced around the room.

"What are you looking for?"

She gaped at him. "A phone. I'm calling the police." Her eyes glistened. "I have to call them. Don't you see that?"

"I can't let you do it."

Cheryl blinked. "Who's going to stop me? You?" She made as if to brush past him, and he grabbed her. "Let go of me." She struggled to free herself, and then….

Oh hell no.

Friday, August 3, 2018

"What happened?" Gary asked in a low voice.

Senator Cain stared at him, tears trickling down his cheeks. "She fell. But she hit her head on the metal grate around the hearth." He swallowed. "I knelt beside her, but she was out cold, blood pouring from her head."

"What did you do?"

The senator regarded him with wide eyes. "I panicked. I knew I'd probably killed her."

"Did you check for a pulse?" Dan asked.

"Yes. It was there but very weak. She lay so still, and there was so much blood. I knew I needed help—*she* needed help—but what could I do? I couldn't let it get out, but I had to do *something*. So…." He sagged in his chair. "I made a phone call."

Gary leaned forward. "Who did you call, Senator?"

"The same person who'd loaned me the Rembrandt—Bruno DiFanetti."

Chapter Twenty-Seven

Gary did his best to maintain a calm exterior.

"That's not a name I expected to be associated with a senator. How on earth do you come to know *him*?"

Senator Cain picked up his glass and drank. "The summer of 1990—July, I think—he called me. He said he had something that might be of interest to me. Well, as soon as I learned who he was, I told him he had nothing that could possibly interest me. Then he mentioned the art collection, and…."

"And suddenly he had your attention," Dan interjected.

He nodded. "DiFanetti said he had its crowning jewel, but that it would come at a price."

"Didn't that set off alarm bells?" Gary asked.

"Of course it did, but my curiosity got the better of me. I told him if he had something to show me, he would need to bring it to the house. I wasn't about to venture into unknown territory, and the house had been shut up for the summer. Cheryl was working at the Athenaeum, and there was no one around." He paused. "You can imagine my surprise when a laundry truck turned up. But when I looked inside…." Senator Cain swallowed. "I couldn't believe what I was seeing. I recognized it instantly. And then a little sanity returned. I told him I couldn't afford whatever he was asking."

Dan stared at him. "Your first thought was to *buy* it? Knowing what it was? Where it came from?"

Senator Cain arched his eyebrows. "I said a *little* sanity. The more I looked at it, the more certain I became that I had to have it. I would have killed to possess it. All those paintings in my collection? Yes, they were good, some even brilliant, but a *Rembrandt*?"

Gary tilted his head. "You've said twice now that it was a loan, but I'm sure Bruno DiFanetti wanted something for it. What was the price he mentioned?"

"He said the people he represented would call on me to fight in their corner. Even get me elected. And sure enough, in 1991, at the age of thirty-seven, I was a senator. But I knew what it meant." Senator Cain set his jaw. "They'd hold it over me forevermore. I was tied to them. If I refused, they'd make sure word got out."

"So you agreed."

"Yes. DiFanetti asked what I wanted to do with the Rembrandt. I had him bring it into the house."

"DiFanetti drove the laundry truck?"

"No, there was a young man with him. I don't know who he was, and DiFanetti never addressed him by name. They brought the painting upstairs and put it in a guest room. And all the while, I was turning over ideas how to conceal it in such a way that *I* could still look upon it, but no one else would know of its existence."

"So DiFanetti left once they'd unloaded the painting?"

The senator nodded. "The following morning, I called him. I asked if he could recommend a carpenter. I figured he would know of someone who could be trusted. He said he'd find one for me. Later that day, Al came. At that time, the paintings were on walls all over the house. I'd called Della, telling her I was having some remodeling done, I'd stay until it was finished, and that it was a surprise. I'd had all night to plan."

"You asked him to construct the pocket doors."

"And a partition wall across the largest bedroom. Al—James—took some measurements. I was impressed. He seemed awfully young but very capable. The following morning he came back, and by the end of the day, the studwork was up. Over the next few days, he built the partition walls and put up the track for the doors. He hung the doors to check everything worked, then paneled the walls with Sheetrock."

Gary tapped his pen on the table. "As a matter of interest, did he ever meet Cheryl?"

"Yes, he did. He met her over that weekend. I said she was an artist and showed him photos of her portraits. He admired her work. I think he was also fascinated by her. She drew a lot of attention."

Dan leaned forward. "Let's get back to your account. James hung the doors."

The senator nodded. "But I'd been watching. When he'd gone, I removed a couple of sides of Sheetrock, removed the braces from the inside of the partition, then replaced the Sheetrock, ready for plaster and paint."

Gary blinked. "*You* did all that?" Then he widened his eyes. "Of course. You worked on a construction site when you were younger."

Another nod. "When they'd finished painting, I added a frame to the edge of the door, then a panel and rollers."

Dan's breathing caught. "So James Sebring knew nothing about it?"

"Not a thing."

Gary made a note. "Back to the night in question."

"I checked on Cheryl. She was breathing, but she was in a bad way. And then she came around. I cleaned up her head. She tried to talk, but she wasn't making much sense."

"And then you called Bruno."

"Yes."

"But why him?" Dan wanted to know.

"I don't know why I called him, to be honest. I-I wasn't thinking straight. I simply knew I needed help, and he was the first person who came to mind. He told me to sit tight and that he'd get to me as fast as he could. I spent the intervening time holding her hand, trying to stem the bleeding, to keep her talking."

"Could she talk?"

"Yes, but still nothing that made any sense. And then finally, two cars arrived. DiFanetti was driving one of them."

"Who was in the other?" Dan asked.

"I didn't know at first. DiFanetti told me later that it was his son. I never saw him. Not that I cared who he was. All I wanted was for DiFanetti to clear up the nightmare situation I'd created." He swallowed. "And for Cheryl to be okay."

Friday August 28, 1992

SENATOR CAIN opened the front door to find Bruno DiFanetti standing on his doorstep.

"Senator. Where is she?"

"Upstairs in my office. It's the room facing the one where you put the painting."

"She's still alive?"

"Yes, but... she's in a bad way."

DiFanetti gave him a reassuring smile. "Don't worry. We'll get her to a doctor. She won't be connected to you."

"But—"

DiFanetti glanced at the other car and then pointed up toward the second story of the house. Then he returned his attention to the senator. "Let's have a drink."

Senator Cain stared at him incredulously. "A… drink?"

"I think you could do with one. I know I could. How about you show me your wonderful library, and we can have a drink and a chat. She'll be taken care of, I promise."

There was nothing to do but follow instructions.

The senator led him into the house. "This way, Mr. DiFanetti."

"Please, call me Bruno."

Senator Cain opened the door to the library. Bruno followed him inside and closed it behind them. The senator's hands shook as he removed the crystal stopper from the whiskey decanter, and he had to hold it with both hands as he poured. He handed a glass to Bruno, who was seated in one of the armchairs by the fireplace, then sat facing him.

"What you said about no one connecting Cheryl to me, I…."

"It cannot come out where she was when she had her accident. That would raise too many questions. No, she needs to recover somewhere far from here. And she *will* recover."

Senator Cain raised his gaze to the ceiling. "Who's up there?"

"My son. He's taking care of her." He gave the senator a reassuring smile. "Don't worry. I won't let anything happen to her. I know she's important to you."

"But she'll say what happened. She'll talk." He was torn between fear of discovery and fear of losing her. *If she'll ever speak to me again after this.*

"You let me worry about that. Now," Bruno said, leaning back, "drink your whiskey."

They sat in silence, the senator straining to hear anything from beyond the library door. After a few minutes, Bruno's phone rang once. He removed it from his jacket pocket and glanced at the screen.

From outside came the sound of a car engine.

He smiled. "She is on her way to receive medical help. All will be well." Bruno gestured to the glass in the senator's hand. "Finish your drink. I'll stay until you do."

"You don't have to," Senator Cain protested.

"Nonsense. You need to calm down. I won't leave you when you're in such a state."

And he was. All he could think about was Cheryl.

I should have gone with her.

Too late for that.

About ten minutes later, his calm restored, the senator was ready to bid goodbye to his guest. "When will you know how she—"

Bruno's phone rang again, only this time it was a call. "Excuse me," he murmured. He stood and left the room. Senator Cain heard the low rumble of his voice but couldn't make out what he was saying.

The library door opened, and Bruno came back in.

One glance at his face and the senator's heart sank. "What is it? What's happened?"

Bruno's voice betrayed genuine sympathy. "I am so, so sorry, Senator, but the call was from my son. Cheryl must have been in a far worse state than you'd thought."

"What… what do you mean?"

No. No. Not Cheryl.

Bruno lowered his gaze. "She's dead."

Friday, August 3, 2018

THE SENATOR'S hand shook as he raised the glass of water to his lips.

"I'm ashamed to say my first thought was that they would never let me off their hook after this. And then it hit me. She was gone, and it was all my fault." His voice cracked.

"What happened next?" In that moment, Gary felt sorry for him.

"Bruno left, saying he'd take care of the… body."

"Did you trust him?" Dan asked.

Senator Cain's smile grew bitter. "I didn't have much choice. I told him she'd be missed. Her father…. But Bruno said people disappeared all the time." He ran his finger around the rim of the glass. "He told me to play my part, act like the worried friend, call the police, search for her. Basically, he told me to pull out all the stops. Once he'd gone, I did what he said, but in the hours, days, weeks that followed, I was a mess. Cheryl was dead, and not only could I not grieve for her, I had to keep up the pretense that she was just missing, that she'd reappear one day. And all the while I kept waiting for Bruno's next call, the next demand." He met Gary's gaze. "But it never came. Then I understood. They were waiting until I had more political clout."

"And eventually there *were* demands?" Gary surmised.

The senator nodded. "Bruno had an uncanny knack of being aware of everything that crossed my desk. I suspected one of my staff was his informant, although I could never work out who it was. Then the demands started. Not big, no overt pressure… and not at all what I'd expected."

"What do you mean?"

"They wanted me to vote *in favor* of stricter gun laws." Gary stared at him, and Senator Cain nodded. "A man like him… wanting such a thing. Then another time, they wanted me to endorse someone who was running for governor. I'm sure you know what went through my mind. Only when I looked into it, the candidate was someone I would have supported anyway." He shook his head. "None of it made sense. And then in 2006, Bruno called. The tunnel had collapsed, and he wanted me to deflect attention away from the investigation, but there'd been a death, and people wanted answers. As it turned out, the epoxy that caused the collapse had been supplied to a company run by Bruno's son, Gianni."

"Yes, we know about that."

Senator Cain sagged in his chair. "I can't tell you what a relief this is. It's finally over. I've lived with this for so long, it feels as though it's eaten away at my soul." He frowned. "Not the favors I did for Bruno. I never lent my support to anything criminal, and the bills I tried to push through were for the good of the people. If they had been otherwise, I don't think I could have lived with that." His face tightened. "But Cheryl's death has haunted me. It wasn't intentional, but I killed her all the same." He glanced at Gary. "Will I be tried for manslaughter, along with receiving stolen property?"

"That will be up to the DA," Gary informed him. "In the meantime, you'll be taken to a cell until bail can be arranged."

"I guessed that would be the case." Senator Cain stilled. "I suppose you'll be interviewing Bruno too."

"You suppose correctly."

"Senator?" Dan looked him in the eye. "All the times we interviewed you, the lies you told, one thing was obvious. You loved her."

The senator's face crumpled. "I did. And then she saw that painting and she stopped loving me."

Chapter Twenty-Eight

Friday, August 3, 2018

Dan waited until the senator had been escorted from the interview room before expelling a long breath. "I didn't expect that."

Gary shook his head. "Christ. Bruno DiFanetti—and Senator Cain."

Dan tapped the table with his index finger. "Yeah, I'm a little confused about that part."

"You and me both. I thought I had a handle on that family. Now? I don't have a clue."

"We'll have to bring him in, won't we? If only to corroborate what the senator told us." He stood. "I don't know about you, but I need some coffee. And maybe a little information."

"What do you want to know?"

"You told me about the DiFanetti family, and both you and Travers made them sound really dirty, but"—he frowned—"it doesn't add up. Because the demands Bruno made of the senator...."

"I know." Gary picked up his notepad and pen. "Let's grab that coffee, and I'll fill you in on a little family history. I did some research once Gianni emerged as a possible suspect."

"The coffee will have to wait." When Gary gave him a quizzical glance, Dan arched his eyebrows. "Travers wants to see you, remember? He wants an update." Then he stared at the chair where Senator Cain had sat. "He really was good."

"What do you mean?"

"We didn't think he was involved in Cheryl's death. His concern, his willingness to help us.... I believed him. And yet it was all a performance, one he'd been instructed to give." He sighed. "Except for the part about being in love with her. That felt real. And when he said he'd killed her, he believed that."

"I'd better go report to Travers."

Dan smiled. "I'll have coffee waiting for when you emerge from the lion's den."

They headed for the door, but Gary paused before opening it. "Was it really Lori's phone call that put you on the right track?"

"Partly. Those pocket doors… there was something about them. And when I realized James Sebring had made them, it was all too much of a coincidence. Then there was that intense curiosity I felt every time I handled the negatives and the photos. Not all of them, just the ones connected to the Caravaggio. And finally…." Dan gazed at him. "You remember when I stepped back in the art room to get a better look at the Rembrandt, and I almost fell?" Gary nodded. "Well, in an effort to prevent myself from falling, I put my hand out and touched the hearth."

Gary's eyes widened. "Where Cheryl fell and hit her head."

"Exactly. I didn't see it happen, but I knew something momentous had taken place." Dan shivered. "He sat with her, trying to save her, trying not to panic, while he waited for Bruno to show up."

"He knew it was over between them." Gary huffed. "I'd better go." He opened the door and hurried toward Travers's office.

Dan walked more slowly, his mind turning over the interview with the senator.

He wasn't how I expected a politician to be. He had the potential to be a truly great man, a force for good.

And all of that potential had been wiped out the minute he laid eyes on a painting.

Dan glanced up as Gary entered their office. "So is Travers happy at how our first cold case concluded?"

"Yes and no." Gary went over to the coffeepot and poured himself a cup.

"Let me guess. Yes, because we've solved the mystery of who killed Cheryl Somers. And no, because it turned out to be a senator."

Gary sat at his desk. "That pretty much sums it up. But before you start talking about this case being concluded, I think I'd better point out something you seem to have overlooked."

"Oh?"

Gary looked him in the eye. "How did Cheryl end up in the tunnel, missing her head? Although knowing the DiFanettis, that last part isn't all that surprising."

"What's this family history you were going to fill me in on?" Dan sipped his coffee.

Gary pulled a folder from his desk drawer. "Okay, I think I mentioned before that in the past, the DiFanettis had their fingers in a lot of pies: gambling, narcotics, robbery, loan sharking, extortion, money laundering, smuggling, fraud...."

Dan gaped. "Dear Lord, we *are* talking organized crime. When exactly was 'the past'?"

"I think the sixties was their heyday, but they got going in the forties. The head of the family was Gio, Bruno's father, and popular opinion has it that he was behind all the shit they got up to."

"Sounds like something straight out of *The Godfather*."

Gary chuckled. "Art imitating life, maybe? Anyway, Gio went in '71. Heart attack. Bruno was thirty at the time, and he took over as head of the family." Gary leaned back in his chair. "Now, it *should* have been his older brother, Nico, but he'd been bumped off in 1960 at the age of twenty-two."

"Bumped off? Someone murdered him?"

"That's how it looks. You remember Paul DiFanetti?"

Dan shuddered. "I'm not likely to forget him."

"Well, Paul was the youngest brother. Three years younger than Bruno."

"Wait a minute. The way you just described Bruno's father.... From what the senator said, Bruno doesn't seem to be a chip off the old block."

Gary nodded slowly. "There have been signs that times are changing. From all accounts, Paul is a lot like his dad, but he's had to toe the line." He tapped the folder. "I did some digging. Lately if the DiFanetti name pops up in anything dirty, it's usually linked to Paul, not Bruno. Which is why I found it easy to believe *Paul* might have had Cheryl taken out."

"And now?" Dan could easily have believed Paul to be the culprit.

"After everything I heard in that interview, it sounds as though Bruno is trying to change the DFF group's rep. All that stuff the senator was asked to support? Maybe Bruno is trying to go legit. A lot of people's perceptions of the family are based on the past, and it could be he wants to change all that."

Dan frowned. "Now hold on there. Are you saying the senator and Bruno are *good guys*? Seriously? Then explain the painting. You think Bruno *happened* to have it lying around? Think about the timing. The museum heist took place March 18, 1990. Then Bruno approached the senator in July." He folded his arms. "We need to know what happened after Bruno took Cheryl away from the senator's house."

Gary nodded. "I agree. Which is why we're going to bring Bruno in for a little chat. Maybe he has the answers. Because *we* don't have them all yet."

"When will you bring him in?"

"Tomorrow morning, first thing."

Dan cocked his head. "And when do you think Senator Cain will make bail?"

"That lawyer of his will have him out of that cell before the end of the day. I guarantee it."

"So he'll be free to go back to the house and wait for the hammer to fall. Only this time he won't have his Rembrandt to gaze at." Dan stilled. "I think it lost its luster when Cheryl died. Because can you imagine how he felt every time he looked at it? It would be a reminder of the night he lost the woman he loved."

"He lost more than that," Gary murmured. When Dan gazed at him inquiringly, he gave a sad smile. "I think that night… he lost a piece of his soul."

Chapter Twenty-Nine

Saturday, August 4, 2018
9:30 a.m.

GARY PICKED up his folder, then checked his notepad was in his pocket.

"Breathe, sweetheart," Dan said in a whisper.

He let out a wry chuckle. "That obvious, huh?"

"I was in the bed next to you last night, remember? You didn't sleep well."

Gary bit his lip. "I don't know why. I mean, so what if I'm about to interview the head of Boston's largest crime family? Especially one who's brought his lawyer with him. That doesn't bode well."

"You said it yourself. They *were* Boston's largest crime family once, but maybe not anymore. Now if you were interviewing *Paul* DiFanetti, then yes, I'd be worried. That man is…." Dan shivered.

There was a knock at the door, and Travers walked in, his eyes gleaming.

"I know I said you still had work to do on this case, but *Jesus*, Gary. You just caused a commotion downstairs."

Gary flashed Dan a smile. "I guess our interviewee has arrived."

"Have you arrested Bruno DiFanetti?" Travers demanded.

"Right now he's helping us with our inquiries. We'll see what the state of play is when we get through with him."

"When I suggested you start with this case, I had no idea it would lead to Senator William Cain confessing to manslaughter. When did he make bail?"

"This morning." Gary held up the folder. "And Bruno is here to add a few more details."

Travers glanced at Dan. "You'll be in on the interview too, right?"

"You bet he will." Gary gazed at Dan, his chest bursting with pride. "He's provided us with some considerable leads so far."

Travers smiled. "Sounds as if I was right to put you two together. You make quite a team." He cleared his throat, then gave Gary a mock glare. "So what are you waiting for? Go interview *Mr.* DiFanetti."

They followed Travers out into the hallway and headed for the interview rooms. On the way they passed officers and detectives who patted Gary's back and shoulders, murmuring noises of approval. Will Freeman met them outside Interview Room One.

"I'll say this about you two." He grinned. "You've got balls."

Gary rolled his eyes. "He's just a businessman who's going to answer a few questions."

Will snorted. "Yeah, right, and I'm the Easter Bunny."

Gary gave a wave of his hand, then pushed the door open. Dan followed him inside.

Bruno DiFanetti sat at the table, wearing an immaculate dark blue suit. His receding white hair and beard spoke to his seventy-seven years, making him look like a kindly grandfather.

His cool gray eyes, however, belied that impression. Eyes that were fixed on Gary and Dan.

Eyes that indicated intelligence.

Next to him sat a man who was roughly the same age, also dressed in a smart suit, a large notepad in front of him.

Gary took a seat. "Thank you for agreeing to come in today." He glanced at the lawyer. "I'm Detective Gary Mitchell, and this is Dan Porter, who's working with me on this case."

The man handed over a business card. "Luke Martin. I've been Mr. DiFanetti's attorney for more than forty years."

Dan frowned. "I thought we'd met the family lawyer—Mr. Stillwater?"

Mr. Martin coughed. "He works for Paul DiFanetti. But he does *not* speak for the family."

Bruno said nothing. He was too busy staring at Dan.

"Is there a problem?" Gary inquired.

"I saw the reports in the media on the Ludlow case." Bruno's brow furrowed. "This is the psychic who helped catch him."

"That's correct," Dan said with a smile.

Bruno's frown deepened. "Then what are you doing here? You're not a cop."

"I'm now working for Boston PD, specifically on cold cases."

"And starting with the case of Cheryl Somers," Gary added.

Bruno gave a dismissive wave. "Yeah, you said as much on the phone. I've gotta say, I'm curious. How does this concern me?" Another gaze flickered in Dan's direction.

Gary saw no reason to delay the conversation. "Mr. DiFanetti, you're here to provide a few missing details related to our case. But this is where I should point out that we know everything: the Rembrandt, your hold over Senator Cain, you and your son coming to the senator's aid that night—"

"Whoa there." Bruno held up his hand. "What makes you think you know *everything*?"

"We interviewed Senator Cain yesterday. He went through the events of August twenty-eighth, 1992." Gary deliberately kept things vague.

Bruno picked a piece of lint from his jacket and dropped it onto the floor. "Good for him."

"He told us how Cheryl discovered the Rembrandt, their quarrel, their struggle, and her fall." Gary opened the folder. "Then he says he called you. He told us how you came to the house with your son, how you took Cheryl away to get medical attention, and how she subsequently died from her injuries before she could get that help. So you see, we know the whole story."

Hook baited. Now all Bruno had to do was take it.

Bruno folded his arms.

"A story that begins with the painting you stole," Dan said in a firm voice.

"Okay, stop right there." Bruno held up a finger. "Point number one. I didn't steal it, so don't go around saying stuff like that unless you want me to sue your ass."

"But you do know who stole it," Gary countered. "And you used it to your advantage."

Bruno said nothing. He stared at the tabletop, his arms refolded.

"Don't you think it's time for the truth to come out?" Dan suggested.

Finally Bruno raised his chin and heaved a heavy sigh. "Yes, I do think it's time. Maybe that's the real reason I chose to accept your *kind* invitation to an interview. That and the fact I was curious to discover how much you knew."

"The real reason we invited you was because we knew we didn't have all the answers." Gary gave him a frank stare. "Okay, we don't have a *lot* of the answers. And we need your help."

Bruno met his stare. "You know, I thought I was dealing with a stupid detective, but you're not, are you? In fact you're pretty astute."

Gary smiled. "I've learned never to jump to conclusions."

Bruno leaned back. "What do you want to know?"

"Let's start with the Rembrandt." Gary leaned forward. "Who stole it?"

"Before I get to that part, there's something I have to say." Bruno gestured to Mr. Martin. "I've asked Luke along today for two reasons. Only an idiot talks to the police without a lawyer present. And…." He hesitated.

Gary's scalp prickled, and he had no clue why.

Mr. Martin laid his hand on Bruno's arm. "I'll handle this part." He met Gary's gaze. "My client is willing to answer your questions, and of course, whatever he tells you will need to be verified. But in doing so, my client will be placing himself in danger. As such, he will require protection until such time as… you have apprehended the perpetrator."

Gary blinked. "Witness protection?"

Bruno's eyes widened. "Hey, if I'm going to give up all this information, then I have to know you're going to take care of me. I think the *least* you can do is offer me witness protection."

Goose bumps broke out on Gary's arms. "What you have to tell us is that explosive?"

Bruno took a deep breath. "I'd be willing to bet you know *nothing* of what I'm going to tell you. We're talking about more than Cheryl's death, okay?"

Gary folded his arms. "I can't see Senator Cain coming after you, threatening you." He didn't think the senator had that in him.

Bruno arched his eyebrows. "Who says I'm talking about the senator?"

That stopped Gary in his tracks.

"Well?" Bruno locked gazes with him. "Do we have a deal?"

"I'd need to check with the DA, but if your information is as damning as you claim, then I can't see any reason why he couldn't offer you witness protection."

"Not good enough." Bruno leaned forward. "I'm not leaving this precinct until I *know* you're going to protect me. That means when we're done, you take me someplace where there's a cop within a few feet of my door."

Gary got out his phone and called Travers. He recounted the conversation so far and Bruno's demands. "Can we protect him?"

"I'll go see the chief right now, and he'll get onto the DA. Tell Bruno we'll do it." There was a pause. "This sounds way bigger than a skeleton in a tunnel."

Gary had a feeling he was correct.

"Thanks." He hung up, replaced his phone in his pocket, then clasped his hands on the table. "We have a deal."

Bruno glanced at Mr. Martin, who nodded. "You asked who stole the Rembrandt." Bruno took a deep breath. "That would be my son, Gianni."

Dan blinked. "How old was he in 1990? He had to have been in his twenties."

"Twenty-five years old, and yet he masterminded the theft of millions of dollars of art." Bruno pursed his lips. "Not that this was my first indication of what he was capable of. But yeah, Gianni stole it— and all the rest of the stuff from the museum—and I saw an opportunity. William Cain had political aspirations. No shocker there. It runs in the blood, I guess. But I knew I could get him into the senate, even at his age, and use him for good. And once I read up on his family and learned about that collection of his?" He smiled. "That's when I knew the Rembrandt was my lever."

Gary nodded. "And when he killed Cheryl—well, when he was responsible for her death—that was another lever."

Bruno straightened in his chair. "And there you go again, proving you don't know everything. The senator didn't kill Cheryl."

Gary stilled. "Then who did?"

Bruno's eyes locked on his. "Gianni."

Chapter Thirty

The more Gary tried to get his head around Bruno's revelation, the less sense it made.

"But why? What reason would he have to kill her, unless it was to silence her because she knew about the Rembrandt." And even that made no sense. "You *told* him to get her to a doctor."

Bruno's face was grave. "Yes, I did. What I didn't know at the time was that Gianni had his own agenda. That night when I got the call from Senator Cain, I didn't ask Gianni to come with me. He offered, which surprised the hell out of me." He sighed. "And as for *why* he killed her, I only found that out later. *Then* it all made sense. By the time I discovered what had led to her death, Gianni had already disposed of the body."

"Did he tell you what he'd done with her?" Dan asked.

Bruno shook his head. "He kept telling me I didn't need to know. Then in 2006 when the tunnel collapsed… *then* I knew." He snorted. "Talk about irony. Gianni was the reason for its collapse. At least, the company that supplied the epoxy was, and he contracted them to do the job." He peered at Gary. "I'm not telling you anything you didn't already know, am I?"

"Yeah, we knew that part." That was public record. Gary leaned forward, his hands clasped. "You give every indication that you're trying to steer your family onto the path of legality. How do you square that ambition with doing nothing about Cheryl's murder?"

For a moment Bruno said nothing, his face dark. Finally he expelled a long breath. "I can't, and that's going to haunt me for the rest of my days. My only excuse was that I was protecting my son." He huffed. "At least, I thought he was my son at the time."

Gary said nothing but arched his eyebrows.

Bruno met his gaze. "You look surprised. No more than I was, I assure you." He glanced around the room. "Do you think I might have a glass of water?"

Before Gary could apologize, Dan got up, walked to the door, and spoke quietly with the officer outside, then returned to the table. "On its way," he murmured.

"Thank you." Bruno cleared his throat. "I married my wife, Talia, when I was twenty." He gave a shrug. "It was a good marriage. We celebrated our fifty-sixth anniversary last year." His face contorted. "Last year she was also diagnosed with pancreatic cancer, and not long after that, she was on her way out. So there I was, sitting with her in the hospital, holding her hand while she was dying right in front of me, and she told me Gianni wasn't mine. She said she'd known she was pregnant when she married me."

"Did you believe her?"

Bruno's face tightened. "What man wants to believe such a thing? Fifty-six years of marriage? I thought I knew her. But a deathbed confession? She said it had been eating away at her for years. And once she'd said it, once the idea was there in my mind… well, it answered a lot of questions." He grimaced. "All the questions I'd dismissed over the years because I didn't want to think about them."

"Do you have a photo of Gianni?" Dan asked.

Bruno took out his phone and scrolled. "That was him the last Christmas before I lost Talia." He handed Dan the phone.

Dan studied the image, and Gary's skin tingled.

He's doing more than just looking.

After a minute or so, Dan handed the phone back to Bruno. He took a deep breath. "Your brother Paul is Gianni's father."

Bruno froze, his mouth open. "How did you…? There is no *way* you could have known that."

Dan gave him a sympathetic glance. "I know because you do."

His breathing hitched. "Stupid of me. I'd forgotten about your… abilities." Bruno gave Dan an appraising glance. "I guess all the news reports weren't hype after all." He gazed at the photo. "I asked her why she hadn't married Paul. She said she knew I'd be the head of the family one day—Nico was gone—and that I'd have more to offer." He swallowed as he stared at the photo. "They even look alike. I don't know how I didn't see it long before. Me and Gianni, we're not alike in looks or temperament." He pocketed his phone. "Funny thing is, Gianni always felt to me like he was a cuckoo in the nest, something not quite right about him."

"But why are you telling us all this now?" Gary's head was reeling. "He's still your nephew after all. Still a blood relation."

Bruno nodded, his eyes suddenly cool. "And I've been cleaning up his messes for far too long."

Dan tilted his head. "Like James Sebring's murder?"

Bruno blinked. "You know about that too?" Another heavy sigh rolled out of him. "That one was partially my fault. After the tunnel fiasco, I moved Gianni, gave him control of the housing construction company." His face tightened. "Except he messed that up too. When James put the bite on him, I told Gianni to pay up and then retrofit the radon barriers. He assured me he'd put it right."

"And then James Sebring fell to his death," Gary concluded.

The door opened, and an officer brought in a jug of water and a glass. He placed them on the table, then retreated. Bruno poured himself a glass and drained half its contents.

He set the glass down on the table. "When I learned about the accident, I knew Gianni had murdered him." Bruno stared into the glass. "Then there were two murders under his belt."

Gary coughed. "Possibly three."

Bruno jerked his head up and stared at him. "What?"

"There was another headless corpse found in 2007. We have reason to believe that was Gianni's handiwork too."

Bruno let out a slow breath. "Kevin Donaldson. Of course."

"Did you know him?"

"Let's say I knew *of* him. Kevin was the head of another family in—"

"When you say 'family,'" Dan interjected.

Bruno nodded. "A rival family might be a better way of putting it. At least Gianni saw it as such. He was certain they were trying to take over from us." He rolled his eyes. "Take over." Another shake of his head. "We might be the same blood, but me and Gianni, we see the family so differently." He scowled. "We're not the *mob*," he said, air-quoting. "Problem is, that's still how we're perceived, and it's that perception I'm fighting to change. So here we are, locked into a power struggle that's gone on for far too long. Gianni wants to go back to the 'good old days,' and he probably has my brother's backing to do just that. So I'm not fighting one DiFanetti, but two. But as long as Gianni sees this family as the 'mob,' then I need to stop him. At all costs."

"And now you understand why my client is concerned for his safety," Mr. Martin added. "You met his brother?"

Gary nodded.

"Then you must realize he and Bruno are nothing alike."

Gary recalled his evening "visitor" with a shiver. "You're right, they're not."

Bruno took another drink from his glass. "Gianni said we needed to do something about Kevin Donaldson. He said we needed to cut the head from the body to put a stop to them." He shook his head. "At the time I thought he was talking figuratively. I told Gianni we should simply step aside and let them do whatever the hell they wanted, but I was wasting my breath. I suspected him of having something to do with Kevin's death, but I couldn't prove it. And he denied it, but he always did deny everything, even as a child. Then someone else owned up to it, so I thought I was wrong."

Gary nodded. "Frank Wyler owned up to it—*after* a visit from Gianni."

A dark cloud rolled across Bruno's face. "And *this* is why I have to put a stop to *him*."

"You do realize my client has no proof Gianni murdered Kevin Donaldson? Or that he killed Cheryl Somers and James Sebring?"

Bruno stopped Mr. Martin with a hand to his arm. "Which is why I'm here." He finished his water, then looked Gary in the eye. "If you need me to be a witness, I'll do it."

Gary strove to keep his face straight. "You'd help us put him behind bars?"

"Yes. Because someone has to help you do it, and I know where all the bodies are buried." His eyes gleamed. "Again, figuratively speaking. But if you want Gianni, you're going to have to move fast."

"Why?" Gary's pulse quickened.

Bruno glanced at his watch. "Because around about now, he'll be at Midway in Chicago, ready to board a flight to Boston, and once he lands and gets wind of this, he'll turn tail and be on the first plane out of here. Probably someplace where you can't find him. Or extradite him." His expression grew grim. "Unless he knows already, and believe me, that's a distinct—and unfortunate—possibility." He shuddered. "Which is why I want to be someplace he can't find me."

Gary made a note. "We'll meet his flight." He leaned forward. "I do have one question left."

Bruno arched his eyebrows. "I thought we'd covered everything. I assume you know why Gianni removed Cheryl's head—to make identification difficult. I don't suppose he ever believed her body would see the light of day, at least not for a very long time."

"Yes, we came to that conclusion too."

"What happened to the heads?" Dan asked. "Kevin's was also missing."

Bruno shrugged. "I can hazard a guess. My bet is that one day in the future, they'll turn up in a pile of rubble when someone tears down one of Gianni's building projects. Either that or he threw them into the ocean, weighted down. Pouring concrete over them makes more sense. That way, it's less likely some fisherman will come across them."

"I have a question." Gary met Bruno's inquiring gaze. "Why?"

Bruno frowned. "Why what?"

"You took over a powerful family with its roots in organized crime, and then you did your best to change its direction. Why? What happened to bring about such a drastic change?"

For a moment Bruno said nothing. He stared at his laced fingers, his breathing steady. Finally he raised his chin. "When I was nineteen years old, my brother Nico was murdered." He held his hand up. "Yes, I know you already know that, but what you *don't* know is how profoundly his death affected me. At the time it made no sense. I asked my father who could possibly have wanted to kill a twenty-two-year-old man who had never harmed a fly."

"What did he say?" Dan appeared spellbound by the conversation.

"He didn't answer. It wasn't until he was dying that I learned the truth." Bruno's eyes darkened. "Do you know what he called Nico's death? Collateral damage. Some tit-for-tat killing linked to his various… enterprises." He swallowed. "When they placed my father in the ground, I vowed never to be the man he was." He poured himself another glass of water and drank several mouthfuls. "Gianni was six years old when his grandfather died. He only remembers him through the stories Paul told him. But I looked at my little boy and swore I would never see him the way my father saw Nico. So I decided the DiFanetti family would cast off its blood-stained garments of the past and take on new clothing." Another drink from his glass. "However, it wasn't the easy task I'd anticipated. For one thing, I had opposition."

"Your brother Paul," Gary said in a low voice.

Bruno nodded. "I'd given him control over some of the companies my father had set up. It wasn't until much later I learned what was really going on. He'd carried on where my father had left off, totally ignoring my instructions." He bowed his head. "I should have been stronger, but… I let things slide, until finally, in the mideighties, I couldn't take it anymore."

"What brought you to that point?" Dan inquired.

Bruno sighed. "Gianni. I saw the kind of man he was becoming, and I knew I had to do something. As it turned out, something drastic."

"What did you do?" Gary asked.

Bruno's face tightened. "I told my brother I wanted nothing more to do with him as long as he continued on the path he'd chosen. We fought— verbally, I should add. It was a long, acrimonious battle, and at the end of it, he told me I'd brought shame to the family, and he was through. What I hadn't expected was Gianni's reaction."

"He sided with his uncle." Dan tilted his head to one side. "Does he know Paul is his father?"

"If he does, he's never mentioned it. And I couldn't see him keeping something that momentous to himself. But then again, Talia never told me if Paul knew the truth." Bruno adjusted his tie. "I won't come out of this unscathed. I realize that. I'll be charged. Accessory after the fact. Receiving stolen goods."

"That will happen once we've finished this conversation," Gary informed him. "But I *will* pass on everything you've told me to the DA."

"Detective Mitchell?" Bruno locked gazes with him. "I want to make amends if I can." His Adam's apple bobbed. "Cheryl would have recovered. She came around in Gianni's car. Please, you *must* let Senator Cain know."

Dan's breathing caught. "Gianni told you that?"

"And more besides."

"We'll tell the senator." Gary would see to it.

Bruno stared at his laced fingers. "All my efforts… it will come to nothing. The senator will be tarnished, his reputation lost…."

Gary tapped his notepad with his pen. "If you had truly wanted to change your family's reputation, you could have used the senator for good without making him an accessory."

Bruno's expression grew pained. "My intention was always to give the painting back to the museum. I have no idea what became of the rest of the stolen works, and Gianni never told me. The senator only had it on loan. The ironic part of all this? It was Gianni's idea to have a senator in his pocket. That was the only reason he told me about the art heist. He was going to bribe William Cain." Bruno straightened. "What he hadn't counted on was me. I suggested approaching Cain. I persuaded Gianni that it would be better coming from me. He agreed. And once William Cain was *Senator* Cain, I was the one calling the shots."

"So Gianni's plan backfired."

"Yes." Bruno paused. "There's something else you need to tell Senator Cain. He won't like it, but he has to know." He gestured to Gary's notepad. "You need to write this down."

As Bruno talked in a low voice, Gary wrote quickly, stopping now and then to ask questions. By the time Bruno was done, Gary's head felt bruised.

I thought we'd gotten all the surprises out into the open.

Not even close.

Gary closed his notepad. "Will you make a statement before you leave—I mean, before you're taken to a place of safety?"

Bruno nodded. "That might take a while."

"And I will see all this gets to the attention of the DA." Gary stood, went to the door, and spoke with the officer. He turned to face Bruno. "The officer will take you to a detective to give your statement."

As Bruno passed them, Dan held out his hand. "I appreciate you were trying to steer your family on a different course."

They shook. "And maybe by putting a stop to Gianni, I'll have accomplished that. We shall see." He gave Gary a nod, then left the room.

Dan stared at Gary. "We need to talk to the senator." His face was grave.

"I know." It was a conversation Gary did *not* want to have.

This will kill him.

CHAPTER THIRTY-ONE

Saturday, August 4, 2018
11:30 a.m.

GARY PUT down Bruno DiFanetti's statement. "I think I've read this three times."

It didn't get any better with each fresh reading.

"Me too." Dan appeared gloomy.

The sergeant at the front desk had called to let them know Senator Cain had been brought to the precinct and was on his way to the interview room.

"He didn't go back to the house in Lenox when he was released?"

Gary shook his head. "I told him to stay in Boston." He paused. "You know, Lori Dettweiler called this morning? The Rembrandt is already back at the museum." He stood as the door opened.

Senator Cain looked exhausted.

And he's about to feel a lot worse.

"Senator, please, take a seat."

The senator frowned. "When you called, you told me I wouldn't need my lawyer with me."

"It's not that kind of interview."

Gary would be doing all the talking.

Senator Cain peered at him. "I don't mean to be rude, but you look awful. I'm the one who'll be facing manslaughter charges, not you."

Gary cleared his throat. "Except you won't."

The senator blinked. "What are you talking about?"

"Cheryl Somers didn't die as a result of her head wound."

Senator Cain frowned. "What do you mean? She died on her way to a doctor from injuries *I* inflicted."

Gary shook his head. "Her death was the result of strangulation, inflicted by Bruno DiFanetti's son, Gianni."

"Strangled?" The senator widened his eyes. "Why would he do that? It doesn't make any sense. Unless I was right, and he did it on his father's instructions because he wanted me to *think* I'd killed her, to have a hold over me."

"I don't doubt that was what Gianni wanted, but that wasn't why he killed her. And actually, it makes perfect sense—once you have all the facts."

"Bruno DiFanetti told us the whole story in a statement," Dan added.

Senator Cain sagged into his chair. "Then you'd better tell me."

Friday August 28, 1992
Just before midnight

BRUNO STOPPED his car at the gate and wound the window down. "Is Gianni back yet?" he asked the guy on duty. There'd been nothing from Gianni since the call to say Cheryl Somers had died on the way to a doctor. Bruno had called him several times after leaving Lenox, but there'd been no answer.

"Not yet, sir."

What is Gianni playing at? He should have been back by then.

Bruno thanked him and drove through the gate. The house sat in darkness, apart from one light on the first floor, which meant Talia had already gone to bed. Sure enough, the space where Gianni's car usually sat was empty.

Where are you?

Bruno switched off the engine and grabbed his phone. His call went straight to voicemail again. "Gianni, call me when you get this, okay?" He hung up.

Christ, what a mess.

Everything he tried to do to improve his family's reputation and bury the past seemed to backfire. He'd attempted to help the senator because there was one guy who could do a lot of good.

But not if he's tarnished by an affair—and manslaughter.

Bruno went into the house and headed for his den. He needed a drink.

He switched the lamp on, poured himself a shot of whiskey, then sat in his armchair, his mind turning over the evening's events.

Why did she have to up and die on us?

Bruno firmly believed they could have paid her off. From what he knew of her and her father, Bruno could have set them up in a different state with no money worries. *Anything* to keep Senator Cain in Bruno's pocket.

It's not as if I wanted to use him for some nefarious purpose, Bruno reasoned with the Lord. *Couldn't you just give me a break here?*

Bruno had a feeling God was *not* on his side.

He heard a car engine and glanced at the clock on the mantelpiece. Twelve forty-five. *What's he been doing?* Bruno listened for Gianni's key in the door, but instead of coming to find him as he'd expected, he caught the creak of the stairs.

Hell no. There was no way Gianni was going to bed.

Bruno wanted answers.

He switched off the lamp and quietly closed the door to the den. He crept upstairs and went to Gianni's room on the third floor. As he reached for the door handle, he heard running water, and he scowled. Talking to his father took precedence over a shower, especially in the circumstances.

Bruno entered Gianni's room and stopped dead at the sight of his crumpled clothes, lying on a sheet of plastic.

The patches of red made his stomach roil.

Oh God, what have you done? Bruno sank onto the edge of the bed and stared at the stained heap of clothing. Then he breathed easier. He was overreacting. Of course there'd be blood. Cheryl had a head wound; the senator had said so.

What troubled him was the *amount* of blood.

"Dad?"

Bruno jumped. Gianni stood in the bathroom doorway, a towel wrapped around him. Before Bruno could get a word out, Gianni scurried over to the clothes, bundled them up in the plastic, and shoved them into a bag.

That oily feeling in Bruno's stomach worsened.

"Where is she?" he demanded in a low voice. His and Talia's bedroom was directly below Gianni's, and he didn't want her to wake up.

"Better if you don't know."

"But I *want* to know."

Gianni snorted. "Trust me, you really don't. What do they call it—plausible deniability? If someone starts asking questions, you can say in all honesty that you know nothing."

"Since when do you know anything about the law? And before you start throwing such terms about, you'd better check your facts, because I don't think that phrase means what you *think* it means." Bruno's heartbeat quickened. "She did die the way you said she did? Because of her head wound?"

Gianni dropped his towel and put on his robe. "Sure. We'll go with that."

He sprang to his feet. "No, we'll go with the truth."

"And what if you can't handle the truth?"

Bruno had heard enough. "I think you're forgetting who you're talking to."

Gianni scowled. "That's the problem. You're not the man I thought you were. You've gone soft. If Grandpa could see you now, he—"

Bruno's laugh sounded bitter to his own ears. "'Grandpa' makes him sound like a sweet old man, but we both know better, don't we? Now sit." He pointed to the bed. "And start talking. Because I'm not leaving this room until you've told me everything."

Gianni flopped onto the bed with a sullen expression. For a man of twenty-seven, he behaved like a child sometimes, petulant and stubborn.

But no child possessed his cunning, his malice.

"I settled an old score tonight, that's all."

Bruno frowned. "What old score?"

Gianni was quiet for a moment. "What if I was to tell you Cheryl Somers wasn't born with that name?"

Bruno rolled his eyes. "I know you think I'm ancient, but I'm not stupid. Even I could work out she was transsexual."

Gianni nodded. "Yeah, but what *I* discovered was, before she was Cheryl, her name was Benjamin Raskin."

Something began to clang in the deep recesses of Bruno's mind. "Why do I know that name?"

"Because nine years ago, Benjamin Raskin killed my best friend."

Shock thrummed through him. "Connor?"

Another slow nod. "Raskin was the other driver."

"But—" Bruno wracked his brains for the details. "—it wasn't his fault. Connor caused the accident that killed him, not Raskin. Everyone said so, the witnesses, the police."

Gianni gaped at him. "Seriously? And Raskin's dad just *happened* to work for a wealthy family that was able to pull a few strings, even pay people off?"

Bruno's stomach plummeted. "Gianni, listen to me. I know you and Connor were close, but—"

"Close?" Gianni's eyes were huge. "He was my best friend. He'd *been* my best friend since we were five years old, when you took us to stay with Uncle Paul in Nantucket for the summer."

The Brightmores' summer home was next to Paul's, and the two small boys had been inseparable. If ever Gianni couldn't be found, Bruno had known to look no further than the house next door, and Connor spent as much time with them as he did playing with his sisters.

"How did you find out about Cheryl?"

That earned him another snort. "You wouldn't believe me if I told you. I knew I had to make him pay. I used to call him, telling him he hadn't escaped justice, that I'd get him in the end."

"When was this?"

"For two years after Connor died."

Bruno's mouth fell open. "You... you were eighteen." Eighteen years old and making death threats.

Cold flooded through him. Bruno had the feeling he'd never known what his son was capable of.

But I'm learning fast.

"And then suddenly—nothing. Raskin disappeared off the face of the earth." Gianni narrowed his gaze. "No phone number, no address.... Took me another five years to learn the truth."

"But *how*? How did you discover it?"

Saturday, August 4, 2018

"That's what I want to know too." Senator Cain regarded them with a bewildered expression. "How could he have found her? Cheryl never used her dead name after 1985. She obliterated all traces of Benjamin Raskin."

Gary's chest tightened. "Gianni found out via an informant. Someone who was reporting back to him on anything that crossed your desk."

"This informant discovered Cheryl's previous identity in 1990, Bruno told us," Dan added. "Not that he knew anything about them. He'd always wondered how Gianni managed to glean so much information about you."

The senator's expression grew sober. "I think I mentioned to you that I suspected it was someone working for me, although I could never prove who."

Gary's throat seized. "Not *working* for you—it was your wife."

Senator Cain paled. "No. You've made a mistake."

Gary's heart went out to him. "I'm sorry, but it's true. There's no doubt."

The senator stared at him with pain-stricken eyes. "But why would she do that? More importantly, how could she have anything to do with the DiFanettis?"

Dan's voice was soft.

"Because she *is* a DiFanetti."

Chapter Thirty-Two

Senator Cain's throat worked, but no sound escaped his lips.

Dan could feel his anguish, see the pain in his eyes, and hear his labored breathing.

"I know this is hard to take, but you need to hear it," he murmured.

The senator stared at him. "Then tell me." The words came out as a croak.

Dan glanced at Gary, who nodded. "When Bruno found out Gianni had strangled Cheryl, and then learned why he'd done it, he demanded to know how Gianni had discovered the truth."

"He strangled—" Senator Cain's eyes glistened.

"Cheryl apparently came around in the car," Gary told him. "Bruno thinks she didn't last long, however."

"That bastard."

Whatever else Dan wanted to say was lost when the senator broke down, tears trickling down his cheeks. Dan grabbed the box of Kleenex and handed it to Senator Cain.

The senator plucked a tissue from it and wiped his face. "I'm sorry. I can't stop thinking about how scared she must have been, coming to in his car, thinking she'd be all right…."

"Gianni told Bruno how he'd learned the truth about Cheryl."

Senator Cain met Dan's gaze. "She isn't a DiFanetti. That cannot be true."

"Gianni told Bruno she'd been adopted."

The senator shook his head. "It's a lie. Della would have told me if she was adopted, and she never mentioned it, not once, in all our years of marriage."

"There's a reason for that." Gary looked him in the eye. "She didn't know."

Senator Cain frowned. "Now wait just one minute. When I was running for the senate, there were background checks—on *both* of us. They would have turned up something like that. Besides, Della comes from one of the oldest families in Boston. We're talking Boston blue blood, for God's sake."

"No, she was adopted *into* one of the oldest families in Boston," Dan corrected. "She only found out in 1990 when Gianni approached her."

"But how can she be part of that family?"

Dan glanced at Gary, who held up Bruno's statement. "Mrs. Cain's mother was dating one Nico DiFanetti, Bruno's older brother."

Senator Cain's brow furrowed. "But Bruno is the oldest."

"He is now. Two years after your wife was born, Nico was murdered."

"But why?"

Gary shrugged. "Rivalry? Ambition? Greed? Take your pick. But his death was part of the reason Bruno decided to go legit."

"Mrs. Cain's mother got scared, and with good reason," Dan told the senator. "In the forties, fifties, and sixties, the DiFanettis were at the heart of organized crime in Boston. She decided she didn't want her unborn child having anything to do with its father's family."

"But she didn't want to lose the baby either," Gary added. "So she 'went away' to have it, and after Della was born, she put her up for adoption."

"And Gianni found out the truth," Senator Cain concluded.

Dan nodded. "He clued her in on her real family. What he proposed then was a little blackmail. She was to send reports on you or her parentage would be revealed to anyone who'd listen. In the media, in politics...."

The senator looked haggard. "Now I understand why she came back to Lenox with me this month—not once but twice—when she could so easily have stayed with our family."

"And why she turned up in Boston the day we interviewed you," Gary added.

"Exactly. She couldn't let you come alone in case she missed something vital that could be passed along to Gianni." Dan went over to Senator Cain and laid his hand on the senator's arm. "If it's any consolation, I had the impression she would rather have stayed away."

"I had the same feeling," Senator Cain admitted.

"Senator, when did your wife learn of your affair with Cheryl?" Gary inquired.

He swallowed. "In 1990. We'd managed to keep it secret for a year, but...." He gazed at them. "I don't have a clue how she worked it out, but she did." The senator paused. "Wait. You said she only found out she was adopted in 1990?"

Gary consulted his notes. "Yes. That was when Gianni approached her."

It was as if some invisible weight was pressing down on Senator Cain's shoulders. "Then maybe it wasn't just learning of the affair that changed her." He glanced at them. "Yes, she changed. Before then she took little notice of politics and my campaign for the senate. She gave public appearances when it was required of her, but that was all. After? Suddenly I had a wife who was interested in my work, who asked questions." He sighed. "And now I know why. I never put two and two together."

"I know you said she tolerated the affair, but that wasn't the truth, was it?" When the senator stared at him, Gary sighed. "Gianni told his father that she was very bitter." He glanced at the statement. "According to Bruno, she could have stomached you having an affair with an intern or a secretary—a female secretary, however. But finding out her husband was sleeping with—and Bruno quoted Gianni—'A woman with tits and a dick' was more than she could bear."

"She said that?" The words crept out as a whisper.

"Our first visit to Lenox, you said yours was not a regular marriage," Dan commented.

"No, it was more a marriage of convenience. My parents chose her because of her family, her social status…. They told me I'd grow to love her, just as my father had grown to love my mother. And when that love didn't materialize, I accepted the situation and vowed to make the best of it. When we discovered she couldn't have children, she was the one to suggest adoption." He shuddered. "That was why I said she tolerated my affair with Cheryl. She and I… we were no one's idea of soul mates. But I had no idea she felt so badly about it."

Gary nodded. "She told Gianni about Cheryl, but more importantly, she told him who Cheryl had been."

"Gianni had been looking for her for five years, except he'd been looking for Benjamin Raskin. And now that he knew exactly where to find her, he bided his time, waiting for the perfect moment." Dan gazed at him with a heavy heart. "And you, Senator, handed it to him."

Senator Cain's shoulders slumped. "I've lost everything. Cheryl, Della, my reputation…." Gary opened his mouth to say something, but the senator held up his hand. "Oh, the public might not know anything *now*, but this will get out, I assure you. Once the media gets hold of what you've discovered." Then he straightened. "Speaking of which, look what the two of you achieved. Gianni did his best to prevent identification, but he failed. You know how she died, and why. You solved the case." His eyes shone. "And somewhere, she knows it."

Tears pricked the corners of Dan's eyes. "You're right." He felt that with every sense he possessed.

The senator's chest heaved. "I don't see how I can make amends. But I *will* try."

Dan nodded, wiping away the moisture from his cheeks.

Cheryl was finally at peace.

"What will happen to Gianni?" Senator Cain asked.

Gary's breathing hitched. "Thank you for reminding me." He glanced at Dan. "We need to get out of here. Now."

Dan stilled. "Yes, we do." He clasped the senator's hand. "You'll have to excuse us, Senator. We have a plane to meet."

This was one flight arrival he did *not* want to miss.

CHAPTER THIRTY-THREE

Saturday, August 4, 2018
12:45 p.m.

LOGAN AIRPORT'S Terminal C had been heaving as they arrived, a sea of passengers armed with heavy suitcases and roll-ons, children clutching toys, parents looking haggard, business travelers with laptop bags....

Gary checked his phone. Gianni's flight had just landed and was taxiing toward its gate. He and Dan stood at the huge window, watching as the plane crawled closer. Behind them were two uniformed police officers.

"He's definitely on this flight?" Dan asked.

Gary nodded. "I checked with Chicago." The plane came to a dead stop, and the air bridge moved into position. "Okay, showtime."

They walked past the waiting passengers to the open doors. Gary flashed his badge to the gate agents, then took a step back. It wasn't long before the first passengers appeared, some strolling, others almost running, undoubtedly trying to make their connections. Gary spotted Gianni, and he stilled.

"He isn't alone."

Gianni was smiling as he walked, casually dressed in jeans and a black shirt open at the collar, in conversation with his fellow passenger.

"Who's with him?" Dan peered past Gary. "Isn't that Paul's lawyer, Aaron Stillwater?"

Gary didn't reply. He blocked Gianni's way, holding his badge aloft. "Gianni DiFanetti?"

Gianni came to a halt, his smile fading. "Yes? What do you want?"

Bruno had been correct—he and Gianni didn't resemble one another in the slightest.

But damn, he looks like Paul.

"You're under arrest for the murders of Cheryl Somers, James Sebring, and Kevin Donaldson." Gary paused. "And for the theft of thirteen works of art from the Isabella Stewart Gardner Museum."

Gianni's mouth opened, but then he snapped it shut. A bored expression stole over his face as Gary Mirandized him. He glanced at Aaron Stillwater, rolling his eyes as if he found the process entertaining. When Gary was through, Gianni flashed Stillwater a grin.

"Over to you, I think."

Stillwater coughed. "Well, I must be on my way. Excuse me, gentlemen."

"What the fuck?" Gianni grabbed his arm. "Where do you think you're going?"

"To my office. I have a meeting with a client."

"And what am I?"

Stillwater arched his eyebrows. "Paul DiFanetti's nephew—and *he's* my client. I don't represent you."

"Fine." Gianni snarled. "I don't need you. Luke Martin's *twice* the attorney you'll ever be." He turned to Gary. "And that's all you're gonna hear from me until I get to talk to Luke." He smiled, his expression smug.

One of the officers held out a pair of cuffs, and Gianni, still wearing that same smile, stood there as they were fastened around his wrists. Then the officers led him along the concourse, Gary and Dan following, past passengers who stared, pointed, and whispered.

All Gary wanted was to watch the smile vanish from Gianni's face.

"I GET a phone call, right?" Gianni demanded after they'd finished with the paperwork at the main desk. "Because I'm not talking to anyone until my lawyer gets here."

Dan leaned in. "I need to make a call. I'll be in the office," he informed Gary under his breath.

Gary nodded. "I'll be there in a minute." Dan hurried away. Gary pointed to the phone. "It's all yours, Mr. DiFanetti."

"What's the number?" Sergeant Rob Michaels asked Gianni. "I'll dial it."

Gianni pulled his phone from his pocket and scrolled. He handed it to Rob. "There. Luke Martin." He glanced at Gary over his shoulder and smiled. "The best damn attorney in Boston."

"I swear, he was smiling all the way over here," Officer Lomax muttered to Gary. "Every time I looked in the rearview mirror, there he was, like the cat that got the cream."

Gary doubted he'd be smiling by the time they were through.

Rob handed the phone to Gianni, who took it and held it to his ear. "Hey, Luke. The cops have arrested me. … Three charges of murder… theft too. I need you to get over to the precinct ASAP." He paused. "Hang on." Gianni stared at Gary. "What was your name again?"

Gary said nothing but held his badge up for inspection.

"It's a Detective Gary Mitchell." Another pause. "Sure." Gianni held the phone out to Gary. "My lawyer wants to speak to you."

Gary took it. "This is Detective Mitchell. Hello again, Mr. Martin." Gianni blinked.

"Detective, I will *not* be representing Gianni DiFanetti. And there's something else you need to know."

Gary listened intently, careful to keep his expression neutral. "I'll be sure to pass that on." He handed the phone back to Gianni. "He wants to talk to you."

Gianni took it. "So how long will it take you to … What?" His face darkened. "You can't do this. What do we pay you for? … You get your ass over here and get me out of this place." He scowled. "Now wait just one goddamn—" Gianni gaped at the receiver with undisguised astonishment. "He hung up."

Rob took the phone from him. "A lawyer will be appointed for you."

Gianni pointed at Gary. "You call my father. *He'll* send a lawyer."

Gary kept his face straight. "I don't think so. Who do you think gave instructions to Mr. Martin?"

Gianni's jaw dropped, and there was no hint of a smile as he was taken to the cells.

Gary shuddered out a breath. There was still a long road to travel, but he had faith in the system.

Cheryl Somers's killer would *not* escape justice.

He headed for the office, but at every turn, there were murmured remarks of approval, pats on the back, and wide grins. Gary shook his head. "It never fails to amaze me how fast news travels around this place."

Dan was pouring coffee when he entered the office. "You had a call. Riley Watson. He's on duty guarding Bruno, isn't he?"

"Yes." Gary removed his phone from his pocket and dialed. "Hey, Riley. Everything okay?"

"Relax. Everything's fine. But there's someone here who wants to talk to you."

There was a pause; then Bruno spoke. "Detective Mitchell?"

"Mr. DiFanetti. I was about to call you. Gianni has been arrested."

He caught Bruno's exhalation. "You were on time. I'm glad. And thanks for letting me know."

"That wasn't why I was going to call. Gianni got a bit of a shock at the airport. Mr. Stillwater, your brother's lawyer, dropped him like a hot potato."

Gary's instincts told him Bruno had something to do with it.

"Ah, did he indeed?"

"And then he got another shock when Mr. Martin also refused to represent him. As per your instructions."

"Yeah, that must have rocked Gianni's world to its core."

"Okay, what did you do?" Dan arched his eyebrows, and Gary mouthed *Later*.

"Me?" Bruno gave a good performance of sounding surprised.

"Surely Paul would have wanted Gianni to have representation."

"Very possibly." There was a pause. "Except... I called him last night. I told him what Gianni had done—the murders of Cheryl and James—and that he'd gotten away with too much for too long. It was time to face the music. *Then* I told Paul it wouldn't be in his best interests to provide Gianni with legal representation." Another pause. "I reminded him of how much I knew."

"No wonder you wanted protection. Why didn't you tell me this when I interviewed you this morning?"

"Because when I'd finished talking to him, Paul said he'd think about it, so I wasn't certain how things would go. He wasn't happy, I can tell you that. I know why. He hated the idea of Gianni swinging in the wind without the family money to protect him."

"What do you mean?"

"Gianni doesn't have a personal fortune that would allow him to hire some big-shot lawyer. Well, he did have, but not anymore." Bruno snorted. "And right now, I'd be willing to bet he's sitting in his cell, wishing he'd saved some of the money he'd spent on his fast cars, his horses, his houses, his women...."

"You mean, he assumed the family money would be there for him, so he saw no need to save any of his own," Gary concluded.

"Exactly." Bruno paused. "Detective Mitchell, now you've got Gianni on the hook… please, don't let him go. I'll help in any way I can, but he can't walk away from all this."

"We will do everything within our power," Gary assured him. "And we'll keep you safe until he's where he belongs—behind bars."

"I'm counting on it. Will he make bail?"

"After being charged with three murders and with a court-appointed lawyer? I doubt it. He can sit in the cells for tonight."

There was a pause, and then Riley was back. "Well done, boss. Sounds as if you've had a result."

"It's not over yet, but it's looking good."

Better than that—it was looking hopeful.

Saturday, August 4, 2018
4:00 p.m.

GARY WALKED into the morgue to find Del Maddox putting on his jacket. "It's a little late for you, isn't it?" If Del worked a Saturday he was usually gone by midday. Gary had been surprised to learn he was still there.

"Yeah, well, I wanted to clear my backlog. I've got an out-of-state wedding to attend, and I wasn't about to leave my fridges full."

Gary scanned his surroundings. The stainless-steel surfaces gleamed, everything in its place. "You'd make someone a wonderful husband," Gary remarked.

"So I'm neat. Bite me." Del arched his eyebrows. "Have I suffered a lapse of memory? I didn't think I was working on one of your cases." He frowned. "In fact, I thought I wouldn't be seeing you for a while, now that you're dealing exclusively with cold cases."

"Your memory is fine. I called ahead, and they told me you were just finishing." Gary smiled. "I'm here to take you for a drink."

Del's eyebrows almost disappeared into his hairline. "To what do I owe this honor?"

Gary took out his wallet and removed a photo. "I have a story to tell you, one I think will interest you. One you're already familiar with, at least part of it."

"Now you really have piqued my interest." Gary handed him the photo, and he studied it. "Beautiful woman. Who is she?"

"The first time you laid eyes on her, she was a body wrapped in plastic."

Del's eyes widened. "And now you know how she came to be there?"

Gary nodded.

Del beamed. "Then by all means, buy me that drink. This is one story I want to hear."

Chapter Thirty-Four

Sunday, August 5, 2018

DAN CLEARED away the dishes from lunch, and by the time he returned to the table with the coffee, Gary still hadn't moved. He sat with his water glass between his hands, rolling it slowly back and forth. Dan stood a few feet away, watching.

"If you don't tell me what's wrong, I may have to kill you," Dan quipped.

Gary jerked his head in Dan's direction. "Hmm?"

Dan sat beside him. "You've hardly said a word all morning. What's on your mind?"

"All you have to do is touch me and you'll probably have the answer to that question."

Dan smiled. "It may interest you to know that I try not to do that where you're concerned." When Gary frowned, Dan covered his hand, lacing their fingers. "When we touch, I make a conscious effort not to open myself up to my gift. The only time I ignore this little rule—" He leaned in and kissed Gary on the lips. "—is when we're making love." Another slow kiss. "Being physically—and mentally—connected to you is mind-blowing."

Gary's pupils enlarged a little. "Maybe that explains why we spend so much time having sex."

Dan knew the signs. "Before you get that let's-go-to-bed look in your eyes, why don't you tell me what's wrong?"

Gary hesitated for a moment, then leaned back. "It's this case."

"The case we just solved?"

Gary's mouth went down at the corners. "The more I think about it, the more convinced I become that it's not going to be easy to convict Gianni."

"Convicting him isn't your job."

"I agree, but for others to convict him, they'll need evidence."

Dan reached for the notepad and pen Gary had left on the table. "Okay, so what do we have? What's our most damning evidence?"

"Bruno's testimony. Gianni told him he'd killed Cheryl, and why. He also told us Gianni was behind the artwork heist at the museum. But it's his word against Gianni's."

Dan made a note. "What else?"

"Chris Reed can place Gianni on the roof rafters with James Sebring. He heard them talking. Not only that, it seems likely Gianni *was* talking about Cheryl." He sighed. "This assumes Chris is still alive when it comes to trial."

Dan nodded. "My thought too."

"And finally we have Frank Wyler, who *might* testify that Gianni asked him to put his hand up to the Kevin Donaldson murder." Gary bit his lip. "I say might because he didn't sound too happy about fingering Gianni the last time we spoke."

Dan paused in his notes. "I think you're overlooking something."

"What's that?"

"Think about what happened at the airport with Paul's lawyer. It seems as though Gianni doesn't have Paul's support in this. So if he's got Bruno against him, *and* Paul…." All Dan's instincts were telling him one thing. He smiled. "I have a feeling that once word gets out, the tide is going to turn. Maybe more witnesses will crawl out of the woodwork. And there's something else. The first artwork from the Isabella Stewart Gardner heist has been found. All those people who bought the remaining twelve pieces may suddenly decide they're too hot to handle now that the case will be back in the public eye. Don't forget, the FBI reward for information is, what, ten million dollars?"

Gary chuckled. "Have I told you lately how much I love the way your mind works?"

"No, you haven't. So maybe we need to rectify that." Dan stood. "In bed."

Gary followed him out of the room, still chuckling. "We can always make more coffee later."

Monday August 6, 2018
8:30 a.m.

As SOON as Gary walked into the department after roll call, he knew something was up. He couldn't put his finger on it, but there was a trickle of electricity in the air, a buzz of excitement. He glanced at Dan and noted his alertness, the way he scanned their surroundings.

He feels it too.

Will Freeman's eyes gleamed as Gary approached him. "Travers wants to see you two, ASAP."

"Then we'd better not keep him waiting." He dropped the bag containing their cinnamon rolls onto Will's desk, then gave him a warning glare. "They'd better be there when we get back."

Will guffawed. "Yeah. Good luck with that."

Gary and Dan headed for Travers's office. It was in its usual chaotic state, the desk buried beneath a mountain of paper, the air filled with the enticing aroma of freshly brewed coffee.

Travers beamed as they entered. "Good morning."

Gary chuckled. "Someone got out of bed on the right side."

"Trust me, you'll be smiling too when you hear my news." Travers gestured to the two worn leather chairs facing the desk, and they sat. "First thing this morning, we received an anonymous call. The caller suggested we might want to take a look at the case of Jason Phelps. And that wasn't all he said." He handed a sheet of paper to Gary. "This is what we've turned up so far."

Gary scanned the first few lines. "A cold case murder from 1991?" Then he read lower down, and he gaped. "You have *got* to be kidding me."

Travers nodded. "If any of what they claim can be substantiated, then this is dynamite. Not only that, it's also the first real break in the Isabella Stewart Gardner case since 2003."

"What happened in 2003?" Dan asked.

Travers sat, coffee cup in hand. "The FBI believed all the artwork was moved through several organized crime networks to Philadelphia. That was where the trail went cold in 2003, and there's been nothing since." He pointed to the sheet in Gary's hand. "But if this turns out to be true...."

"Who is Jason Phelps?" Dan inquired.

"He was already a career criminal by the time he was killed in '91," Travers told him. "He'd been in prison for drug dealing in the mideighties."

"And it definitely *was* murder?"

Travers chuckled. "I think two shots to the back of the head is pretty categorical, don't you?" He glanced at Gary. "I recommend interviewing Phelps's sister, though. If our mystery caller is correct and she's still with us, she can support some of their claims." Travers stared at them. "Well?

What are you waiting for? Get this all checked out before you interview Gianni DiFanetti." He grinned. "I may have to watch this one on camera. I want to see the look on his face."

"You *know* he's not going to admit to any of this," Gary informed him.

"That doesn't matter. What *does* matter is we might have found more nails for his coffin." Travers's face darkened. "Yes, it's a case of innocent until proven guilty, but in *his* case, we know he's guilty. Now we just need to prove it."

Gary held up the sheet. "And this might be exactly what we need."

It was a start, at any rate. And Travers was right. They had a lot to do before they walked into that interview room.

4:30 p.m.

GARY HAD assessed the situation correctly. Gianni was *not* talking.

He'd sat through the interview so far with a sullen expression, and every now and then he'd glanced at his appointed attorney, who'd intoned, "No comment," at regular intervals. Gary hadn't missed the momentary frisson that had rippled through Gianni, however, when he'd learned his father had provided a lot of the information.

Gianni had to be feeling awfully lonely right then.

The door opened, and an officer entered. He handed Gary a piece of folded paper, then withdrew.

Gary opened it, doing his best to school his features as he read it. He showed it to Dan before meeting Gianni's bored gaze. "Some interesting news." Gary told him. "When the stock exchange opened this morning, your uncle sold all his shares in DFF group companies. Now why would he do that?"

Gianni's eyes widened slightly; then he gave his attorney another glance.

"No comment." Mr. Ellis shuffled his papers. "Does that conclude your evidence against my client?"

"Not quite." Gary turned the page in his notepad. "We haven't talked about the art heist at the Isabella Stewart Gardner Museum yet. Are you familiar with this event, Mr. Ellis?"

"I recall reading about it, a long time ago."

"Twenty-eight years ago, to be exact. March eighteenth, 1990. The stolen works have been valued at hundreds of millions of dollars by the FBI and art dealers."

Mr. Ellis made an impatient noise. "I am aware you have charged my client with the theft of the artworks. I am also aware this comes from information given to you by his father. But if that is all you have to connect my client to this heist, then—"

"Not all," Gary assured him. "But my story starts the week before the heist." He consulted his notes. "Sunday, March eleventh, to be exact. An ex-drug dealer by the name of Jason Phelps went to visit his sister."

"I fail to see what this has to do with my client."

Gianni's bored expression morphed into a look of faint alarm.

"Mr. Phelps told his older sister, Trish, that he had something big coming up, only he wasn't sure if he was going to do it. At the time she thought he was referring to selling cocaine."

"And?" Mr. Ellis tapped his pen on the table. "How does this connect to my client?"

"I spoke with Trish Adams this morning. She told me her brother used to work for your client. That he spent a lot of time at Gianni's home in fact. I'm sure that can be corroborated."

Mr. Ellis folded his arms.

Gianni stared at Gary.

"In February, 1991, eleven months after the art heist, Mr. Phelps was letting himself into his apartment in Lynn, Massachusetts, when an unknown assailant shot him twice in the back of the head. The lightbulb above the door had been removed. The crime remains unsolved to this day."

Mr. Ellis arched his eyebrows. "Is this another cold case murder that you're trying to pin on my client?"

"According to information we received today, just days before he died, Mr. Phelps was reportedly heard bragging about the fact that he had in his possession two of the stolen artworks, and that he'd hidden some more of them." Gary looked Gianni in the eye. "The informant also stated you were the one who shot Jason Phelps, and that they are willing to testify to that."

Gianni paled. "No comment."

Gary closed his notepad. "And *now* we're done." He gave a nod to the officer standing against the wall. "Mr. DiFanetti is ready to go back to his cell." He glanced at Gianni. "Tomorrow morning, you'll be taken to the Suffolk County Jail to await your trial." He smiled. "See you in court."

And with that, Gary walked slowly from the interview room, to be met by Dan and Travers.

Dan's eyes shone. "You were awesome."

Gary smiled. "You should have been in there with me. After all, you helped put him in that room."

Dan shook his head. "My part in this case is done."

Travers patted Gary on the shoulder. "Well done."

"Thank you, sir."

"When the media gets wind of this case, you two will be in the headlines again. Talk about a high-profile case." Travers smiled. "Good start."

It was the opening Gary had been hoping for. "I wanted to talk to you about that, but… could we go to your office?"

Travers blinked. "Sure."

They filed through the hallways, and yet again Gary and Dan were greeted with comments and smiles from their coworkers, in stark contrast to the day they'd learned of Dan's new role in the department.

Amazing how a little success can change people's opinions.

They reached Travers's office. Travers closed the door, and before Gary could speak, he got in first.

"I think I know what this is about. You want to find your brother's killer."

Gary stared at him. "You know about him?"

Travers's expression was solemn. "Of course. I knew the day you walked into this precinct."

Gary hastened to explain. "I'm not asking for his case to be investigated—he died in Springfield, Mass, not Boston—but I want permission to follow leads if any turn up." He gestured to Dan. "If Dan helps with the case, that's entirely possible."

Travers rubbed his jaw. "Yes, I can agree to that." He smiled. "You two work well together."

Gary glanced at Dan. "I think we make a great team."

Dan beamed. "I agree."

Travers cocked his head. "Are you still living at Gary's place?" Both Gary and Dan blinked, and Travers's eyes twinkled. "Paperwork, gentlemen. Little things like mailing addresses."

"Yes, he is," Gary confirmed, his stomach clenching.

Travers nodded. "I don't suppose he has any plans to move out. Just don't let it interfere with your job."

Gary stilled. "Sir?"

"You think I don't know what goes on in this precinct? Who is seeing who?" He chuckled. "A mouse farts in the store cupboard and I get to know about it."

Gary couldn't get his mouth to work.

Travers met his gaze with arched eyebrows. "You expected intolerance?" Before Gary could respond, he took his wallet from the pocket of his jacket and removed a photo. He handed it to Gary, who studied it.

Two women smiled at the camera, their arms around each other's waists.

Travers pointed to the figure on the left. "That's my daughter, Teresa, and her wife, Mandy." He replaced the photo in his wallet, then gave Gary a frank stare. "Just be careful. I know Lewis was not the most tolerant officer, but there are others like him around here. Whether they'll show their hand remains to be seen." He set his jaw. "But if they do, I'll have something to say about it." Travers glanced at his watch. "But now you need to go home. You're done for the day."

"We're not going home," Dan interjected. "Gary is taking me to dinner at our favorite restaurant."

Gary had to laugh. "Oh I am, am I?" He felt light.

"Yes, you are."

Travers laughed too. "Enjoy. I'll see you both first thing tomorrow—when we'll discuss your next case."

They left his office, Gary's head in a whirl.

What filled him was a welcome emotion. Hope.

Chapter Thirty-Five

Saturday, September 22, 2018

DAN SIPPED his champagne. "This is better than the last time I was here."

"Why?" Gary looked edible in a tux. Dan couldn't keep his eyes off him.

He rolled his eyes. "Are you kidding? I stayed here and ended up on the front page of every newspaper in Boston."

Gary chuckled. "You mean like earlier this month?" When the news broke about Senator Cain and Gianni DiFanetti, for one whole week a day didn't go by without some journalist or other calling them, asking for an interview.

Dan gazed at the Fairmont Copley Plaza's Grand Ballroom, with its mirrored doors that reminded him of the palace of Versailles. Above each door were gold-covered moldings, and graceful arches led the eye to the ornate ceiling. White-cloth-covered round tables filled the space on three sides, with a dance floor in the center. Candles flickered, and the flower arrangements' sweet fragrance filled the air. At the far end of the room was a long table, groaning with items brought for the raffle at the end of the night.

"What did you bring for the raffle?" he asked Gary. "I know Sean asked you to bring something." When Gary flushed, Dan gazed at him with interest. "Now you *have* to tell me."

Gary coughed. "Floppy disks."

Dan laughed. "Seriously?"

"Well, Sean's email said bring something from their college years, so I took a look around Brad's room last time we had lunch there. I found a box in his drawer." He took a drink from his glass. "I was never much of a fan of champagne, but this tastes great."

Dan chuckled. "That's because it's the good stuff. I took a look at the bottle when the servers were refilling the glasses."

"It should be the good stuff, knowing how much the tickets cost."

Dan took another sip. "It's for charity." He sighed. "It was sweet of Pete Raskin to come see us today." Pete had visited the precinct to thank them, and to tell them he'd had a letter from Bruno DiFanetti. He and Senator Cain wanted to create a gallery dedicated to Cheryl, to showcase the work of new artists.

Dan saw the gesture for what it was—both men trying to make amends.

"I guess Bruno will be happy once Gianni gets to trial. He must want his life back," Gary commented.

"Only if he can live without forever looking over his shoulder."

For that to happen, Gianni needed to go away for a long time.

Music poured from the speakers, and many of the guests took to the dance floor, the beat pulsing through the floorboards, the lights winking on and off, reflecting in the mirrors around the room.

"Want to dance?"

Dan smiled. "I'm not really much of a dancer." He let his gaze drift slowly around the ballroom. They'd met a lot of people that evening, so many that Dan had difficulty recalling individual names and faces. Brad's former classmates came from all walks of life, some successful, others less so, but all happy to meet Brad's little brother, even if he wasn't so little anymore. Everyone appeared friendly, and the one thing Dan could say for certain was that they held Brad in high regard.

Gary shifted his chair closer. "Well?"

Dan knew what he was asking.

"Well, apart from getting to know Sean a whole lot better and meeting some really nice people, I think this is a bust."

"You didn't pick up on anything?"

Dan shook his head. "Maybe Sean's right. Maybe Brad's murderer *wasn't* one of his classmates." He hadn't met anyone who'd set off his radar. All he'd felt was warmth, affection, and pleasure to be amongst friends once more.

"We knew it was a long shot," Gary murmured.

Dan squeezed his arm. "Maybe, but I wanted to give you something to work with."

The music died, and Sean's voice filled the air. "If I can interrupt your dancing and chatting for a moment? Please take your seats."

It wasn't long before the dance floor was empty, and Sean stood in front of the raffle table, a wireless mic in one hand.

He grinned. "And now the moment you know you've all been waiting for. It's raffle time, so have your tickets handy." He narrowed his gaze. "And if you haven't bought any yet, shame on you. This is for charity." That grin was back. "So I'll wait while you let the moths out of your wallets and buy a strip of tickets."

Laughter echoed around the ballroom.

Dan removed his tickets from his pocket and placed them on the table. "If I win those floppy disks, *you're* going home in a taxi, and *I'm* sleeping in that beautiful room upstairs."

Gary chuckled. "After the way you looked at that big tub in the bathroom? I think that would be cutting your nose off to spite your face."

"Never mind the tub—that bed looked wonderful."

There was something about hotel rooms that always made Dan horny.

Sean tapped his wineglass, and silence fell. "Thank you to everyone who contributed a prize. We asked you to bring something that reminded you of our fun-filled years in college, and boy, you delivered." He peered at the sheet in his hand. "Although I have to ask…. Whoever brought the box of floppy disks?"

More laughter ensued, and Dan gave Gary a dig in the ribs with his elbow.

Sean consulted his list again. "There's also a Walkman, a compact CD player, VHS tapes…." He peered at his audience. "Really, people?" Chuckles and snorts erupted. Then he gave them a mock glare. "And who brought Pogs?" A wave of laughter rippled around the room. Sean narrowed his gaze. "*Now* I understand why some of you were behaving so furtively when you left your prizes." Then he smiled. "But what this collection really shows is that our greatest pleasure was… going to the movies." He gestured to the table. "Most of you brought DVDs of movies we all went to see back then." He grabbed one and held it up. "*Thelma and Louise*, anyone?" He replaced it on the table and held another aloft. "*Four Weddings and a Funeral*?"

"How are we doing this?" a voice called out.

"I'll get a volunteer to draw the first ticket," Sean told him, "And if your number is called, go to the prize table and pick something." He grinned. "I'm betting at the end of the night, the Pogs will still be there." He scanned the tables. "So, can I have a volunteer to draw the tickets?"

A woman yelled, "Me!" Everyone laughed.

Sean beamed. "Bev, I knew you'd be the first."

Bev turned out to be a short woman with bright red hair and an infectious smile. She came up to the mic, and Sean pointed to the large bowl behind him. Bev drew a ticket from it, handed it to Sean, who called out the number.

Dan peered at his strip of ten tickets. "Listen out for anything between one hundred and one hundred and nine."

Gary chuckled. "Got your eye on anything?"

He smiled. "I think I'll play safe and grab a DVD."

Fifteen minutes later the numbers were still being called out, and Dan was starting to think his luck wasn't in. He loved the laughter that accompanied each winner's visit to the prize table.

Bev handed Sean the next ticket. "Number one hundred and seven," he announced.

Dan grinned and held up his ticket. "That's me!" He glanced at Gary. "And you're coming with me. You can help me choose."

They walked over to the table, and Dan scanned the remaining items. There were plenty of prizes left to choose from. He chuckled. "Decisions, decisions."

And then he froze.

Gary moved closer. "What's wrong?"

"I think this one has my name written all over it, don't you?" Dan pointed to a DVD of *Cape Fear*.

"I think you're right." Gary rubbed his arms and shivered. "And now I've got goose bumps."

Beside Dan, one of the female guests shuddered. "That movie gave me the creeps. Mind you, the book was just as creepy."

Dan paused, his hand outstretched toward it. "*Cape Fear*'s based on a book?"

She nodded. "It was written by one of my favorite authors, John D. MacDonald. Different title, of course."

Ice crawled over his skin. "What was the title?" He stared at Gary, silently willing the next words from her lips not to be the ones he was dreading.

"*The Executioners*." She nodded toward the DVD. "But hey, if you want it, you take it." She grabbed the DVD of *Thelma and Louise*. "Now *this* one is more *my* kinda movie." She walked away from the table.

Gary's eyes were huge. "Don't touch it."

Dan took a deep breath, dismayed to realize his hand was trembling. "You know I have to." He picked it up and staggered, falling against the table. "Oh God," he whispered. He couldn't stop shaking.

"What is it?" Gary supported him. "What do you sense?"

Dan straightened, making an effort to get his emotions under control. "He's got guts, I'll say that for him." He shivered. He scanned the room, first in one direction, then in another. "He's here. He's one of them."

"He? Who?"

"Brad's killer. And I don't have a clue who he is."

Then a thought occurred to him.

"If he knows who I am, and he *still* left that DVD there…." Dan looked Gary in the eye. "So it's to be a game, is it?"

"What are you talking about? What kind of game?"

Dan took a deep breath. "Cat and mouse."

Keep reading for an excerpt from
Out of Sight
Second Sight: Book Three
by K.C. Wells

PROLOGUE

November, 2014

EVERYTHING SEEMED to be happening in slow motion.

The casket team met the hearse, then carried the flag-draped coffin to the graveside. They lowered it with reverence to the stands provided before taking a step back while the firing party moved into position, everyone moving with slow military pace and precision.

The wind was so cold, it bit into the bone.

The casket team stood guard, having moved to a position several feet from the grave, their faces impassive as the ceremony took place.

Did some of them know him?

The words of the service barely registered, and all of a sudden it was over, and those who'd carried the casket lined up on either side of it, facing each other. Silence fell, only to be shattered by a loud command. Three rounds pierced the air, and somewhere a bugler played taps.

It was "lights out" indeed for the casket's occupant.

The casket team began to fold the flag, starting with the red-striped end, passing it precisely on each fold to the next two soldiers, a ballet of nimble hands that folded the fabric until no red was visible.

At last it was handed to the officer in charge, who stepped forward to stand in front of the row of black suits and dresses. The words were spoken quietly, competing with the icy wind that stirred hair and clothing alike.

"I present this flag to you on behalf of the president, the secretary of the Army, and with the thanks of a grateful nation for his service." The officer then released the tightly folded flag to the family and saluted before taking one step back to rejoin the casket team.

And then it was over.

Another life lost.

Only one thought dominated.

This has to stop.

Chapter One

Saturday, September 22, 2018

DAN PORTER paid no attention to the luxurious hotel room with its king-size bed, the window, framed with opulent drapes, overlooking the park, or the fluffy robes they'd laid out on the comforter before heading down to the charity ball. Not that he deliberately paid no attention—he simply didn't see any of it. His mind had launched itself down a tight, dark rabbit hole, and daylight—and escape—had become a pinprick of light way above him.

His stomach churned, and his throat seized.

Brad's killer is downstairs, right this second.

And Dan didn't have a fucking clue to his identity.

He'd left the ballroom where all the past alumni were sipping champagne, chatting, and dancing. Dan was in no mood to take part in such activities, not once he'd found that DVD. He couldn't suppress the notion that the killer had hoped Dan would find it.

He'd have known Gary and I would be there. We were on the guest list. And that pointed to only one conclusion.

He's baiting me. Us. Hell, he could have been one of the guests who was selling the raffle tickets.

Dan had stood at the prizes table, scanning the faces of everyone around them, searching for some kind of recognition, anything that would give them a break, but….

Nothing.

Then his imagination had gone into overdrive. Suddenly all those happy expressions morphed into far more sinister glances, eyes glinted with evil intent, and it was as if every voice clamored inside his mind, all saying the same thing.

Me, Dan. It was me. I killed Brad. I ripped his heart from his chest and placed it in his hands, then left him there on that picnic table to be found.

Now catch me—if you can.

Before I rip your heart out.

"Will you just take a minute and breathe, for God's sake?" Gary's strong arms enfolded him, and Dan leaned into them, grateful for their support. Gary's warm voice settled on him, dispelling the ice that had crept under his skin and seeped into his bones.

Dan shuddered. "How can you be so calm about this?" Surely knowing he'd been in the same room as the psychopath who changed the course of Gary's—and his parents'—life had to have taken some effect.

Then realization sank in.

"You don't think I can find him, do you?"

Because if Dan had lost faith in his own gift, it stood to reason Gary had to feel the same way.

I couldn't see past whatever mask the killer was wearing. And it had to be a supremely effective one. Dan hadn't gotten so much as a whiff all night. All he'd sensed was warmth and affection, the delight of renewed friendships....

Gary's arms tightened around him. "Cross that thought right out of your head, Dan Porter. You hear me? We knew this was a long shot before we came."

"That's what you said earlier. And I'll repeat what I said—I wanted to give you something to work with."

"And you will. In fact, you already have."

Dan frowned. "What exactly have I given you?"

Gary managed a smile. "We came here hoping to find more information. That maybe one of Brad's classmates might know something, however small, that would lead us to the killer." He trailed his fingertips over Dan's cheek. "And now what do we know? I'll tell you. One of those people downstairs in that fancy ballroom looks like everyone else, but inside they're a psychopath." He kissed Dan lightly on the lips. "After all these years of having no clues to work on, you just handed me a list of suspects. All we have to do is whittle it down. To my mind, that sounds like you've accomplished something. Now it's my turn to run with this." Gary pulled Dan close, molding him against his body, sending a wave of affection and love rolling over him. "This is going to take both of us, okay?"

Dan knew Gary was trying to lift his mood, but he wasn't there yet. "But how?" He breathed in Gary's comforting scent.

"Hmm?"

"How do you suggest we whittle it down?"

"As much as I don't want to even contemplate this… what if Brad wasn't the only victim? What if he was just the first? Or even the second?"

Dan crumpled a little at the thought. It felt as though a heavy weight dropped in his stomach, and something sour was on his tongue. "As much as I hate to admit it, that's a reasonable assumption."

Gary nodded. "So we could look for unsolved murders bearing the same characteristics. Cross-check any we find with the whereabouts of everyone on that list."

"We're talking nearly a hundred people," Dan remonstrated. "We can't do this alone."

"I agree. We're going to need help. Leave that part to me."

"You're amazing." Dan's throat grew thick. "I thought you'd be broken up about this, but you're much more resilient than I expected."

Gary kissed his forehead. "I've had twenty-three years to work on my resilience, remember? And although I might not be showing it right now, what you did tonight has lit a new fire under me. We're going to find this guy. I know it." His voice rang with confidence.

Dan glanced at the bed. "Before I picked up that DVD, all I could think about was getting you naked between silken sheets and making love all night long." Then a pleasurable shiver ran through him. "Seems I wasn't the only one." He opened himself up to Gary's emotions, and despite his stomach-churning fears, Dan's cock sat up and took notice.

"We need to leave this evening behind us—for now," Gary whispered, his lips soft on Dan's neck as he kissed a path to his collarbones. He stopped at the bow tie. "And you need to get out of this tux."

"To quote you, I'm going to need some help."

Gary cupped Dan's chin, tilting his face upward. "Can you forget about it? For tonight?"

Dan smiled. "I'll try." He meant it.

That rabbit hole was way too dark.

"Then I'll do my utmost to make it all go away for a few hours."

A few hours wouldn't hurt.

Monday, September 24, 2018

DETECTIVE GARY Mitchell barely had time to sip his coffee before the phone rang.

"My office, when you have a minute."

He smiled to himself. Lieutenant Travers didn't believe in wasting his breath. "Coming now, sir."

Coffee would have to wait. So would the cinnamon rolls, unfortunately.

"We're wanted," he told Dan, who'd already begun sifting through the folders on his desk, his cup in one hand. "We can choose a new case once we've spoken with Travers."

Dan squinted at him, his eyes lit with a twinkle of mischief. "Remember what happened last time we did that? Actually the last two times. He sent us off in a totally different direction."

It had been Travers who'd suggested the case of the body in the tunnel, and for most of September, they'd pursued another case he'd shoved in their direction. Not that it mattered, as long as they were solving cases that had once seemed impossible.

Thank God for technological advances, DNA testing—and Dan Porter's extraordinary gift.

Gary was also grateful for the previous day. They'd done very little except sleep, eat, and snuggle. He'd wanted to lighten Dan's mood, and if that meant staying in bed the whole day, Gary could take one for the team.

Sex was a fantastic distraction.

They headed for Travers's corner office. Gary smirked at the usual chaos that greeted them. "You know, legend speaks of a desk under all that crap."

Beside him, Dan stifled a snort.

Travers narrowed his gaze. "I was about to pay you two a compliment, but now I'm not so sure." He gestured to the two worn leather chairs in front of his desk, and they sat.

"Aw, go on, sir. Throw us a bone. We don't get too many of those," Gary quipped.

"Before I get to the main reason for me wanting to see you—" Travers consulted a desk diary. "—you're both good to go for October sixth."

Dan frowned. "And what's happening then?"

Travers arched his eyebrows. "Aren't you going to a wedding or something?" He gazed at Gary in bewilderment. "Have I got it wrong? That was the date on the request for time off, wasn't it? The request you put in back in August? I know I took a while getting back to you—my apologies for that, by the way, but there were a lot of requests, and yours got buried—but I figured you'd need to know. After all, it's less than two weeks away."

It took a moment for his words to sink in.

Gary gave Dan an apologetic glance. "I totally forgot. It's Nina and David's wedding. I accepted for both of us." His chest grew constricted. Back when he was in high school, Nina had been his best friend's aggravating little sister, and ever since Cory's murder, she and Gary had stayed in touch, cementing their connection.

The knot in his belly tightened.

Cory's little sister is getting married, and Cory won't be there to see it.

The thought deflated him, and he knew Cory would have called him out to see him indulge in such melancholy.

Called me out? He'd have kicked my ass.

Then he smiled to himself.

Yeah, I wouldn't put it past him to turn up as a ghost, complete with a glittery Pride suit.

The quiet hit him, and he became aware of being the focus of attention.

Dan pointed at him. "I think we need to work on our communication."

Travers laughed. "Do yourselves a favor and don't say stuff like that too often around here." When Gary blinked, Travers bit back a smile. "You can't hear yourselves, can you? You really are starting to sound like a married couple. Take it from someone with quite a few decades of married life under his belt. And as for why I wanted to see you…." He grabbed a folded copy of the Boston Herald from on top of the filing cabinet and tossed it in front of them. "We made ink. Fortunately, this time it was the right kind."

Dan peered at it. "Obviously not enough of the right kind for the front page."

"So what did we do to merit being written about?" Gary opened the newspaper, searching for the article. "Ah," he said before Travers could reply. "The painting."

"It reads well. Thankfully the journalist—what's his name again?"

Gary looked closer. "Jonathon Wilmer." He recognized the name. Wilmer's pieces were usually supportive of the Boston Police Department.

"Yeah, he doesn't mention Senator Cain. Just talks about the painting being recovered and back on show at the Isabella Stewart Gardner

Museum. There's a bit in it about Lori Dettweiler too. She's the expert who handled its return, isn't she?"

Gary gazed at the photo of the painting, Christ in the Storm on the Sea of Galilee, by Rembrandt. Goose bumps slid along the back of his neck. "This doesn't do it justice, you know," he said in a low voice. "So much more impressive when you're standing in front of it." There were moments when he understood Dan's lost-for-words appreciation of it and the power it had held over Senator Cain.

Then he recalled the events set in motion by its acquisition, and a chill crawled over his skin.

Cheryl Somers died because the good Senator wanted to look at it on a daily basis. James Sebring died because he knew too much.

"It's all going to come out sooner or later," Dan said with a dejected sigh.

"Can't hide a story like that for long." Travers sat in his high-backed chair, elbows on the arms, fingers laced. "So… what's next for Batman and Robin? Or do you prefer the Dynamic Duo?"

Gary jerked his head back. "Excuse me? Where did that come from?"

Travers chuckled. "I thought you hadn't seen it. Our mystery cartoonist strikes again." He shifted papers on his desk, then tugged a sheet out from under them. "I found this pinned to your office door this morning."

Gary couldn't resist. "This morning? And it already got buried?"

Travers glared. "Any more comments about my organizational skills would be ill-advised." He glanced at the sheet before handing it to Dan. "That is you dressed up as Batman, right?"

Gary gaped. "Hey, wait just one goddamn minute. If anyone's gonna be Batman, it should be me."

Dan smirked. "I don't claim to be an eccentric billionaire, but I can live with this." He grinned. "Personally, I like it. A short Batman. It's cute." He took one look at Gary's face and burst into laughter. "For God's sake, it's just a drawing." He shifted on his chair, all trace of mirth gone. "Why don't you tell Lieutenant Travers what we've discovered? About Brad?"

Gary cleared his throat. "We made—well, Dan made—a bit of a breakthrough Saturday." He told Travers about the charity ball and Dan's revelation. "The ball's organizer, Sean Nichols, was Brad's boyfriend back in college. We called him yesterday morning and told him what we knew. He was horrified to think one of his former classmates could be Brad's killer, but he sent us the list of everyone present."

Travers cocked his head to one side. "I'm assuming there's something you want from me."

Gary nodded. "I'd like to give the list to Barry Davis, if that's okay."

"Our tech whiz kid?"

"Yeah." Gary outlined his idea. "But he'd work on it on his own time, of course, and I'd pay him."

Travers snorted. "Good luck with that. Barry's good people. He won't let you pay him." He leaned back. "Yes, I can agree to that. I hope he turns something up." Another smile. "So… what's your next case to be?"

"We were trying to decide that when you called and asked to see us," Dan remarked. "I'd like a really meaty case. Something to tax our brains."

Travers laughed. "Be careful what you wish for, Mr. Porter."

K.C. WELLS has an active imagination. Sometimes it produces rainbows and unicorns, but occasionally something darker emerges…

She lives on an island off the south coast of the UK where her favourite writing spot is the Lighthouse. The waves crash against the rocks, the wind howls, and she lets her imagination loose to follow its convoluted path, meeting diverse characters with stories to be told – and twists in the tale…

If you want to follow her exploits, you can sign up for her monthly newsletter: http://eepurl.com/cNKHlT

You can stalk – er, find – her in the following places:

Email: k.c.wells@btinternet.com
Facebook: www.facebook.com/KCWellsWorld
KC's men In Love (my readers group): http://bit.ly/2hXL6wJ
Amazon: https://www.amazon.com/K-C-Wells/e/B00AECQ1LQ
Twitter: @K_C_Wells
Website: www.kcwellswrites.com
Instagram: www.instagram.com/k.c.wells
Book Bub: https://www.bookbub.com/authors/k-c-wells

IN HIS SIGHTS

K.C. WELLS

His psychic powers could help find the killer——unless the killer finds him first.

Second Sight: Book One

Random letters belong on Scrabble tiles, not dead bodies. But when a demented serial killer targets Boston's gay population, leaving cryptic messages carved into his victims, lead detective Gary Mitchell has no choice but to play along.

As the body count rises, Gary gets desperate enough to push aside his skepticism and accept the help of a psychic. Dan Porter says he can offer new clues, and Gary needs all the insight into the killer's mind he can get.

Dan has lived with his gift—sometimes his curse—his entire life. He feels compelled to help, but only if he can keep his involvement secret. Experience has taught him to be cautious of the police and the press, but his growing connection to Gary distracts him from the real danger. As they edge closer to solving the puzzle, Dan finds himself in the killer's sights….

www.dreamspinnerpress.com

A GROWL, A ROAR, AND A PURR

K.C. WELLS

Lions & Tigers & Bears: Book One

In the human world, shifters are a myth.

In the shifter world, mates are a myth too. So how can tiger shifter Dellan Carson have two of them?

Dellan has been trapped in his shifted form for so long, he's almost forgotten how it feels to walk on two legs. Then photojournalist Rael Parton comes to interview the big-pharma CEO who holds Dellan captive in a glass-fronted cage in his office, and Dellan's world is rocked to its core.

When lion shifter Rael finds his newfound mate locked in shifted form, he's shocked but determined to free him from his prison… and that means he needs help.

Enter ex-military consultant and bear shifter Horvan Kojik. Horvan is the perfect guy to rescue Dellan. But mates? He's never imagined settling down with one guy, let alone two.

Rescuing Dellan and helping him to regain his humanity is only the start. The three lovers have dark secrets to uncover and even darker forces to overcome….

www.dreamspinnerpress.com

DSP PUBLICATIONS

visit us online.
WWW.DSPPUBLICATIONS.COM

Made in the USA
Las Vegas, NV
20 October 2023